THE PLASTER FABRIC

Martyn Goff was born in 1923, the son of a Russian fur dealer who had emigrated to London and established himself with great success. As a youth, Goff read prodigiously, and at 19 he was offered a place at Oxford to read English, but he joined the RAF and served in the Second World War instead. After the war, at age 22, Goff decided to become a bookseller; in 1946, he opened his first shop and before long opened others.

Goff published his first novel, *The Plaster Fabric*, in 1957, at a time when homosexuality was still illegal in Britain and authors who wrote openly about it could find themselves prosecuted. However, the book earned a rave review from the popular poet and critic John Betjeman, and, as Goff has said, "After that, the authorities could hardly condemn it." He went on to publish several other novels; three of these—*The Youngest Director* (1961), *Indecent Assault* (1967) and *Tar and Cement* (1988)—dealt with gay themes. He has also published a number of non-fiction works, including books on collecting vinyl records.

Goff is credited by many as one of the most significant figures in modern British fiction for his involvement with the Booker Prize, which he helped to create and oversaw for its first 36 years. Little noticed and even jeered at in its early years, the Booker under Goff's chairmanship grew into one of the world's major literary awards, attracting an annual media frenzy and guaranteeing huge sales for winners and shortlisted novels. As Goff approached retirement in 2002, John Sutherland wrote in *The Guardian*: "The current health of English fiction can be explained in two words: Martyn Goff."

Martyn Goff lives in London with his partner, Rubio Lindroos; the two met in the late 1960s after the latter, then a student, wrote a fan letter to the author after reading *The Youngest Director*.

Martin Dines is Senior Lecturer in English at Kingston University. He is the author of *Gay Suburban Narratives in American and British Culture: Homecoming Queens* (Palgrave Macmillan, 2010) and the co-editor of *New Suburban Stories* (Bloomsbury, 2013).

Cover: The cover of this edition is a reproduction of the original jacket art by John Minton (1917-1957) from the 1957 Putnam edition. Minton was a talented gay artist and a friend of Goff's whose career was cut tragically short by his suicide in January 1957, shortly before the publication of *The Plaster Fabric*.

By Martyn Goff

The Plaster Fabric (1957)*

A Season with Mammon (1958)

A Sort of Peace (1960)

The Youngest Director (1961)*

Red on the Door (1962)

The Flint Inheritance (1965)

Indecent Assault (1967)*

The Liberation of Rupert Bannister (1977)

Tar and Cement (1988)

* Available from Valancourt Books

THE PLASTER FABRIC

A novel by

MARTYN GOFF

With a new introduction by
MARTIN DINES

VALANCOURT BOOKS

The Plaster Fabric by Martyn Goff
First published London: Putnam, 1957
First Valancourt Books edition, 2014

Cover art by John Minton, reproduced by kind permission of the
Royal College of Art. The Publisher is grateful to M. S. Corley for
digitally restoring the copy used for this edition.

Published by Valancourt Books, Richmond, Virginia
Publisher & Editor: JAMES D. JENKINS
20th Century Series Editor: SIMON STERN, University of Toronto
http://www.valancourtbooks.com

ISBN 978-1-941147-09-2 (*trade paperback*)
Also available as an electronic book.

All Valancourt Books publications are printed on acid free paper
that meets all ANSI standards for archival quality paper.

Cover by John Minton
Set in Dante MT 11/13.2

INTRODUCTION

A pivotal and enduring figure in the publishing world, Martyn Goff (b. 1923) worked tirelessly throughout his career to instil in others his passion for books. After serving in the War he threw himself into the business of selling them, with his first bookstore opening in St. Leonards on the Sussex coast in 1946. Two and a half decades later Goff became director of the National Book League (now Booktrust). For eighteen years at the helm of this charitable organization whose remit still is to promote books and literacy, Goff instigated myriad initiatives—including the 1971 Bedford Square Bookbang, a two-week-long open-air (and rain-soaked) festival to encourage reading which attracted nearly 60,000 visitors. During this period he also reviewed fiction for the *Daily Telegraph* and the *Evening Standard* and had his own weekly broadcast on LBC radio. Goff's other executive positions are too numerous to list in full, but his most prominent and influential role was undoubtedly to oversee the running of the Booker Prize from 1970 to 2006. In these thirty-six controversy-strewn years he transformed the institution from being something that resembled a genteel reading group into a major annual media event that has reshaped the publishing trade.

While operating as an *éminence grise* in the publishing world Goff found the time to write numerous books. *The Plaster Fabric*, his first novel, was published in 1957; eight more followed alongside as many non-fiction books (several of which were on the topic of collecting classical music LPs). Notably, four of Goff's works of fiction—his debut novel, *The Youngest Director* (1961), *Indecent Assault* (1967) and *Tar and Cement* (1988)—closely deal with homosexual experience. Early in his career such material was considered risky. Goff's publisher at Putnam warned him shortly before the release of *The Plaster Fabric* that "this book could land both of us in the Old Bailey." It didn't; Goff suggests a prompt, sympathetic review in the *Telegraph* by John Betjeman helped head off condemnation from the authorities. Actually, there is little in the novel to frighten the horses. Indeed, one of the things that Betjeman commends in his review is the convincing manner in which the novel's sensitive protagonist is exposed to but ultimately overcomes physical temptation. Quite possibly it is this triumphing over homosexual desire which helped render *The Plaster Fabric* palatable—in fact, the book received a glowing review penned by Goff's local vicar for a parish magazine from the depths of suburban Surrey.

What, then, might this novel offer a contemporary reader interested in the queer fiction of earlier eras? In his introduction to a 1996 reissue of Rodney Garland's debut novel *The Heart in Exile*, first published in 1953, Neil Bartlett declares that he has rather developed a taste for the neurotic homosexual characters that appeared so frequently throughout the 1950s. *The Plaster Fabric*'s somewhat awkward bookseller Laurie Kingston certainly has much in common with the protagonists of, say, Mary Renault's *The Charioteer* (1953), Audrey Erskine Lindop's *The Details of Jeremy Stretton* (1955), and James Courage's *A Way of Love* (1959). Perhaps some pleasure, or at least interest, can indeed be found in becoming familiar with the generic contest between temptation and denial, and the strict demarcation made between good and bad homosexuals—the former just able to resist their desires, the latter entirely beholden to them. For sure, these clear-cut distinctions altogether work in support of the case for the partial decriminalization of sex between men: an invisible majority of homosexuals, these novels suggest, live as restrained, respectable and productive lives as everyone else. The only difference has to do with their sex lives, which reassuringly take place behind firmly closed doors.

But *The Plaster Fabric* starts off much more promisingly—dangerously even—with what is, quite brazenly, a pick up scene between two men. On the fog-bound streets near Marble Arch, Laurie runs into the impressive figure of Guardsman Tom Beeson. Their early interaction follows a well-worn course—a request for a light leads to small talk and their retirement to a pub for drinks (paid for of course by Laurie), followed up by Laurie's suggestion that he might like to paint the Guardsman's portrait the next time they meet. If Laurie's eyes, which are excited by desire, give away his intentions before either has a chance to speak, Beeson's are twice said to be "calculating". It is not clear whether he is anticipating sexual opportunity or material gain; for sure, as historian Matt Houlbrook has discussed in *Queer London: Perils and Pleasure in the Sexual Metropolis, 1918-1957*, more than any other figure, the Guardsman had a reputation in queer circles for being easily bought, but also for proving to be less than a bargain. Whether or not he has designs to "tap" the young bookseller, one thing is clear: Beeson, who initiates the encounter, knows the score.

Perhaps this is what is most interesting about the novel—it reveals (and therefore also perpetuates) such a wide-scale aware-ness of queer desire. Laurie is in fact often the last to learn that his needs and behaviour follow a long-established pattern. The Italian teenager who picks him up on the sultry streets of Flor-ence remarks "knowingly" that a lot of English authors visit the city. Even a priest comments that Laurie is just one of a long line of homosexual tourists intent on seducing the local boys. Partly to mortify his desires, Laurie abandons the more obvious queer locales of London and Florence for rural Sussex. But even the simple life gets complicated. Laurie is obliged to share a bed with the comely teenager Martin, whom Laurie tantalizingly sees unclothed. The boy is wise beyond his years: incredibly, he warns Laurie to hold off his advances so as not to be overcome by shame the next morning. Possibly, the novel's depiction of such broad cognizance is a reflection of a growing awareness of homosexuality in the UK. While the period saw increased discus-sion in the British press of sexual matters generally (following the Kinsey reports for instance), a number of sensational tabloid exposés helped focus public attention on the particular "problem" of homosexuality, from Douglas Warth's notorious "Evil Men" articles for the *Sunday Pictorial* in 1952 to a number of subsequent court cases featuring prominent men convicted of importuning or for engaging in homosexual activities. With a criminal act so thoroughly demonized, how would it be possible to imagine not feeling anything but guilt the morning after?

Yet even though *The Plaster Fabric*, like so many queer novels of the period, succeeds in retreating from the dissolute and dangerous city into a more secure and respectable domestic setting, Laurie never manages to free himself from temptation or scrutiny. His interactions with Beeson become less risqué once the Guardsman falls in with Laurie's best friend Susan. But then, as Eve Kosofsky Sedgwick and other scholars have noted, in literary love triangles it is the bond between the two men which is almost always the most intense; their dealings with the female character tend to deflect attention from their feelings for one another. Goff's novel is no exception, though some mileage is made out of the difficulties Beeson and Susan encounter from being across class and religious divides. Laurie also attempts to sublimate his desire by way of art. Whereas initially he exploits his interest in painting as a sexual ruse, he goes on to try to elevate his baser passions through genuine artistic expression. But his portrait of Beeson succeeds only in reproducing the Guardsman's "calculating look", thereby invoking the very kind of interaction he is trying to distance himself from. In a similar fashion, Goff's novel cannot fully manage the desires it steadfastly insists it can contain. The sheer physicality of Beeson impresses itself throughout. The Guardsman's powerful hands—rendered as great rough-hewn paws in John Minton's illustration on the cover of the first edition—never leave Laurie's mind, in part because they so often leave their mark on his body: he is repeatedly grasped (or wishes that he were) and, finally, is groped "unambiguously". These various grapplings seem to have a much longer afterlife, for this reader at least, than their ultimate repudiation. The novel's title, then, might be seen to be unintentionally appropriate, with its "moral" conclusion proving little more than a flimsy fabrication plastered over more visceral flesh and blood.

MARTIN DINES
Kingston University

April 8, 2014

THE PLASTER FABRIC

To the memory of
JOHN MINTON
a friend of many years

CONTENTS

PART I

LONDON

[1]

Laurie first saw Beeson at Marble Arch. It was an early winter's day at lighting-up time. Faint mounds of mist clung to the high trees, and the air smelt of fog. Outside the Park ordinary people hurried to ordinary houses, while the traffic edged slowly forward. By the gates were barrows piled with fruit, decked with deceptive signs: a large figure "one", followed by the shilling sign and the symbol for a pound weight. Closer inspection revealed a tiny figure "six" on the other side of the shilling, invisible, it seemed, until the fruit was in the bag. But no one was buying, and the barrow boys, mostly little old men at this hour, were talking in clipped phrases or striking their hands across the chest to keep warm.

Inside the Park there was no hurry and little that was ordinary. Small groups of people, looking vaguely displaced, cluttered round cranks who spoke of Immediate Doom or Immaculate Birth; while larger, less displaced crowds listened to spirited orators who leaned dangerously from soap-boxes and railed against the Jews, the Government or the colour-bar. Laurie moved restlessly from group to group, never listening to more than a word or two, uneasy and made excited by the threat of fog, the Park beyond and the proximity of so much eccentric human flotsam. Then he crossed the road and passed outside the Park.

Along Tyburn Way there were two fruit barrows, some Irish labourers who had come to work for Wimpeys and stayed to live by their wits, and Beeson. Beeson stood alone. He was a Guardsman and in uniform: tight, rough battle-dress and a flat cap that reached almost to his large, calculating eyes. He was at once threatening and stupid, to be distrusted and protected. He was tall and well-built, and he stood with a natural grace, his weight on one leg, his eyes travelling slowly up and down the traffic, across the cinema hoardings and back to the fruit barrows. In the mixture of twilight and yellow lamps his face was deathly white and quite smooth. His nose was slightly arched and the large eyes were brown. He and Laurie studied each other carefully, but the two sets of eyes, the one calculating and the other excited, skirted each other like boxers stalking round a ring.

"Match?" It was Beeson who spoke. His voice was deep and sharp.

Laurie tried to answer but no words came. He felt in his pockets for a box, found them and struck a match for the Guardsman. The soldier pulled sharply on the cigarette, then looked up, staring at the civilian. The glance lasted a second, but to Laurie the second was infinite. All else was blotted out. Then—

"Thanks, chum."

Like switching on a television set, Laurie first heard, then saw the traffic; and the mist and the smudged yellow lights disappearing down the Bayswater Road. Beeson turned away for a moment. Laurie felt an impulse to kick the Guardsman on his round, jaunty behind. But the mad desire passed, and ridiculously he wondered whether he could have kicked that high.

"Bloody cold!"

He agreed with Beeson. It was cold. He wanted his voice to sound strong and casual, but it seemed hollow. He suggested a drink. Beeson looked at him slowly and carefully, for a moment more stupid than threatening, then nodded.

"Where?"

Laurie tried to remember a local pub, but instead thought of that July day fourteen years earlier. It had been hot and an acrid smell of dustbins pervaded the tiny garden. He remembered the huge vans parked opposite the house. The Smiths were moving out to Watford, and the removal men sweated as they pulled and pushed the ugly Victorian wardrobe across the short lawn, down the steps and into one of the vans. Chairs, a coal scuttle and a ribbed leather golf bag were stacked in the road. Against the bag leant a drawer and from it one of the men took a tiny mauve and white envelope. Someone said: "Durex for safety", and they all laughed. Laurie rushed to meet Tony as the older boy sauntered down the pavement towards him, and impulsively he queried the mauve and white envelope and the laughter. For answer Tony took him to a toolshed behind the church, and there Laurie was born, aged ten, into his first private hell.

"Where?" he repeated finally.

"I know a pub," said the Guardsman, and started off towards Park Lane, Laurie accompanying meekly.

"You a regular?"

The Guardsman sniffed, then nodded.

"Been in long?"

"Four year."

They crossed Park Lane, and Mayfair seemed less foggy and romantic. The streets were quiet and new fears tormented Laurie. He saw the Guardsman turning on him, attacking and robbing him. A Bentley stopped at the kerb in front of them, and a broad man in a bowler hat stepped out. A taxi cruised slowly past them.

"Long to do?"

"Three year."

"It's jolly damp tonight."

"Yep."

"Like the Army—I mean the Guards?"

"It's better'n prison, I suppose."

They were in Grosvenor Square. Blue-kitted American sailors hurried past or lounged against the doors of chromium-ribbed cars parked at the kerb. They crossed to Brook Street.

"What did you do before you went into the Guards?" A furtive glance accompanied each question, but Beeson's eyes looked straight forward from under the long, curving peak.

"Operator."

"What sort?" For a moment the word "operator" conjured up log-rolling or crane-driving. He even had time to see a brawny navvy with calculating, brown eyes working a pneumatic drill, before Beeson answered "Cinema."

Laurie smiled. "Like it?"

"Better'n this mob."

The pub was empty. Last year's cheerful barmaid was stroking an overfed cat. A gas fire hissed a little cheer into the barren room, the slight flames reflecting in the brass rail. Some of the fog from outside and a square little man with a brown cap would have completed a Ruskin Spear scene. As it was, the frail smoke from the Guardsman's cigarette left the atmosphere clean and furniture-polished.

"Yes, gents?"

"What'll you have?"

"Brown Split."

"Mine's a Worthington," said Laurie, "and my friend's is a———"

"Brown Split."

"One light, one Brown Split," the barmaid repeated cheerfully. "Awful night, gents?"

Beeson studied her legs and apron. "Needn't be," he said.

She poured the drinks and put them on the counter, then looked disappointed as Laurie made for the corner farthest from the bar. The seats were high-backed and covered with red velvet.

"What'll you do when you come out of the Guards?"

The routine of the conversation seemed neither to bore nor amuse Beeson. If he had heard a hundred similar ones, his lean answers carried no overtones to remark it. If this were a new experience, he seemed equally unimpressed. He was interested in his drink and, to the extent that more drinks might be forthcoming, its buyer. If there were a mine to be discovered rather than a few bits of coal, he was content for this to be discovered to him rather than actively to start prospecting.

"What do you do most evenings?"

Beeson shrugged his shoulders. "I don't go much for the women round here."

"Where do you come from?"

"Mitcham."

"Oh, you're a Londoner?" But the Guardsman was intent on a painting of a haystack, two hedges and a field, high up on the wall opposite them. There was a ladder leaning against the haystack with perhaps an inch or so of air between it and the hay.

"Are you interested in painting?" asked Laurie.

The Guardsman nodded affirmatively, then stared hard at Laurie as if searching for a hidden meaning in the question. Laurie avoided the other's eyes. The drink was making him feel unusually light-headed. He felt a sinking sensation in his stomach and a sourness in his throat.

"I paint," he said, suddenly conscious that the barmaid was listening. "As a hobby, I mean. I like to go out on Sundays. You know, just a few sandwiches and the old drawing-book. You ought to try."

"This Sunday?" asked Beeson, taking the invitation literally, translating it into known coinage.

"Why not?" The overfed cat and the barmaid and the room were hazy. Laurie felt a little wild. If only Sunday was the next day!

"I 'aven't any civvies."

"I'll fit you out. We can meet early on Sunday morning. What time can you get out?"

"Nine."

"And go back to my place. My trousers'll be a bit short, but I've got a corduroy pair that are too long for me."

"Corduroy!" The brown eyes narrowed. "Who d'ye think I am? Picasso?"

"Well, I'll find something anyway." Laurie was desperate now. He ordered more drinks.

Beeson drained half the second tankard at one go. Then he leaned back and took off his cap. His hair was short, a rich chocolate colour that looked almost as though it had once been ginger. It reduced the threat but also the stupidity. He became honest-looking, though Laurie shuddered as the word occurred to him. He looked at the rough, strong hand that toyed with the hat and felt secure in his sense of danger. Beeson leant farther back.

"I work in a bookshop." There was no acknowledgement from the Guardsman. "Here in the West End to be precise. Used to work at the same place before the war." Laurie hurried on with his unasked-for information. The chord needed holding. "Must sound funny to you. I mean just selling books. But I like it. You meet all sorts. We had a terrifically well-known racing driver in this afternoon. He bought a gardening book. Sounds funny, doesn't it? You get all sorts of people. That's half the fun. And they get all the titles mixed up and ask for the wrong names, like the heading of a review, that's a common one. You know, the sort of accounts in the newspapers of books. I didn't think I'd get used to it after the R.A.F. That seemed the only life to me then. Flying and——" He paused. "But I've settled down again and now I like it enormously, though it's not very well paid."

"No?"

"Well, not compared to other jobs. But I make a bit out of my painting."

"A lot?"

"Well, not much. I'm not terribly good yet. I've always painted, since I was a boy. I wasn't very happy at home." He glanced at the Guardsman. "My father left us when I was about six. And I used to rush off to my room and paint. My pictures aren't brilliant but one or two people like them. They're sort of easier to understand than most. I mean, I don't paint like Nicholson, you know, abstracts."

"Those you can 'ang upside down?"

"Well, no—yes. That's right! You'll see on Sunday, of course." Laurie paused. "I hope you won't be bored."

"How do you sell your pictures?"

"To friends, or sometimes a gallery takes one or two for their summer bazaar. I do the odd portrait, too." He paused, then plunged: "I'd like to paint you. You've got a sort of interesting face. And your eyes——"

"Nobody's painting me! I'm not the Venus de whatever she was!"

Laurie laughed awkwardly and stared at the barmaid, who went back to stroking the cat. He felt suddenly disappointed. Through a stupid remark he had put the whole outing in jeopardy. His eyes rose from the Guardsman's belted waist to his broad shoulders and pale, slightly pinched face. He avoided the brown eyes and sought for a chlorophyll to kill the taste of the last remark.

"What's your name?" He spoke softly because of the barmaid, but as he spoke the smoked glass door of the bar opened and a shrivelled charlady came in, calling her greeting in a loud, nasal voice: "Evenin' all."

"Tom."

"Mine's Laurie, well Laurence really, but everyone's called me Laurie since I went to Grammar School." He vouchsafed his trust. "My surname's Kingston. Like the town in Surrey."

The Guardsman nodded. "Where you going from here?"

"I've got an appointment," lied Laurie. He only half regretted the lie; a continued meeting was fraught with difficulties and possibilities that he sensed were beyond him.

"A girl?" The Guardsman looked sly and knowing.

"No. Chap I work with. He's working late tonight, but we promised to meet and go to the pictures together. Where'll we meet on Sunday?"

"You know Sloane Square?"

"Yes."

"Tube station at nine."

"Not too early for you?" asked Laurie, for whom it was.

"No. Make the day more interesting."

Laurie stood up. "Coming?"

"No. Not yet. Listen!" The strong fingers gripped Laurie's arm and pinched his skin.

Inconsequently Laurie thought of Plomer's "Self-Made Blonde":

> Hope was running through
> Her heart like sand
> Oh let him stop the flow
> With his strong white hand.

"You listening, Picasso?"

"Yes," answered Laurie, conscious only of the strong white hand.

"Can you lend us something? Just to get a bite with."

Rashly Laurie pulled a ten-shilling note from his pocket and screwed it into Beeson's hand. The Guardsman looked round self-consciously. "That's all right," muttered Laurie, who thought he detected gratitude. "See you Sunday at nine. Sloane Square. Good luck."

He lingered at the door, consciously noting every limb in the sprawling body, every inch of the sallow skin and finally, triumphantly meeting the large, brown eyes. He passed into the street, and as he did so the phrase "make the day more interesting" started to worry him like a rash, and like a rash the more he scratched it, the more it itched.

[2]

"What are you doing on Sunday?" asked the girl. She was small and dark. She wore a tight black jumper and tight black trousers; and a fringe across her forehead.

"Going sketching," answered Laurie.

She put her head on one side and smiled. "Can I come?"

"I'm leaving very early," Laurie replied.

"Please!" The girl jumped off the high stool and put her arm round his waist. "Please!" She drew out the word like a string of chewing gum. "You know how I hate staying at home on Sundays. Mummy drives me mad. Do this, do that, dress up, put on a clean blouse, take off that sweater. And all those awful bores she keeps trying to marry me off to. Please, Laurie."

The Club was almost empty. Upstairs at street level the pubs were open, and the students, the needy and the mean were not prepared to pay the Club's prices for drinks. Farther down the long counter a gaunt man with a strong red beard stared at the girl behind the bar. With the face and manner of a tart, she looked incongruous balancing customers' accounts, but just this she continued to do without seeming to notice him. Everyone who came there made a point of telling everyone else what an easy "lay" she was. It was a Club legend, and as far as anyone with first-hand knowledge could prove, a legend it remained.

"No," said Laurie at last.

"Why not?" The girl squeezed him tightly. The touch of her body excited him, but he turned from the scent of her powder.

"Because I'm going with a friend."

"Who?"

"Just a friend."

"Would I like her?"

"It's a him."

"Then I'll come. What could be more exciting than two men?"

Laurie was silent.

"Do I know him?"

"No."

"How do you know?"

He was becoming irritated. He liked Susan. Usually she was friendly and intelligent; and she could talk sensibly. They had met a year earlier at the Club; and ever since only at the Club. He suspected that she would have liked something more than their casual meetings, but of this he was frightened. When he wanted to leave the Club at the end of an evening, he said: "Just going to the you-know. Back in a second," and never returned. He thought that taking her home might lead to complications.

In one way he would like to have taken her with him on Sunday. It would be safer. Yet no sooner was the word realized than he knew that it was just the thought of danger that made the day so exciting. Besides, intelligent people like Susan had a way of high-lighting the shortcomings of the Beesons of this world.

"Done any painting?" he asked abruptly. He always changed the subject to art when he felt the conversation with Susan was getting out of control. She was an art student, and though not a very good one, her painting had become a symbol of revolt against her parents and their background; and so was vital to her.

"No," she replied, "have you?"

He shook his head. "I keep wanting to. I get terrific ideas until I pick up a brush. Then they go."

"Why don't you just paint—and to hell with ideas?" she demanded, getting back on her stool.

He took a sip at his beer. "Sometimes I do," he said. "That doesn't work either." He looked round him at the bottle-green armchairs and dark, round tables. In one corner a negro played chess with an unkempt, fidgety man whose glasses were lopsided. "The other day I painted a telephone," Laurie started. "I wanted it to convey so much. I put it in an empty room—with a hand visible on the arm of a chair in the left foreground. If it rang it could suddenly connect its owner with a fragment of the world outside. It could please or upset him. It could be a key to goodness knows what or lead to a jail sentence. Or bring love or hate. It seemed symbolic of the unexpectedness of everyday life. It might ring and it might not. It sort of symbolised all our insecurity." Laurie was silent.

"And?"

"By the time I finished the bloody thing it looked like a telephone that had never been connected to anywhere."

"I hate telephones," said Susan. "People hide behind them."

"I always think it's the police," he said; "that is, when I'm not expecting a call."

But she did not hear his provocative remark and the tiny spark that could have flared into confession was snuffed.

"Let's go to the Jazz Club," she said brightly.

"I'm not a member."

"I am."

Laurie hesitated for a moment. "I'm not keen on jazz."

"Then I'll go alone." She finished her drink and slid off the stool. He followed her without a word. He had never had much to do with girls, and never quite knew how to adopt the easy, confident attitude that came so naturally to others. So much of his leisure in his early schooldays had been spent with his mother. He had hardly bothered to make friends and the other boys had resented it. When his mother had suddenly turned all her attention to the man who had become his stepfather, he had abruptly retreated into a shell. Only in the Air Force had he gloriously, but all too briefly, found companionship for the first time. And even then he had finally been betrayed. So now he trailed after Susan, eager to please, but not really sure how to set about it.

In the street it was cold and dark. Italians in American-style clothes hurried along close to the buildings, while the girls perched on high heels deep in shop doorways, hobbling forward only when they saw an unescorted male approaching. Restaurants looked steamy and full. A pavement violinist played Mozart's "Turkish Rondo" atrociously, and lost his place altogether when someone threw a sixpence into his hat. A waiter, running from a pub with three lagers on a tray, laughed and shouted a greeting to the musician as he passed.

"I love Soho," said Laurie after they had walked some way in silence. "It's got a vitality that makes the rest of London seem like a morgue."

"Can't see it at the moment," answered Susan.

"Eyes have they . . ."

"Oh, you always want so much out of life," she said in mock disgust.

"Only way you get anything."

They crossed Oxford Street. In a couple of minutes they were descending the stairs to the Jazz Club. While they waited silently in a queue Laurie remembered the *Empire Story*. There had been four hundred of them in the hold. They had slept on mattresses on floors and tables, and in hammocks slung close together. Ventilators were erratic. It needed a definite act of courage to pass through the single, slim door into the stench of unwashed feet and sweaty bodies.

"A penny for them," said Susan, smiling.

They had stopped at the bottom of the stairs behind a crowd of young people waiting to pay. Through the doorway came the strident tones of brilliantly played jazz, and in an atmosphere made blue with cigarette smoke the dancers could just be seen. Laurie's glasses were instantly steamed up.

"I was thinking of the *Empire Story*," he answered, taking them off and wiping them.

"Hans Andersen?"

"No, a boat."

"A boat?"

"Sort of smell in the hold that scratched your senses in an unforgettable way."

"And?"

"The smell here—it's about as bad."

"All part of the atmosphere—and your vital way of living." She laughed. "Come on, pay up. They're waiting." She had already put her own money on the table, and moved forward without him as he hastily replaced his glasses.

The huge basement was full. At the far end, barely visible through the smoke, was the band, a small group of men and boys in shirtsleeves. In rows around them sat youngsters, mostly male, in two-tone pullovers, jeans and moccasins, their hair cut in the latest crew style. Few had jackets and these were cut low to the navel. Fewer wore ties. Against the centre of the longest wall was a clear oblong of floor, and here they danced.

The boys on the floor mostly had their shirts open to the waist and the girls wore sleeveless blouses. Everyone danced with an intensity that was ferocious. Eyes dilated, staring straight ahead, they flung each other this way and that, under the arm and round again, until perspiration trickled freely down their faces and chests. The deafening music created an orgiastic tension as taut and frightening as the final moments of an Arab wedding.

Susan's small eyes were bright. "Let's dance."

"Not me."

"Come on, spoilsport."

Laurie shook his head vigorously. Susan turned to a group of boys standing near them. The oldest was about eighteen. He had a huge head and a mass of wavy, ginger hair. His broad shoulders were permanently hunched.

"Dance?" asked Susan, raising her eyebrows.

For answer the boy grinned and took hold of her. In a moment they were seized by the fanaticism of the music and the mood on the floor. It was like a spiritual meeting even to the eerie quality of the trumpet ever winding higher and higher. Laurie's attention was taken by a young soldier who was flinging his partner away with one hand and catching her with the other. The soldier was lithe and supple, and each time he pulled the girl to him he arched his spine and threw back his head. Laurie was fascinated. He watched them as they moved slowly round the floor: fling, catch, arch, fling, catch. It was like a ritual. The basic rhythm and heat and smoke combined with the sheer animal grace of the dancers gradually to envelop him. He, too, felt seized by it. He wanted it to go on and on.

The soldier reminded him of Tim, but Tim had come from an upper-class family. They had met at Flying Training School, having accidentally discovered their mutual interest in drawing. The hot-house of wartime conditions had helped their friendship to blossom quickly. Tim's assurance, background and interest in him had given Laurie a new outlook on everything. His terror of flying, which was equalled only by his terror of having to give it up through fear, had been transmuted into exhilaration and excitement through their friendship. It had lasted only eight months, eight months that had seemed simultaneously a lifetime and a prelude to one. Then one night, when they were on leave together, Tim had failed to keep an appointment. Later he told Laurie of the smashing girl that he had met, but Laurie had never understood. Even now watching the soldier who looked a little like Tim, he felt again the deep despair that Tim's explanation had invoked that night.

"Laurie!"

He came out of his trance. It was Susan. She and the ginger-headed youth were dancing near him. The boy was squeezing her tightly. She was struggling to free herself. She seemed caught between the hunched shoulders and huge head. His chin was just above the level of her head, pressing down on it. "Laurie!" She was red in the face now and screaming his name. The ginger-haired boy was grinning. "Laurie!" No one else seemed to notice. Laurie stared straight ahead of him at the band. "Laurie!" He glared at the trumpeter and tapped his fingers on a pillar next to him in time with the music. The rhythm was getting faster. Couples on the floor were shouting. "Laurie, please!" He glanced. They were dancing away from him, still locked together. Then the music stopped. The applause was deafening.

"Laurie! Didn't you hear me?"

Susan was beside him. She was sweating and there were tears in her eyes. "I shouted for you. That brute was killing me." The words came in gasps. "I thought you saw!"

Laurie looked pained and puzzled. He put his hand on her shoulder, then took it away. He started to mouth an apology. Then he saw the soldier talking to the ginger-haired boy. They were pointing at Susan, who had her back to them, and laughing.

"Let's go," said Susan. "I need a drink."

Oxford Street was cold and very quiet. The pavements were almost deserted. They walked quickly without talking. Laurie tried to think of something to say but was frightened of striking the wrong note. When Susan spoke her voice was soft.

"'Bout Sunday. I just remembered I couldn't make it in any case, Laurie. We've got some relations coming."

He said nothing. He wanted to take her arm and beg her to come. He remembered the bitter way in which she had said, "I thought you saw", and he remembered too the young soldier who had arched his spine and thrown back his head as he had pulled his girl towards him. He had borne quite a resemblance to Tim.

[3]

Laurie lived in a basement flat in Smith Street, Chelsea. During the last few months of his four and a half years in the Forces he had often wondered whether he would live at home again or find a flat of his own once out of uniform. Within two days of his return he knew: he must live alone. As a youth his mother's abasement before his stepfather disturbed him at a level which he felt rather than understood. He had become suddenly aware of this man when he was sent off on his own for one, then two, then every evening of the week. The relationship must, he supposed, have started casually, gradually. He had only become aware of it when it was full grown. Now at twenty-four it was all too clear at both levels, and more than his eyes and love for her could bear. So he spent half his gratuity on the premium for a flat and moved in the day before starting work. His Auntie Pam had arrived for tea just as he was about to drive away in the removals van.

To supplement the bed and wardrobe given him by his mother, he spent the rest of his gratuity on various pieces of second-hand furniture. The flat had three rooms, the largest being unfurnished as a studio. He lived in the second largest, which was the front room. The top two feet of its oblong window allowed a narrow view of the railing that bordered the street. Through it he would watch the innumerable legs as they hurried or sauntered to and from the King's Road, while he sipped a cup of black Nescafé which usually completed his supper. His coffee finished, he would go to the back room to paint, the early strokes raining on the canvas until gradually his energy and enthusiasm flagged, and the painting was transformed from a masterpiece to just another "still life".

Usually on Sundays he slept late, then lay on his bed in his dressing-gown, reading the *Sunday Times* or *Observer*. About eleven he would make some coffee and eat cornflakes with milk, finishing his breakfast with brown toast and Cooper's marmalade, a relic of Tim's influence. Then the bath or "The Critics" would claim him; and finally the necessity to dress in a hurry if he were going to his mother or some friends for lunch. Only when he was going out sketching for the day did he break this routine. Then, jerked into life by an alarm clock, he would have a long hot bath to adjust himself to a waking state, eat a quick breakfast and dress before the Sunday "heavies" arrived. On those days he would ration himself to Eric Newton and Neville Wallis, "Comment" in the one paper and Schwartz in the other. Then straight to Victoria station, leaving the rest for the evening and that state of mental exhilaration induced by four or five drawings of the country, still, by their nearness to creation, authentic and inspired.

On the morning of his appointment with Beeson he spent too long in the bath and had to leave the papers wedged in the letter box. Even so it was five past nine when he arrived at Sloane Square underground station. It was a cold morning, but a faint haze and promise of a blue sky beyond it augured well. There were few people about. Men still unshaven and women without make-up hurried from Pimlico streets, bought a paper and hurried back the way they had come. Empty buses drove slowly round the Square, while taxi-drivers read the *News of the World* and *Sunday Pictorial*. They hardly seemed to expect a fare, and the porter from the Royal Court Hotel had to rap on their offside windows to obtain attention. There was no sign of Beeson.

Suddenly Laurie saw a Guardsman approaching. Excitement and fear seized him. He wanted to rush back to his basement flat, unmade bed and unread papers. As the tall figure marched coolly towards him, he rehearsed his greeting. He would be quite friendly but not particularly pleased that the appointment had been kept. Then he saw that it was not Beeson. It was another Guardsman, an ugly, uninteresting oaf who marched past him into the mouth of the underground.

He recalled other Sunday mornings when they went to live in Highbury. He used to leave the house early to avoid his stepfather, who seemed to start by being too pleasant and end by teasing him for his loneliness. He used to wander round the drab streets until lunchtime, avoiding boys from his school, especially Tony, who would twist his arm until he agreed to go to the toolshed behind the church. Later, when he might have wanted to go himself, Tony always pretended not to understand what Laurie meant. And then there was the Sunday when he had come back with his aircrew badge over his tunic pocket. Even his stepfather had bought him a beer that day. But his mother had cried.

It was a quarter past nine. Laurie tried to think of other things, but in vain. He wondered whether perhaps Beeson had been put on guard or was under detention. Beeson was not the sort to stand any nonsense and a sharp reply to a stupid N.C.O. was in keeping with his character. He might, of course, just be on duty, longing to come out and warn Laurie. Or had he perhaps joked when making the arrangement? Worse, was he frightened that Laurie might ask for the ten shillings back? He cursed the loan. But why had Beeson accepted the invitation with such alacrity if he had had no intention of coming? He remembered, though, that that was before he had accepted the money. Then suddenly Beeson was there in front of him and Laurie was confused.

"Hullo. I began to think you weren't coming. On guard or something." He held out his hand which Beeson shook briefly. "You never know in the Forces. I had nearly five years of it myself."

"Which one?"

"The RAF."

"Did you fly?"

"Yes."

Beeson appeared impressed, then changed the subject. "Any grub at your place?"

"Yes of course," Laurie answered. "Haven't you had any breakfast?"

"No."

"Up too late, I bet. Well, we've got to go back to the jolly old dungeon—I call it that because it's a basement—to get you some civvies, so we'll get you something to eat at the same time." They walked to the bus stop. "It's a nice day for going out, anyway. At least I think it's going to be, don't you?"

"Don't know that I can go out."

"Oh?"

"Meetin' the girl at six."

"The girl! Oh well! We can arrange it so as we're back by then." He paused. They were alone at the bus stop and even now there were few people about.

"I thought you didn't like London girls," commented Laurie at last.

"They're orright in the dark," said Beeson. He stared at Laurie, who immediately felt the same tightening, sinking sensation as on their first meeting. "Wouldn't touch any of 'em," he added on second thoughts.

"No?"

"Knew a rich bit that lived over there." He pointed his nose at Sloane Street.

"And did you *touch* her?" Laurie treated the word like a live coal.

"Not 'arf!" said Beeson, and gave one of his near smiles.

The bus came and they boarded it. Laurie exulted in the idea of Beeson subduing women left and right. He drew a perverted pleasure from the mental picture of Beeson seducing innocent, white-faced girls. He had always believed in the tale of wealthy women wanting brute navvies or hefty soldiers as occasional substitutes for their well-bred, less manly husbands, and felt at once that the casting of Beeson for such a role was perfect. Long before they left the bus, his imagination had run complete riot. Only the need to start a conversation as soon as they were alone cut short his mental extravaganza.

"Live 'ere alone?" asked Beeson, as Laurie closed the front door behind him.

"Yes," answered Laurie. The Guardsman seemed enormous in the small flat. Laurie led him into the living-room and told him to sit down. Beeson took off his battledress jacket and sprawled in one of the armchairs, his eyes making an inventory of everything in the room.

"Who done them paintings?" he asked, indicating with a sweeping gesture the three pictures in the room.

"Like them?"

"Orright."

"I did." Laurie tried in vain to sound casual.

"Did you?" The surprised tone was welcome.

"I'll make you something to eat." Laurie turned towards the door. His eyes were caught by the Ronson lighter. He wished he had removed it before going to meet Beeson. It was not so much that he distrusted the Guardsman, which he did, but that he believed that honesty was relative to temptation and need for most people. He had left temptation lying about, and if Beeson pocketed the lighter while he was in the kitchen, he would never have the nerve to demand its return. He had bought the Ronson for his mother on his return from the Forces. But he had planned to give it to her only. When he found that it still meant giving it to his mother and stepfather, he had kept it for himself and bought her three pairs of nylons instead.

Briskly he made the breakfast. He wondered what the Guardsman was doing, but was afraid to keep running into the living-room in case he showed the distrust he felt. When he did go in to ask Beeson whether he wanted coffee or tea, the huge Guardsman was idly flicking the pages of an old *Lilliput*, his face expressionless.

"Tea or coffee, Tom?" He savoured pronouncing the name as if he were tasting a three-star brandy.

"Tea."

"Right."

When Laurie brought the eggs and bacon, Beeson ate quickly and enthusiastically, large spoonfuls of jam on hunks of bread completing his meal. He sat back satisfied and completely relaxed for the first time.

"You do yourself well 'ere," he remarked to Laurie, who had had two cups of tea to keep him company.

"I try to." Laurie wondered whether to broach the subject of the outing yet, but thought it better to wait. "Don't you go home on Sundays?" he asked.

"I don't give a f—— for any of 'em."

"Oh!" The language bruised slightly. Laurie was used to it from his own Service experience and it fitted his conception of Beeson. Yet hearing people swear violently or being kissed by his mother or having to discuss the movements of his bowels always made him feel uncomfortable, as if he had put on a laundered shirt before it was properly dry.

Beeson seemed to guess at once. "You don't swear, do you?" He grinned. "You used Brylcreem instead in the RAF."

"When the occasion demands I swear like the rest," Laurie answered on the defence at once, "but I don't believe in all this indiscriminate f——ing this and f——ing that. It doesn't mean anything any more, does it?" He sounded unconvinced. "It's only mental laziness, after all. Too lazy to look for the right adjective." The moralist was coming out and he wanted to withdraw. "There's no harm in it, of course, except if it's too much of a habit it might slip out at the wrong moment. A chap in a unit I was in did that." He finished his tea. "He went home on leave. Came from a nice home, too. One day at tea he asked for the butter. Nobody heard him, so he asked again. Still nobody replied. 'Pass the f——ing grease,' he called." Laurie shouted the words self-consciously. "Everyone nearly had a fit and he went very red." He paused. "That's sort of what I meant," he concluded lamely.

They were silent for a while. Beeson took out a cigarette and lit it, putting away the packet. After taking a few puffs he brought out the packet again and offered a cigarette to Laurie. The Guardsman piled the plates at one end of the table, then sat back studying the paintings.

"Not selling these?" he queried finally.

"If someone wants them, I'd certainly sell them."

"What's it like at the London Gallery?"

"Do you mean the National Gallery?" asked Laurie.

"One in Trafalgar Square."

"Very interesting. Have you ever been there?"

Beeson shook his head. "Not part of a Guardsman's training. Is it open today?"

"After lunch."

"Might be an idea."

"Jolly good one. We can have lunch somewhere in the West End, then go on afterwards."

"I'm meeting the girl at six."

"Yes." Laurie felt the pain again, as acutely as before.

In the end they went to the Tate Gallery. They ate lunch at the Green Parrot on the Embankment, and walked by the river towards Westminster until they reached Millbank. Beeson was wearing a pair of Laurie's flannels and his new sports coat, his older one being too small for the Guardsman. The flannels were too short and exposed two inches of olive green sock at the bottom of both legs, and only the lowest button of the jacket fastened without pulling, yet the general effect was to soften Beeson. He seemed now like any garage hand or house painter on his day off, and even his manner warmed. Laurie felt safe now that they had left the flat, though every time he met the Guardsman's eyes the sinking sensation made him catch his breath.

Beeson was greatly impressed by Rodin's *Le Baiser* and he examined it carefully, a little self-conscious as he circled it. "They're enjoying themselves," he said at first. Later he added: "Can't believe it's in stone." But Laurie's favourite painting, the *Green Tree Form* by Graham Sutherland, left the Guardsman cold. Twice he moved on to other pictures and was bored when Laurie called him back and tried to explain.

"You'll come to him," he said trying to laugh, but the Guardsman was already studying Nash's *Totes Meer*, seeing, in the shapes of twisted metal, objects whose being Laurie had never suspected, but refusing discussion; and hurrying on instead to an Edward Wadsworth.

Out again in the cold, wintry sunshine Laurie lamented that it was almost impossible to obtain tea in London on a Sunday, then suggested the Club. Beeson was dubious, but finally agreed after reminding Laurie about his date at six.

When they arrived the Club was nearly empty. The owner was playing chess with the man whose glasses were lopsided, and a young man in a lumber jacket and check shirt was doing a cross-word while sipping coffee. In the farthest corner from the door Susan sat reading. As they came in she looked up.

"Hullo, Laurie."

"Hullo, Susan." He felt rather proud. "This is Tom, a great friend of mine." He knew that the "great" must sound incongruous to the others, but could not resist it.

"I thought you two were going sketching?"

"We went to see other people's sketches instead," Laurie replied.

"Meaning?"

"We've just come from the Tate."

"Oh." She turned to Beeson, indicating a green leather armchair beside her, then smiled. "Your first visit?"

"Yes."

Laurie sat on the other side of Susan. How had she guessed that Beeson had never been to the Tate before? What else did her intu-ition enable her to surmise? He felt uncomfortable and frightened that either Susan would ask questions or that Beeson would let him down. Susan had suddenly shrunk from the picture he had always had of her as the broad-minded, friendly girl. He had let her down that night at the Jazz Club and now she would get her revenge.

"I've not seen you here before?"

"No," agreed Tom, "I've not been 'ere before."

Being Sunday the bar was still closed, so when the waitress came to take their order Laurie asked for three coffees. He felt an urgent need to keep control of the conversation, but could think of nothing to say.

"And what," asked Susan, smiling, "did you think of our Tate?"

"I liked the stone thing of the couple kissing. Quite real." Beeson helped himself to a cigarette, then offered her one.

"Oh, you darling! I've quite run out. First thing I thought of when I saw you and Laurie coming in. Thanks." She drew a light from his match. "The Tate, of course, is such a mixture. I mean all those eighteenth-century English landscapes and the Impressionists and the Moderns. Do you paint?"

Beeson shook his head. "Only Nissen 'uts." He paused. "Never had the chance to do the real stuff."

"Now you ought to. To express yourself." She studied his hands, seized one and looked at it closely. "What strength!" she muttered.

"I like dancing better," he said, warming to her. "Not just the Palais stuff but the real thing."

"Have you ever been to the Jazz Club?" she asked. "It's one of my passions."

"You mean the dive in Oxford Street?"

"Yes," she said.

"No," he replied. "Some of the chaps back at barracks 'ave spoken of it."

"You're a soldier?"

"A Guardsman."

"Then," she continued with a flourish, "I shall take the first Guardsman I've ever met to the Jazz Club!"

"What a good idea," put in Laurie. "When shall we go?"

"Tom and I will go tomorrow, if Tom can manage it," she replied gaily. "You're not invited."

"Not invited?" Laurie repeated.

"No," she said very strongly. "When I took you last time you hated it. So you shan't be bored again." She paused. "But I'll look after your friend, won't I?" Her question was directed to Beeson not Laurie.

"Not 'arf," he said, and smiled broadly.

They were silent for a moment. The coffees were brought and Laurie paid for them. He looked at his watch.

"Tom, it's nearly six."

The Guardsman looked at him. "What of it?"

"Your date."

"What date?"

"You know——"

The Guardsman laughed. "I 'aven't no date. Whatever made you think I had?" He turned back to Susan. "He's got women on the brain."

[4]

"It's R/P, Laurie."

"Thanks."

Laurie closed the catalogue and turned to the customer. "I'm so sorry, Madam, but it's reprinting."

"December, I think," Eccles called across the shop.

"It's reprinting in December, Madam. Would you like to put it on order? We'll send you a card when it comes in."

"No, thank you," said the woman briskly. "I only wanted to look at it." She turned away and walked slowly down the shop, not bothering to answer Laurie's "Good morning, Madam."

Laurie put away the Whitaker's and returned to his dusting. The woman had irritated him by not ordering the book. Eccles had irritated him by knowing all the answers. Or was it that since the previous day he had been irritated by nearly everything? Yet the Sunday had exceeded his expectations, and had perhaps shown how far his expectations had fallen short of his inner needs. He pushed back one book and dreamily took out the next.

Susan, Tom and he had stayed at the Club until seven, then had gone to the Continentale to see a stupid French film whose title he had already forgotten. Fernandel was its star and Fernandel annoyed him. Or did his annoyance come from the suspicion—he had seen nothing—that Susan and Tom had been holding hands all through the film? Afterwards they had had a snack, then parted,

Beeson going with Laurie to collect his uniform, while Susan caught a bus home. He flicked a film of dust from the top of a book with a small, dry paintbrush. Again, perhaps it was the way that Susan's eyes had lit up while she and Beeson were talking. Laurie had been out of hearing at the time, paying the bill for their snacks. It all made this Monday particularly irritating.

"Have you the *Vicar of Bullhampton?*"

Laurie turned round. "Any special edition, sir?"

"*Everyman* or *World Classics* will do."

Laurie fetched one, showed it to the customer, then started to wrap it.

The man sighed. "Strange. No one writing like that these days." He sighed again. "What an age that was! What characters that man created! Hundreds of 'em! All alive! And the chap wasn't even a full-time writer, I don't believe."

"No," agreed Laurie, "he wasn't."

The man put down his money, turned to go, then hesitated. "Do you read him?"

"I have done," answered Laurie.

"Try him again now you're older," said the man inconsequently. "Good morning."

"Good morning, sir."

Eccles came across the shop as the door closed. "You ought to read more Trollope, Laurie. 'Specially now you're older."

"Oh, shut up! Can't stand him. If he was alive today, he'd be turning out serials for *Woman's Own*. The Great Pot Boiler himself!"

"And on that Fourth Programme note, let us to lunch."

Laurie followed without answering. He wondered what Eccles would say if he knew that he had spent all yesterday with a Guardsman. He glanced sideways at the round face with its puffed, "churchy" look. He pictured the expression of disgust on it if he even tried to describe the excitement of preceding the tall Guardsman into the darkened flat. They stood on the crossing in the centre of the road, marooned in a slowly shifting mass of taxis and buses, cars and vans, with here and there a deft errand-boy weaving his way swiftly through, but Laurie felt only the huge figure behind him as he fumbled for the living-room switch. For that part of a second during which his hand grasped the switch before the light came on, their bodies touched, and Laurie felt the momentary agony of a man attacked or a woman ravished. Then the light came on and he was left with the cold fear that Beeson might turn nasty. Even as Eccles said "now's our chance", he remembered catching Beeson's eyes on the Ronson, but the Guardsman had replaced the lighter as soon as he had lit his cigarette.

The café was crowded, but upstairs *their* table was vacant. Eccles studied the menu without speaking. It varied little from week to week and they both knew it by heart, but he preserved a sense of dining-out by a quiet consideration of its contents. In their pre-war days at the bookshop they had eaten at a smaller café farther down the road towards Portman Square. Then there had been no choice of main dish.

Laurie had come to the bookshop straight from Grammar School. The Headmaster had wanted him to stay on for another year and try for a scholarship to a university. But his stepfather had said that sort of career was fit for the wealthy; it was time that Laurie earned his keep. For once the two agreed, the boy still being unhappy at school. His Auntie Pam had read in the *Evening Standard* "Appointments Vacant" column that the bookshop needed juniors, and his mother had taken him to be interviewed. He had never been really happy there before the war, but the manager had liked his quiet manner and studious approach, and he had stayed until he volunteered for the RAF.

"What did you do yesterday?" asked Laurie, studying the green plastic cloth.

"Took June to the pictures. The film wasn't bad, but she's in the middle of a you-know. She hadn't mentioned it and I didn't notice anything, so we started back through the park as usual. The moment I started something she burst into tears. How was I to know? I apologised, but that didn't do much good. In the end we both walked in silence until we reached her place. Then she smiled and cried again. They're all the same. They just don't know what they want." He grunted. "Do they?"

"No," agreed Laurie. It was a routine question requiring a routine answer, but he felt as awkward as when people asked him if he was going to get married. He liked to conclude such conversations as quickly and discreetly as possible. Sometimes, though, he felt that it sounded more natural if he made some jovial or casual comment. Either way he was awkward and afraid. A hundred times he had heard Eccles's surprised "Aren't you interested in women or something?" in the split second that he changed a conversation or avoided a question. Yet in spite of all the times that he had imagined the words being spoken, he was still not sure how he would answer if Eccles said them.

"What did you do?"

"Nothing much," replied Laurie. Did Eccles come to town on a Sunday? Had he been seen? How innocent was the question? "Went to the Tate in the afternoon and saw a French film at the Continentale in the evening."

"Who with?"

"A couple of friends."

"Do I know them?" Eccles put down the menu at last.

"I think you met Susan when you came down to my Club with me." He spoke of it as if it were the Athenaeum.

"Oh, that arty girl friend of yours. She struck me as being a bit sexless." He made a crease in the plastic cloth. "Is she?"

Laurie coloured. The waitress came and took their order. His confusion over the question extended to the choice of vegetables, and he wondered whether he could ignore the subject and start a new topic now that a couple of minutes had elapsed.

His stepfather had told him the facts of life when he had left school. He had taken him to a Lyons teashop for lunch one Saturday, his mother alleging a headache and staying at home. The baked beans had been dry and the eggs too hard, and Laurie had spent the awkward half-hour wondering whether the silent people at the next table were listening to his stepfather.

"Does she?"

"Does she what?" Laurie knew his answer was a mistake.

"Grow cucumbers. What do you think?" Eccles wore the expression of a parson on a spree.

"Depends."

"On what?"

Then unusually he lost his temper. "Oh, drop it, Ron, for God's sake!"

The parson returned to his dignity. "I'm sorry," he said, partly offended, partly sincere. "I've never known you to get upset at that sort of talk." He paused. "Sorry."

"It's all right. I'm all on edge today."

"Not well?"

"Oh, I feel all right." He regretted his outburst and wanted to make amends. "I had a funny experience last night and it rather shook me."

The waitress brought their lunch. An enormous, laughing, commercial traveller of a man filled the doorway. For a moment his laughter died when he saw that every table was taken. Then he turned and looked over his shoulder, spoke to someone behind him and burst out laughing again, checking all conversation in the room. The cabbage was watery and the meat was stringy, and Laurie wished that he had not started the story.

"What happened?" asked Eccles, struggling to cut his meat.

"Well, I put Susan on a bus, then caught one to Chelsea."

"Didn't you see her . . ." Then: "Skip it!"

Laurie looked a little puzzled but continued: "As I reached the flat I saw a bloke leaning on the railings outside. He had a khaki uniform on, and a flat cap."

"A Guardsman?"

"Yes, a Guardsman," said Laurie. He felt excited and elated, and tried hard to eat his lunch with studied calm. "He asked me for a light. I said I didn't have one on me, but if he'd like to come down the stairs to the flat I'd get him one." Laurie chewed viciously on a piece of gristle.

"Well?"

"He came down and I got him a match. Then he demanded a quid."

"Demanded?" Eccles sat there, knife and fork at the high port, his mouth slightly open.

"Well, first he asked me to lend him a quid and when I refused he demanded one. Said he'd bash my face in if I didn't give it to him."

"Why didn't you shout for help or hit him?"

"He was about six foot two, a huge, tough bloke."

Eccles looked up from his plate at the last words, and for a moment Laurie was frightened that his voice had echoed his excitement. "I had no choice." He put down his knife and fork. "I just had to give it to him."

Laurie felt weak. He knew that he should never have told the story and was sure that some of the thrill experienced in its telling had been communicated to Eccles. But he also knew that it was an emotion outside the other's range, and so might pass unrecognised. Somehow the tale atoned for his weakness and fear in offering Beeson a pound before the Guardsman had left for barracks the night before. Beeson had been surprised and pleased.

"Did you follow him?"

"No."

"Why not?"

Laurie resented this cross-examination. He had told a story to explain his mood. It was his pound that the Guardsman was supposed to have stolen, so he was entitled to do what he liked. Besides, it was too small a sum to bother about. He would have lost an hour or two's sleep making a statement at the police station. He had almost begun to believe more in his story than in his frenzied pressing of a folded pound note into Beeson's hand when Eccles's voice interrupted his reverie.

"The police would have traced him."

"I doubt it."

"Simple enough. They'd have had an identification parade of every Guardsman known to have been out at that hour. And you'd have picked out the one. That's what you ought to have done, not let the bugger get away with it."

The incongruity of the swearword and Eccles's slightly high-pitched, chanting voice nearly made Laurie smile. It was as if Canon Knowles had used the word "bloody" in one of his unctuous sermons. It occurred to Laurie that now he would probably label the Canon "queer"; in those days he had welcomed his fondling kindness. Then there had been Mr. Johnson, the Maths master, tall and ascetic looking, but given to putting his hands inside boys' shirts and patting their chests.

"No reason for you not to go to the police now," added Eccles. "I wouldn't let the bugger get away with it." He was pleased with his let-justice-be-done air. Crime demanded punishment. Stamp it out. Don't waste time with talk about environment, crowded houses and unmarried mothers. Incant the middle-class equivalent of "Gad, sir, we'll show the scoundrels," and send them to prison. It was that air of satisfied, confident intolerance that made Eccles such a suitable West End bookseller. Sin and Socialism belonged in Charing Cross Road, together with penal reform and psychoanalysis.

But Laurie was already in the forecourt of Wellington Barracks. He was walking slowly up and down lines of tall, tough Guardsmen. Behind him came an officer, a sergeant and a police detective, all waiting for him to say: "That's him!" The reality of his plate, empty now save for the pieces of chewed gristle, hidden behind half a potato, had dissolved into the greater reality of the identification parade. It was a dull day and the cold in his fingers was intensified by the cold, ugly barracks and the rows of silent, motionless Guardsmen who stared in and through him, accusers not accused. He did not even notice that his sweet had arrived, so fearful had he grown that the next pair of eyes, or the one after that, would be those huge, calculating eyes that were Beeson's.

"I'll come with you after we leave here. Won't be too late. If the police ring the barracks straight away they can have a parade this evening. You can always get away early for a thing like this." Eccles chased the last streak of custard round the plate, then licked the back of his spoon, as if accidentally. "There's too much crime these days. We'll show these hooligans, uniform or no uniform."

Two girls at the next table had stopped talking when Eccles had sworn a few minutes earlier. Since then they had strained desperately to catch every word of the conversation. Eccles, or what they could hear of him, sounded like their Sunday newspaper and they felt the comfortable security of his sentiments. But Eccles had also spoken of crime and hooligans and the police; and their senses, trained to respond to the stimuli of the same newspaper's deafening account of the latest crime, were excited. Gradually they leaned more and more towards the two men until the laughing, commercial traveller of a man, who had just returned to see if there was a free table now, might have thought that the two sets of people were one party. His laughter cut the girls off from their contact with life-in-the-raw, and they straightened themselves self-consciously in their chairs. In a moment they were discussing how unfair it was of Ruth's mother not to let her stay at the dance after eleven, but just below the talking level a germ of a story was maturing. By the time they met their boys that evening, Eccles would have become a detective and Laurie an unwilling prosecutor, at least.

Laurie himself only wanted to get away from Eccles. Half an hour earlier he had been a free agent. He could tell the story or keep it to himself. Now he was committed. He had shared his experience and shared his responsibility as a citizen. To refuse to go to the police would mean losing caste in Eccles's eyes. He would almost become an accomplice after the deed. Worse, not bothered by greys and off-whites, Eccles might go to the police himself. Then suddenly, as if stumbling on some original thought, Laurie remembered that the whole story was a fabrication.

A sudden outburst and the need to explain it had led him into this ridiculous situation. Unfortunately the extent of its absurdity did not rule out a sordid aspect. It was impossible for him to confess having made up the whole story and go on working with Eccles. Unless he was prepared to make a much greater confession, few people would have sympathised with his lie, and Eccles was not one of them.

Even the one action in his life which was to have such happy consequences had started from similarly false circumstances. He had threatened his mother so often that he would volunteer for the RAF that when she called his bluff he had felt compelled to implement his threat. He had stalked out of the stuffy dining-room, the stewed apples still unfinished in his dish. He had ignored his stepfather's shouted advice to take cotton wool with him to the Recruiting Centre. And he had been so certain that his slightly defective eyesight would bar him from flying that he had volunteered for it. His acceptance as a probationary radio-observer—the one flying category for which 6:6 eyesight was not required—had cost him two or three nights with hardly any sleep.

"We can skip coffee," proposed Eccles. His delight in the situation made it more dangerous. Here was something new and challenging, a change from selling books or dealing with a girl whose periods always came at week-ends. His parents had a small house and a pre-war Austin Seven: as an only child they would one day be his and he would become a man of property. The sooner he ranged himself on the side of those with property to be protected the better.

The coffee was rarely worth drinking. They ordered it because it entitled them to sit longer at the table. But today Laurie wanted it as never before. His refusal to acquiesce in its abandonment would be the first rung of the ladder of escape. He was not sure whether there would be further rungs. The important thing was to get one foot up first.

"I'm rather thirsty," he announced baldly, but as at the first meeting with Beeson in a slightly cracked voice.

"So am I," said Eccles. "As soon as we've finished with the police we'll slip in the milk bar and have a coffee. There's tons of time."

A bellowing laugh from the commercial traveller of a man seemed to Laurie so perfectly timed as to pretend to a knowledge of the situation. He slipped threepence under his bread plate, followed Eccles to the cash desk and paid his bill. He thought of pretending to faint or of pleading a severe stomach ache, but neither would have carried conviction. He made up his mind to say: "Now look here, Ron. I don't believe in stirring up all this trouble over so small a matter. The boy was probably hard up. He may come from a miserable home where no one has ever shown him any affection. Perhaps he's in trouble." The image of a tough, confident Beeson belied every word, but it was finally his own lack of courage that made him walk meekly beside Eccles, whom he was beginning to hate.

They walked without talking, Eccles wearing his brassy air of a good job done, while Laurie looked pained, puzzled, and resigned by turn. He had spent so much time in his life avoiding trouble. He had lied, camouflaged and drawn complicated veils to ensure a smooth and comfortable life. Now of his own free will he was jumping into a net, each strand of which might set off dangerous traps beyond his escaping experience. This was the moment for refusing to go any farther. If Eccles despised him as a result, then their friendship was in any case not worth the label. He could carry on without Eccles. He could obtain a job elsewhere if necessary. But as he turned to face his friend, as they hurried along, his resolution faded. When they finally halted, they were at the foot of the steps leading to the police station.

"This is it," said Eccles. "You go in and tell them what happened. I'll wait here. No point in my coming in. They'll just wonder who I am."

Laurie nodded. He felt frightened, but his fear was not compounded, as on the previous evening, of terror and excitement. It was a cold, hard fear that made him want to run. He remembered standing outside the Headmaster's door, waiting to be ushered into the study. His relationship with another boy had been unearthed by authority and castigated as indecent. He had already been told that his letters, groping love expressed in groping phrases, might have been written by the scum of the earth. Now sentence was to be passed on his beautiful folly. The moment and the words "scum of the earth" had ever since remained close to the surface of his consciousness, as real whenever brought to the top as they had been on that fateful summer's day. Now as he stood at the bottom of the steps, he knew *that* terror and a fresh one simultaneously.

"Go on," said Eccles, a little irritated.

Laurie nodded again, then started up the steps. At odd moments in his life he had had the feeling that he had been dealt cards well below the average hand. This time he held the Joker.

[5]

They met outside Swan and Edgar on the following Saturday evening. Susan was the first to arrive. She wore no coat and the usual black sweater, but instead of trousers she wore a black, pleated skirt. This made her at once older and more attractive. She watched the people turning the corner from Piccadilly expectantly but not anxiously. He would come, of that she was sure. Yet this was the first date she had ever made outside the art student circle among whom she had spent the last three years.

She was an only child, and had rarely been allowed beyond her mother's short sight. Her school friends had been carefully vetted, their parents' standing and religion being far more important than the girls' own personalities. From the age of fourteen onwards she had wanted to rebel, but her father was only a friendly neutral and her mother all-powerful. Then one day, Miss Sturrocks, her art mistress, had decided that Susan had talent. She had even conveyed that decision to Susan's mother; and from that moment onwards Susan had fought with tears, temper and tantrums until finally she had been enrolled in an Art School.

Piccadilly Circus was normally busy. Crowds moved slowly in all directions, funnelling into cinemas, theatres, and restaurants. A few people stood under Eros and looked at the flashing advertisements. Their garish brilliance brought an air of melancholy and mystery to the unlit corners, and a lone prostitute outside a bank looked extravagantly alluring from the distance of Swan and Edgar.

Susan was sure that Tom would come. She knew nothing of duties and guards, and had she been familiar with them would still have been sure that Tom would circumvent such trivial obstacles. She felt sorry, though, for those waiting round her, and there were many. Some stood in the doorway of the store itself, others waited by the kerb. Nearly everyone carried a newspaper and looked, every so often, at the Stop Press for the nth time. All seemed anxious and prepared for disappointment. An absurdly fat man kept taking the loose change from his trouser pocket, counting and then letting it slip back coin by coin. A girl with greasy, black hair and badly worn heels kept fetching a mirror from her bag and studying her face. Susan turned away as it caught the rays from a lamp and reflected them into her eyes.

Then Tom came, accompanied by another Guardsman. Her relief at seeing him turn the corner showed her certainty to have been only hope, and it smothered any resentment she felt at his not being alone.

"Hullo, Tom." She sounded cheerful and assured, almost brassy.

He took her outstretched hand, then turned to his companion. "Be seein' yer, Bert." He winked.

"Be good!" said Bert, smiling at Susan. He left them.

"What about some grub first?" asked Tom. "I'm starved. Didn't get off till half six. Chased us about all bloody afternoon like a gang of navvies."

"We may as well. We'll need some energy for bopping."

Tom laughed. He had forgotten about the Jazz Club, their reason for meeting. He wondered whether arty girls were free as legend made them. He hoped so.

"Where?"

"I know," she said and took his arm. She piloted him across Regent Street, under the Arch and round, through Shaftesbury Avenue into Great Windmill Street.

She led him into a small Jewish snack bar. The windows were steamed up, and inside it was hot and noisy. Behind a flashy counter four talkative Jewish men in white coats displayed salt beef, gherkins, *gefilte fish*, *sauerkraut*, *lutkas*, eggs and onions, *chraine*, apple strudel and lemon tea that always seemed too hot to drink. Conversation was shot out in all directions by the men in white coats, here and there answered, or if directed over their shoulders, obeyed by white-coated minions who otherwise collected the dirty cups or buttered the rye bread. Round the walls were high swivel stools and mirrors. On the stools sat dark-jowled men and white-faced women. Everyone ate and talked simultaneously and incessantly. Everyone looked more jaded and ugly than usual because of the bright orange light with which the fluorescent strips flooded the shop.

"Vienna and two *lutkas* for Mr. Diamond."

"Sour or sweet, sir?"

"Come on, Hymie, give us some of this second-rate salt beef and leave the gee-gees alone."

"Just bringing you a knife and fork. Where's that *schlemiel* got to?"

"Seen Abe this week?"

"Believe me, if I were his father . . ."

"By my life it's the best smoked salmon . . ."

Tom seemed to be the only Gentile there, surrounded by loud chatter, steam from the coffee machine on the counter and the incessant chewing of chopped liver, eggs and onions and rye bread crammed with salt beef. Through the open doorway he could see people going slowly by in the cold night air: a negro, a group of soldiers, a couple from the North. Inside the noise and activity never relaxed. Beside him, holding his hand, Susan bridged the two. Cool and calm, she shouted her order over the heads of those sitting at the counter on the high stools.

"But what we having?" he asked for the third time.

She smiled at him, defiantly proud of the powerful *goy* who stood beside her. "You'll see," she said and laughed.

Tom was hungry and wolfed the plate of eggs and salami that Susan handed him. His unorthodox methods of eating were unremarkable in the snack bar, and only his uniform and the peculiarity of eating without talking marked him as different from the other customers. He refused a lemon tea and waited impatiently while Susan had hers. Then just as she finished, he noticed some Coca-Cola on the shelves behind the counter, and wanted a bottle of it.

"Get me one, Susan, will you?"

She looked at him over the top of her nearly empty glass. "You ask for it."

He shook his head. "No."

"Don't be silly. You won't get bitten."

For a moment he sulked, then went up to the counter. One of the white-coated men was carving salt beef that had just come from the basement, while the rest were taking money, serving portions of chopped liver or just talking. Tom towered above the other customers but no one appeared to notice him. He turned back to see if Susan was watching. She was.

"Can I have a Coca-Cola?"

His words were spoken unheard. For a moment his large eyes narrowed slightly, and Susan from the side could almost hear the unspoken, anti-Semitic oath by watching them. He was tapping his right foot against the chromium rib at the bottom of the counter. Then he kicked it and stopped. He looked at Susan again and this time she smiled encouragingly. He shrugged his shoulders and smiled back. "Can I help you, sir?"

"What? Oh! A coke, please."

"Certainly! One Coca-Cola for the gentleman in uniform," and a spotty youth came out of a room at the back, carrying the drink already poured. Tom paid for it and for the rest of their snacks before rejoining Susan.

In the street outside they argued about the payment. Susan was used to paying her share. Among the students with whom she went around this was the usual practice. To Tom it lacked the quality of gallantry that he associated with taking out a lady, and by his standards Susan was a lady, not just a better-class edition of the girls who hung round Marble Arch every evening. He was unable to express this and Susan was too inexperienced to understand, so they argued all the way up Wardour Street, stopping occasionally to look in the display windows where the film companies paraded their masterpieces to the very people too blunted to respond: employees of other film companies.

"Did you see that?" asked Susan.

"No. I don't see much of the film when I go to the cinema." Tom looked at her and smiled. "Did you?"

"Yes. It's the sort of thing you'd like. I don't mind seeing it again either. The colour's wonderful and the dancing's awfully good."

"How do you know what I'd like?" It was the same half-aggressive, half-defiant tone of "Nobody's painting me!" Neither Susan nor Laurie yet knew the tender places. They poked blindly like a dentist searching for decay and were surprised when they touched a nerve and the patient jumped.

"Oh, I do," Susan replied knowingly, but blushing and uncomfortable at the same time. She paused, then seized Tom's arm. "And I know you'll let me pay half the cost of the snack."

"You know more'n I do."

"Please!"

"No!"

The boys at the Art School had been so different from the determinedly middle-class boys that her mother was always inviting home. Now Tom was different to both. Her mother's victims would have cars. They would drive her to the Ace of Spades and try to kiss her on the way home. The art students would take her to the New Lindsey and substitute the top of the bus for a car. Neither would have dared the frankness of Tom's remark about the cinema—and she loved it.

Then they saw another film which Susan had seen but not Tom. She made no suggestion about their seeing it together. Only when they came to a window which advertised the most colossal movie ever did Susan suggest their going together. Tom agreed. As they went down the stone steps to the Jazz Club he wondered what Bert had thought of Susan. Nobody in his room had believed in his date. Bert would shake them; and it was Bert who owed him a pint of beer. This would teach everyone to call him a liar! While he thought and triumphed, Susan paid.

The Club was crowded. There were less dancers on the floor than last time, but round the walls groups of boys in American-styled clothes, with occasionally a girl among them, made it difficult to move from one place to another. Over the hubbub of chatter came the strident and brilliant noise of the band. As Susan and Tom made their way to the floor the atmosphere gradually enveloped them, possessing their senses at first tentatively then completely. Even before they started dancing, their feet were tapping and bodies swaying.

They gave themselves to the drug for as long as the band were prepared to administer it. Supple, lithe movements were stitched to the framework provided by an insistent ground rhythm. They felt their way forward with abandon and assurance, as if their highly complicated dance routine had been rehearsed a hundred times. Occasionally they shouted a word at each other, but mostly they danced in silence, faces tense and eyes riveted by a strange fervour. That, too, seemed almost rehearsed.

When the music stopped Tom and Susan were sweating freely. They stood facing one another, smiling and panting, an ecstasy softening into a joint experience. The ease with which they had adapted themselves to each other gave them a feeling of having crossed not one but many streams. The harmony of their steps and movements became a symbol for their feelings. True or false, it had a certain reality at the time. To each of them in a different way it seemed to seal their need of one another.

As Susan wiped her brow she swung round until she noticed the boy with wavy ginger hair and hunched shoulders. He was talking to a soldier and grinning. She watched him calmly, almost daring him to see and stare at her. Laurie had inexplicably let her down. It had been something that belonged to that side of his character that made him make silly excuses towards the end of an evening, and then vanish for the night. She had expected each occasion to be the last she would ever see of him. But at their next meeting he would be as friendly as ever, until the end of that evening. The incident in the Jazz Club had been stranger though, for afterwards he had seemed upset by his failure. Even at that stage he had not offered to go back to demand an apology from the ginger-haired youth.

"Someone you know?" asked Tom, following her gaze.

"Yes," she replied. "Common brute!" she added, then told Tom the whole story in answer to his questions.

"I'll go and fix 'im," said Tom, and Susan was excited by his hard, determined look almost as much as Laurie would have been. But she took hold of his arm and restrained him. "Don't. It's not worth it."

"I'll say it is. Bastards like that oughtn't to get away with it."

"It'll only make it difficult for me down here."

At that moment the ginger-haired youth saw her. He said something to the soldier beside him, who laughed, then sauntered to the edge of the floor. Tom ran his fingers round the edge of his collar. He watched the youth intently.

"Hiyyah, sister! Want a dance?"

"Buzz!" Tom almost spat the word.

"What's that?" The ginger-haired youth faced him, unsmiling now.

"Buzz, I said. And quick. And keep your filthy hands off my girl, see?"

The language was clear and unequivocal. The youth understood. As the music started he walked away quickly and rejoined the soldier. By the time that Susan and Tom started dancing again they had both left, and Susan's intense pleasure was marred by a fear that they had gone to fetch friends to help attack Tom. Tom danced less effortlessly. Once or twice he was not ready to catch or spin her at the right moment, and when Susan suggested a cold drink he left the floor ahead of her.

They edged their way to the bar and drank two orangeades each. Then a good-looking boy in a maroon corduroy jacket came up to Susan.

"Hullo, Sue. Seen Jackie around?"

"No. I haven't seen him for weeks." She paused as if anticipating a refutation, then introduced the two men. "Tom, this is Bernard. He's from the same Art School."

They shook hands. "I finished my two years in June," said Bernard. "How long you got?"

"I'm a regular."

They were all silent, then Bernard said: "Tell Jackie I'm looking for him, Sue, will you? I must be off. So long."

"Who's Jackie?"

"Boy at the Art School."

"Was Laurie at the school?"

"No, at least he used to go to evening classes. I didn't know him then. Some student or other introduced us at the Club."

"You've known him some time?"

"About a year." She studied his face. He looked puzzled or concerned. "There's never been anything between us."

"You didn't need to tell me that."

"What do you mean?" It was her turn to be puzzled.

"He's 'queer,' of course." He spoke with a sneer.

"Laurie?"

"'Course. Didn't you know?"

She knew immediately that she had always known. She understood now the curious departures. She was still puzzled over the incident on the dance floor. Yet even now he failed to fit into the category as sampled at the Art School. There was nothing outwardly feminine or feline about Laurie; there were no whisks of the hands as he spoke, no discreet make-up, no catty remarks about other boys.

"I like Laurie," she heard herself saying, "whatever he is." She had a man now, a tough six-foot-two Guardsman. Laurie was just a friend interested in painting and the particular direction of his sex urge was of little importance.

"He's all right." To Susan the words were slightly mean. They were part indifference, part sneer. In fact, they would have exceeded Laurie's wildest dreams had he been able to measure their harmlessness against the mocking chatter that filled the walls of the Guards barracks whenever "queers" came under discussion. "Queers" at such times were abnormal men who could be robbed or blackmailed, would pay well for their furtive pleasures or offered opportunities for satisfying sadistic tendencies. At other times when thought of, but not discussed, individual "queers" were quite nice men who wanted to do funny things but were willing to pay for their pleasure.

But they soon forgot Laurie and went back to their dancing. Once again they matched each other's movements with effortless harmony. Their minds were freed of worries, opinions and thoughts, and filled with the exciting, noisy music. To its rhythm their limbs answered instantly and smoothly. It was as if one brain controlled both their bodies and limbs, while their minds, apart from acting as reflectors for the rhythmic impulses, merged into a state of intoxication that bound them temporarily into a perfect union.

By the time that they left the Jazz Club they were exhausted on the physical plane and wildly stimulated on the emotional. Tom's grip round Susan's waist, as they walked down Oxford Street, was more than a pleasantly protective hold; it was a strong, sensual grip that aroused Susan to a point where she accepted his offer to accompany her home. She knew that she was acting recklessly, but the stimulation of the dancing took time to wear off. The bus journey sobered her, allowing the knowledge of her rashness to come to the surface.

Tom remained elated. He was only a little irritated because he had proposed to leave his home ground. He did not know whether there was a porch or alleyway near Susan's house and was suddenly shy to ask. He wanted one, too, and his need made him hold her hand tightly and respond when he felt her answering pleasure.

Once off the bus they walked slowly because Susan forced him to a slow pace. He searched eagerly for a recreation ground or dark lane, but all was built-up and well lit.

"You'll know the way back?" she asked.

"'Course." She noticed that his voice was a little higher-pitched than usual and was worried. Then she stopped.

"What's up?" he asked.

"You'd better not come any farther," she said. She was becoming a little frightened and tried to make out his expression, but the nearest street light was behind him. She felt at once alone and unprotected, and at the same time an easy target for every neighbour who knew her mother. Someone would appear round one corner or the other, even though at the moment the road and pavement were deserted. A dry leaf was blown fitfully across the pavement and stuck against her shoe. Tom's fingers were fondling her waist urgently. Now and then he squeezed her whole body against him so that she gasped for breath.

"Tom, when can we meet again?"

"Why can't I see you to the door?"

"In case my people see you."

"Well?"

She wanted to avoid a quarrel. "Please. I must go. I'll explain next time, really I will. It's not easy. They wouldn't understand. Not at first." She tried to draw away, but he held her tightly.

Holding her waist with his right hand, he pulled her towards him with his left and, bending down, tried to kiss her. She resisted for a moment and his lips found her chin, then her cheeks, then firmly and finally her lips. Gradually she relaxed, then tensed again, this time with him. After a few moments they drew apart, the tension and argument lost in the knowledge of each other and the feeling of desire and satisfaction that it gave.

"Susan!"

It was a woman's voice and it came from behind Tom. They both looked round, Susan frightened and Tom annoyed. The small, grey-haired woman in a musquash coat had made a stage entry. They had heard neither footsteps nor the banging of gates. At one moment they were looking at each other, sensually conscious only of each other's eyes and lips and bodies. At the next she stood there, a whole summons of charges contained in the tone of her voice. It was an accusation, not a recognition.

"Tom, this is my Auntie Beck. Auntie, this is Tom."

"A soldier! Good evening! You come home, Susie!" The evidence seen, sentence was pronounced and the little woman walked straight on down the road, not looking back but certain that Susan would follow. She did. After a brief look at Tom she turned and ran after her aunt. In a second he caught her up, held her and kissed her again. Then she ran.

"Day after tomorrow. The 'dilly at seven," he shouted after her.

She looked back just before she reached her aunt. The silhouette of a tall, flat-capped Guardsman was strong against the distant lamp post. His face was in darkness, but in the moment that the look lasted she could see, in her mind and clearly, Tom's eyes, large and warm. As she followed her aunt up the steps of the house she remembered that she had an evening class at half past six on the day after tomorrow. But it was too late to go back: the road was empty.

[6]

Laurie ordered a neat rum. It was rare for him to treat himself to spirits. A Guinness or a milk stout were the strongest drinks for which he willingly paid. He liked alcohol, but compounded his liking with a tinge of guilt: it was a waste of money, the pouring away of coin that would buy him other things: some new shirts, an electric toaster, a copy of *The Studio*. Tonight, however, he drank the price of the magazine without a glimmer of guilt and soon followed it with that of a second copy. For the first time since the nightmare of midday a feeling of ease and comparative security began to spread through him. Another rum still and the incident would have lost all sense of reality and become a horrible dream.

He looked round him. Being early in the evening the Club was fairly empty. At his right a man and woman sipped their drinks in silence. They seemed too suburban for the Club and Laurie wondered briefly how they had come to descend the steps into the basement which belonged, as if by natural right, to the young, the arty and the misfits. The man looked slightly familiar. He had a big head with close-cropped, grey hair and kind, mournful eyes. Then Laurie remembered: he resembled the police sergeant before whose desk he had finally arrived after lunch that day. It had been a moment of torment. He looked into those other kind, mournful eyes, speechless and unable to think. Someone had moved up behind him and he wondered if it was Eccles, but he remained facing the desk.

"Well?" queried the sergeant.

"I've lost my cigarette case. Silver one."

"When?"

He stumbled on, inventing the circumstances wildly.

"Where? What time? Shape? Size?" He answered the questions, forgetting the answers as he gave them.

The sergeant had noted it all down, checked a list in front of him and quietly, sympathetically, told him that no such case had been found. If it subsequently turned up, he would be notified. But it was unlikely, especially as Laurie had explained that there were no initials or other engraving on it. He had turned away to the door, tremendously relieved and yet suddenly and irrationally terrified because his name was now on the books in a police station. Eccles was talking to a uniformed constable as he came out into the daylight.

Laurie turned away from the man with the close-cropped, grey hair and sought the eyes of the girl behind the bar, the same whom rumour placed in everyone's bed. He ordered another rum, conscious now that he was spending too much, but certain that his experience deserved some reward. It would soften the details of his experience and blur the last painful jab, received as he ran down the steps to Eccles.

His fellow worker had turned from the constable as soon as he had seen Laurie.

"Well, what did they say?"

It was an awkward moment. If he lied, the policeman would hear, might become curious and make inquiries from the sergeant within. If he hedged, Eccles might become insistent. He looked at his watch.

"Good Lord, Ron, look at the time! Come on!" He smiled vaguely at the policeman and hurried off down the road, Eccles following closely.

"What happened, Laurie?"

"Whatever you succeed in drowning will float to the top again later." It was a deep, quiet voice that cut across Laurie's train of thought and replaced his answer to Eccles with its amused, friendly tone. The owner of the Club came in, opened a wooden box over the shelf of bottles and pressed down some switches. As Laurie turned to look at the man who had spoken, the basement was flooded with a bright, harsh light.

"Oh?" Laurie's annoyance at the interruption was reflected in his tone.

"As a bookseller you should know that," the man went on, disregarding Laurie's surprise. "I say 'as a bookseller' because we're always supposed to be so intelligent."

Laurie swung round on his stool. "How did you know I was a bookseller?" he asked.

"I've seen you at London branch meetings," replied the man beside him. "Will you have another rum, or is the drowning complete?"

Laurie asked for a beer. The man turned to the girl and ordered two beers. Laurie studied him carefully. It was difficult to gauge his age; he could have been thirty or even forty, rimless glasses and a heavy jowl possibly adding ten years or, as likely, making one think they did. He was immaculately dressed and wore his clothes with an ease that showed their quality and cut to be an experience of long standing. Incongruously he bit his nails, though only at those rare moments when he was not pulling at a highly polished pipe.

The man passed Laurie a beer. "Cheers," he said, then raising his bushy eyebrows, "Crisis over?"

"I think so," Laurie replied, and again he had a desire to tell the stranger the story of the Guardsman, adding, to complete the expiation, that of the police station. The man did not answer at once and, after waiting a few moments, Laurie's mind caught the severed ends of his daydream. He went back to the questioning police sergeant, but realised that his daydream had gone beyond that before the interruption. Then he remembered hurrying down the road with Ron, who badgered him insistently.

"Why couldn't they do anything?"

"No proof."

"If you picked him out on a parade he'd probably confess."

"Probably isn't enough. You can't go about accusing anyone and everyone."

"Did they say that?"

"Yes . . . well . . . yes."

"You sound as though you want to protect the bugger."

The man who had bought Laurie a drink saved him again. "Do you come here often?" he asked.

"Quite."

"Lonely?" The question was accompanied by an intense stare.

"Yes and no," replied Laurie.

"Aren't we all?"

Laurie was suspicious of the way the conversation was leading.

He himself had troubles enough to unburden without accepting the weight of someone else's as well. "Where's your bookshop?"

For half an hour they talked bookshops, then books. Abruptly the man, whose name was Norman Wayne, told of putting a *Kinsey Report* in his window and of customers' objections to it. The conversation slid easily across the points. Laurie was no longer antagonistic. Wayne's deep knowledge of books had stirred his respect and he listened attentively as the older man pleaded for tolerance.

"Tolerance must be the keynote to our lives now the aeroplane had brought us so close together." He revolved his beer glass on the green, leather-topped counter. "Racial tolerance, religious tolerance, sex tolerance. They talk of altering laws, letting negroes into this hotel and that, and accepting 'queers' as normal human beings." He was watching Laurie very closely now, but the younger man allowed his eyes to wander up and down the huge array of bottles without meeting Wayne's. "But legal tolerance counts for nothing, or precious little anyway. The 'queer' will live within the law, but the ordinary man in the street will still despise and ostracise him."

Laurie turned at last to face him. "Does it much matter? 'Queers' have their own little circles. They seem quite happy mostly." He was still chary of committing himself, only ninety-nine per cent certain of his companion. "The law is the thing. Once someone has to live outside it, his whole outlook becomes warped."

"In what way?"

Laurie thought for a moment. "Supposing a chap's 'queer' and has a boy friend. The boy friend goes housebreaking and steals some jewellery. The 'queer' finds out. He's terrified and knows he ought to go to the police. But if he does, what of his own position? If the boy's much younger than him or of a different social class, there'll be raised eyebrows and possibly questions. Besides, the boy could turn nasty, and blackmail's just as effective when not expressed. So the 'queer' turns a blind eye and becomes doubly outside the law." He paused, then added: "He's on his way down."

"Not necessarily at all. Presumably someone who is genuinely homosexual assumes that his condition is an accident of heredity or environment. So the particular law relating to him has no validity for him, is against his nature. So he disobeys it; but that should have nothing to do with his attitude to other laws. He's only using his unfortunate accident of birth to avoid responsibility. If he fails to take some action in answer to the boy's housebreaking, he's giving way to moral weakness and probably a bit of self-pity as well."

Although they had met so recently, Laurie felt that the truth of Norman's words specifically attacked his own way of life. He slid from one slippery rock to the other, always seeking to escape moral responsibility by clutching at anything above water as an excuse for his attitude to life's problems. He had been born an exception. His home life had been unhappy. Even the one real friend he had made in the RAF had betrayed him. In turn he clung to each of these three lifebuoys, knowing deep down that they were slippery and dangerous and that he had much better strike out for dry land. He even guessed that the swim would be less arduous than he liked to imagine; and it would provide its own exhilaration as he went on, each stroke counting towards the eventual success of standing firmly on the dry land of a philosophy and courage that accepted responsibility in every guise. Yet if after two or three strokes the waves threatened or his arm seemed tired, he would grope blindly for one of the lifebuoys and lie on it, safe and full of remorse.

They sat for a while without speaking. Laurie reflected on their conversation. It had been curiously intense, and intimate in that it had the flavour of a late-night conversation carried on between two close friends. Strangers normally indulged in small talk when they first met, then perhaps passed through the pick of their joke repertoire into the tentative, testing stage where vague questions brought vague answers, and the backgrounds began to be filled in. But they were not, at least not quite, strangers. They felt the same bond as two men experience who have never met before, but discover early on that they went to the same school. A whole private code is opened to them and to them alone. Even their language is sprinkled with phrases that only the initiated can understand. A segment of their outlook is identical, however much they differ in every other way or even within the segment. So it was with Wayne and Laurie.

Wayne slid off the stool. "I must be getting along," he said. He held out his hand.

"I'm awfully pleased to have met you," said Laurie. The exclusive mood was dissolved. They were just two men who had met casually in a club, although Laurie wanted to hint that another meeting might be welcome. "Perhaps we'll meet again down here." Wayne smiled for answer, and Laurie added: "Thanks for taking my mind off other things."

Wayne smiled again, turned and walked slowly across the room. At the door he stood and hesitated. He put his hand in his jacket pocket, took out some letters and straightened them. Then he replaced them and came back to Laurie, who had been watching him all the time.

"I just thought I'd mention," he started, "that if you're ever hard up for a job I might be able to use someone like you in my shop." Before Laurie could answer he turned away and left the Club.

[7]

Beeson arrived unexpectedly the next evening. Laurie had gone straight home after a tiring day at the book-shop. He had found it difficult to concentrate, worried and excited by Norman Wayne's proposal. He was not sure what it entailed. It had sounded like a normal offer of a job, but Laurie had heard that offers from men like Wayne were not unqualified. Yet in every other respect the advantages would be enormous. The shop would be small and intimate, and the clientele regular. He would handle all kinds of books instead of those of two departments only. Wayne would doubtless be a sympathetic and stimulating person to work for, and although they had never discussed painting, Laurie felt sure he would be encouraged in his work. As he reached the same stage in his thoughts for the tenth time that day, the bell rang. He glanced at the almost empty canvas with slight disgust, put down his palette and wiped his hands on a dirty rag.

When he opened the door Beeson stepped in. "'Ullo!"

"Hullo, Tom. I didn't expect to see you. Come in." The invitation was offered as the Guardsman came into the living-room without it. Laurie followed. "Fancy a beer? I've got a couple of pints of brown ale hidden away somewhere."

"Your own cellar? I wouldn't mind."

Laurie went to the kitchen and returned with a pint bottle of brown ale. He emptied most of it into a glass for Beeson, and kept the remains for himself. He tried to sprawl in the armchair opposite the Guardsman, but he neither looked nor felt comfortable. Had the Guardsman come for money? Or just to beat him up? His fear was illogical and enormous, the product of being different and all its social implications, not just of the immediate situation. Tom was no longer the magnificent brute with the huge, white hands whom he had met, rashly dated, and met again. He was a tough, dangerous bully capable of hurting Laurie badly and possibly of inflicting wounds whose scars would never disappear. Almost as a reflex to his thoughts he took off his glasses, folded and placed them gently on the small, unpainted table by the armchair; conscious even then that in a struggle, however brief and one-sided, they were still too near the danger area.

"Not expecting anyone, are you?"

"No."

The question and his unthinking automatic answer added to his fear. Why ask that? Why had he answered that no one was expected? Laurie felt a tremendous desire to get up and run, leave the flat to the Guardsman, sacrificing anything and everything that Beeson might take. His eyes caught the Ronson lighter and he glanced furtively at Beeson. The Guardsman was drinking his beer, his large eyes staring moodily into the glass. Laurie looked at one of his pictures and tried to think of something to say. It seemed silly, in his state of tension, to talk of the weather. He tried to remember something that had been said or done on the previous Sunday. Then he remembered Susan.

"Did you meet Susan last night?"

"You bet."

"Did you have a good time?"

"What do you think? She took me to some Jew snack bar for grub, then we went to the Jazz Club."

"Did you like it?"

"It or her?" He licked some froth from the outside of his glass. "I told that ginger bastard where he got off. The one she met when you was looking after 'er. Couldn't bloody well get out of the place quick enough after, either. I'd a' thumped him, too, only Susan said no."

So Susan had told him of the incident. Was that why he had come round? To avenge his treatment of the girl? Laurie was aware of the fantastic air of melodrama with which he engulfed every situation, yet the fear remained. Tom, though, was becoming less the stranger than the powerful complement whose need Laurie again began to feel so strongly.

"Took 'er 'ome after. Lucky enough there's a park round where she lives. She wasn't having any at first, but I soon got her ready for it."

"You mean you——"

"Yeah!"

Laurie became wildly stimulated, excitement compounding with fear until the latter was lost in the former. He became giddy and light-headed, possessed by an intoxicated mood that he had first felt ten years earlier in a clearing on Clifton Downs. Sent to live for a time with his grandmother in Bristol, he had gone to school there, and on Saturday afternoons and Sundays had taken to walking alone on the Downs. There, on a patch of green grass in a short stretch of closely planted woodland, he had come across a lady's handbag. It was in the days when he had started surreptitiously to smoke, buying single cigarettes from other boys with pennies from his grandmother.

The bag had been black and difficult to open. It had lain on its side in the long grass, and after a quick look round to make sure that nobody was watching, he had seized it and started to search rapidly through its contents. He had already framed a mental image of himself at the police station, receiving a huge reward from its owner, when his trembling hand touched the hard, square edges of a box of cigarettes. He had clutched the box and some matches, and stuffed them both into his pocket. Dropping the handbag where he had found it, he had run, as if chased, deep into the wood, stopping at last with the same feeling of light-headedness and intoxication that held him now, took possession of his head and body, and left him at once exhilarated and powerless.

"Were you in the Battle of Britain?"

"No. Just after."

"And you flew a plane?"

"I was the observer in one."

He raised his eyebrows. "Goes to show." He half grinned. "What an Air Force!" He picked up his glass again.

Laurie smiled back.

"'Ow long you known Susan?" asked Tom after draining his glass.

"About a year."

"Any more beer?"

"I'll have a look. I don't keep much in the house. We usually go to the pub round the corner."

"We?"

"Well—anyone who drops in."

Laurie went to the kitchen and returned with another bottle of brown ale which he divided as unequally as the first. His fear of Beeson had abated, yet he was still sure that the Guardsman was going to make some request. For the first time there was something hesitant about Beeson's manner. He was afraid, that was it; he, Tom Beeson, Guardsman, was afraid. For a moment Laurie exulted, then his sense of security vanished as he realised that Beeson's fear was a false one; brute force was on the Guardsman's side, and when one lived outside the law's boundaries, even in only one direction, brute force was the law. So he waited for the blow, not wishing the visit to be curtailed, but hoping that it would come quickly. Once more he tried to think of something to say, conscious that each moment's silence made casual speech between them more difficult. Finally it was Beeson who spoke.

"I'm seeing Susan again."

"Oh?"

"She go with lots of blokes?"

"Not seriously. Art students usually go around in droves and she's no exception."

"There's no one set on her?"

"I don't know about that, but I doubt whether she's very interested in anyone special."

"Perhaps they don't know 'ow to go about it?"

"Perhaps."

Laurie was sure that Beeson was still only skirmishing. He was leading up to something, and Laurie wondered whether he was giving the answers that would help him arrive. It was cold in the room and Laurie turned on the second bar of the electric fire. Beeson at once leant forward in his chair and cupped his hands round it.

"Cold?" asked Laurie.

"Bit."

Laurie finished his drink. He wondered whether it would be a good idea to suggest going round the corner for another. It would serve to get Beeson away from the flat and to reduce the tension between them. In the street it was easier to talk of awkward subjects than it was in a room where looking away became so pointed.

"Is Susan the marrying type?"

Laurie wanted to laugh. So that was it. Beeson had fallen for her, or perhaps it was even more stupid; he just wanted to marry and Susan seemed a fair bet to aid him in his scheme.

"Eh?" The Guardsman waited eagerly for his answer.

"I'd say she definitely was," said Laurie, though in fact he believed the opposite.

"Is she sort of fussy about, you know, education and all that?"

It was hard to refrain from laughing, not just a quiet chuckle but a wild, almost delirious guffaw. "She's very broad-minded, Tom."

Another silence followed.

"'Ow old is she?"

"Your guess is as good as mine."

"'Bout?"

"I've no idea. I'm not much good at guessing ages."

They lapsed into silence for a little, then Beeson tried again. "Is she used to a grand sort of life?"

"Not particularly."

The Guardsman pondered this for a moment, but his expression showed that he was unconvinced. "Can you lend us a suit for me to meet her in?"

"No!" Laurie was surprised by his bold answer, and then afraid of it. "I've only got two and I'll need them both. When one is at the cleaner's——"

"Some other civvies?"

"I'm not very well off in the clothes line at the moment, but——"

"What about lending me some money to get a suit with? I'll pay you back." He looked at Laurie with the eager sincerity of a child. "Really I will."

Laurie was tempted. He had a little put away. He had plans for it: a holiday abroad or a motor bike. But Tom's unexpected thaw, the first complete one that he had witnessed, struck a chord in Laurie. He identified the Guardsman's selfish eagerness with a plea for help to an only friend. He had come to Laurie for assistance. No true friend could refuse. As he was about to accede the bell rang long and shrilly.

The Guardsman's expression froze again. "'Oo's that?"

"I don't know," answered Laurie petulantly. Who was it? Who could it be? He rarely had unexpected callers in the evenings, in fact he was unable to recall a single surprise visit at night since he had lived there. Was it the police? Had they found his cigarette case? He almost smiled as he fell into the trap of his own lie. Had Eccles been to see them and told the whole story? How could he explain a Guardsman to whoever it was? He considered not answering at all, but then remembered that the front-room light could be seen even with the curtains closed. The bell rang again, this time accompanied by a sharp, military knocking.

"What's 'olding yer?" asked Beeson, tense yet taunting the other's tenseness. "Stuck to yer chair?"

"Just going," answered Laurie, getting up slowly from the armchair. "Just going." Should he try to hide Beeson? He went into the hall as the bell rang again, three short, sharp rings accompanied by renewed knocking.

He opened the door. It was Eccles. Laurie stood there looking at his fellow assistant. Eccles had never visited him before. Why now? How would he explain Beeson?

"Well, aren't you going to ask me in, Laurie?"

"'Course, Ron. Sorry. I was so surprised seeing you there. Come on in."

Eccles smiled and crossed the threshold. "I think I've caught you in the act, old man. Who is she?"

Laurie mustered a smile and led him into the living-room.

[8]

Beeson contracted like mimosa in a cold room. At the sight of Eccles he became hard and unyielding. Eccles in his turn lost some of his assurance before a word was spoken. The story that he had heard at lunchtime, coupled with the long delay in the door being answered, made him wonder whether this was the same Guardsman come again to blackmail Laurie for money. But the empty beer glasses and Laurie's continued seriousness despite, or was it because of, Eccles's arrival weighed against this.

"I'll be getting along," said Beeson as soon as the introductions were complete.

"Don't go on my account, old boy," put in Eccles. "I'm only staying five minutes. The unexpected guest. Ha-ha! Laurie told you what happened to him Sunday? One of your——"

"Sunday?" queried Beeson, his large eyes narrowing.

"Sunday it was."

"Laurie was with me Sunday." The Guardsman looked puzzled and a little reproachful.

"After I left you and Susan, Tom. I'll tell you all about it later. Sorry there's no beer left, Ron. You would pay your first visit when we've just drained the last drop. In town for the night?" Laurie was beyond caring how transparent were his efforts to change the conversation. The one need was to do just that. Tomorrow he would invent another story.

"Nasty incident," said Eccles, determined to drop the conversation when he wanted and not when he was ordered. "Police are damned inefficient, too. What do we pay rates for, I want to know, if a man has no protection in his own home?" He paused, realising that he had lost the Guardsman's attention. "How long you in that mob for?"

"I'm a regular."

"Like it?"

The conversation followed almost the same pattern as the very first one between Laurie and Beeson. Beeson's answers were a little slower this time, for he was trying to think while he spoke. When Eccles had come in he was sure that the new arrival was not "queer"; the exposure of one of the usual conversational techniques had caused him to change his mind. Besides, it was probable anyway: "queers" usually knocked around with other "queers". He wondered vaguely whether the visit had been planned, forgetting that his own call had been unexpected.

Laurie waited for the situation to blow up. It was beyond fear or worry. Sooner or later some hint would be given, and Eccles would understand what he was and that the whole of the police station incident had been a pointless, lying story. He was not sure whether Eccles would become rude and walk out, or just present a quiet, oh-so-English ultimatum: either you resign from the shop or I shall tell Mr. Moore what you are. All this, or so it seemed at the moment, because he had invented a stupid lie to excuse his brusqueness.

He knew that he ought to concentrate on the conversation between Eccles and Tom, especially as Eccles was asking questions, but he was more worried by the situation for its example than for itself. He hated lying, yet always ended by lying, even to himself. It had started way back with the need to pretend that he had been reading a book in the church toolshed on that hot July day; that he had caught at a boy's waist in the gym to stop himself slipping; that he went out with girls. He wanted to tell and live the truth. He wanted to be a whole person, not just half a one and the rest filled in with lies, exaggerations and imagined virtues. From time to time he strove sincerely to achieve his wish, but the plaster fabric of his life hung over him always, and sooner or later a flake would chip from it, flutter down and mar his new-found honesty.

"Do you do guards at the Palace?"

"Yeah."

"Must be quite a thrill."

"Blow that for a lark!"

Or was he incapable of being honest all the time? Was there something in his make-up that precluded honesty? The thought alarmed him. Such a vision of himself, were it true, would mean that he would never be at peace with himself. Whenever he might feel secure in his work, home or art, even in his sex life given sufficient integration, there would always be the scratching of his conscience, maddening in its quiet destructiveness of everything beautiful and settled. Truth must be there for all, needing only the action of acceptance. Nobody was excluded by birth or circumstance from it. Nobody! It needed only courage and willpower, and given these, the treacherous years, the years of lies and inventions, half-truths and exaggerations could finally be erased.

"What happens when you're on guard if a kid comes up and touches you?"

"Put your tongue out, if no one's looking. Keep still, if they are."

"And if you move?"

"You've had it if you're seen."

Tomorrow he would tell Eccles the truth, tomorrow he would explain that he had invented the story of the cigarette case to excuse his sharpness, told it as one might tell a dream, and like a dream it had not actually happened, only could have or still might. Tomorrow he would confess that by some accident of birth or environment he was not like other men, not like Eccles. He was different and non-conformist, but this difference in no way made a decent life impossible. He had no designs on minors or innocent youths, nor did he want to misbehave in public places. He wanted his friends to know the truth and respect him in spite of it. Then Eccles asked: "How long have you known Laurie?" and even before the Guardsman could reply, the bubble burst and he knew that tomorrow itself was a lie, the latest in the endless, dreary series.

"Not long."

"Where did you meet?" This time the question was aimed at Laurie, who sat on a hard chair facing Beeson to the left of Eccles. Like the other questions it was spoken without special emphasis, as if simply to make conversation.

"Marble Arch." He would try the truth.

"What's the time?" asked Beeson.

Eccles and Laurie both looked at their watches. "Quarter to nine," said Eccles.

"I must be getting along." Beeson stood up and nodded to Eccles, then smiled at Laurie. "Be seein' you, I expect."

"Yes, any time you like. Always drop in when you get bored. I'll tell Susan I saw you."

"I'm meeting 'er tomorrow."

"Where?"

"Outside Swan and Edgar's." The Guardsman picked up his cap. "Half six." He adjusted his belt thoughtfully, then put on his cap. He looked at the two men in turn, smiling the while in a knowing way. "Say," he started, addressing Laurie but intending the message for Eccles as well, "if your friend sort of wants a friend, I could fix him up with a pal of mine. You know." He nodded.

They all knew at once: Eccles the truth, Laurie its cost and Beeson that he had said the wrong thing. He froze and without a further word turned to the door. Laurie followed and opened the door for him. The Guardsman passed through it without looking back, leaving Laurie with the small comfort of a "Sorry, mate," as he made his way back to the sitting-room. The Guardsman's steps sounded clearly on the pavement outside, loud at first then getting fainter in the distance.

Eccles knew now, but he wanted confirmation, for with it would come the satisfaction that the hunter always feels when he has the scapegoat in his power. It is his chance to avenge his pride. If he had been more perceptive and knowledgeable, he would have known long ago. Instead he had been led up the garden path and his credulity demanded compensation. By the time that Laurie was seated on the chair vacated by the Guardsman, Eccles was once more smiling and sure of himself.

"Nice bloke."

"Yes," agreed Laurie.

"Rather quiet, too. You'd expect him to be the big, blustering type."

"Yes, you would."

"Is he interested in painting?"

"Yes."

"That how you came to know one another?"

"Sort of. I wanted to paint him. Strong, masculine type." He stopped, conscious that the lies were beginning to mount.

"Cigarette?"

"Thanks."

"What did he mean when he said if your friend sort of wants a friend I could fix him up with a pal?" His tone was sharper now.

"I don't know really."

"You don't what? Come off it, Laurie."

This was the truth. This was going to hurt. There was to be no retreat from here, no clinging to lies or vague remarks about art. The moment had come. He waited for Eccles to follow up his advantage, but the other was in no hurry. Self-pity was welling in Laurie, overrunning his desire to state the cold, simple truth. He wanted to throw his accident of birth at Eccles's feet, squirm there with it and bleat until his friend sympathised and pitied him. If only Eccles would be sensible and allow him to tell the truth!

"What was all that nonsense at lunch yesterday? Eh? You perverts are all the same. You try and seduce decent, ordinary blokes like that Guardsman, then squeal when they make you pay."

Laurie stood up and leant on the mantelpiece. "What do you mean—perverts? Can I help how I was born? It might have been you or me or Beeson——"

"Born! Everyone's born the same. I heard that story when I was in the Army. You haven't the guts to go after a woman in the normal way, so you sneak round boys. But don't bring me into it, see?" He was showing anger now. "Don't tell your friend I want to get fixed up with his filthy pals." He stubbed out his cigarette. "And keep away from me—and the shop. We don't want your type polluting the atmosphere, dragging every schoolboy into a corner to show him filthy sex books."

"But, Ron——"

"Don't 'Ron' me either!"

"What about countries where it isn't against the law? Like France? What about all the famous people who've been 'queer'? They've given the world something even if they were perverts, as you call them. What about Michelangelo, Leonardo da Vinci——"

"They didn't go about chasing boys. They controlled themselves —and, anyway, there weren't half so many of them as perverts like to make out. They suppressed the filthy side of themselves and created things—instead of inviting half-wit Guardsmen to secret drinking parties."

"Listen, Ron! Listen! That's all I ask. Just let me say this and then you can go. You needn't see me again. I won't come back to the shop. But just listen."

"I'm listening. Go on." Eccles stood up and faced him, his hand on the mantelpiece, almost touching the blue and grey pottery ashtray, a present to Laurie from the shop's manager. There was hate and contempt in his expression.

"Listen, Ron. What's the difference between the 'me' you're talking to now and the 'me' of a quarter of an hour ago? Eh? I'm the same person and you know it."

"Quarter of an hour ago I didn't know you were a pervert. That's all and that's enough."

"But I haven't changed, Ron."

"Nor would you bloody well have changed if I'd have just found out you were a murderer. What I know is what *has* changed, see? And it makes me feel bloody sick to think of the time I've spent with you." He moved closer and put his hand on Laurie's shoulder. For a moment Laurie thought that Eccles was going to strike him. "Now just get this straight, Laurence Kingston. If you ever set foot in that shop or cross my path again, I'll mash you within an inch of your life." He stopped as if searching for the phrase that would clinch his ultimatum. Finally he turned, spat in the grate, and muttering "Filthy little pervert", walked quickly out of the room and house without closing either door behind him.

For a few moments Laurie stood by the mantelpiece, his left hand feverishly tracing its bevelled edge, quite numb. Then he began quietly to cry.

[9]

Susan was as late at their second meeting as the Guardsman had been at their first, but Beeson showed no sign of concern. Girls had always kept the dates they made with him. Girls in fact had only one interest: to get a man, and then marry him. Normally it was up to a man to allow the first but evade the second. This time, however, Beeson was interested in both. The Guardsman had a picture of Susan waiting outside the barracks for him each evening, while Guardsmen going off duty whistled inwardly and asked each other whose missus she was. Perhaps his father would lend him enough to buy a decent ring; it would glitter in the lamp-light as she stood waiting for him.

Beeson lived in Battersea, not Mitcham as he had once told Laurie. To him Mitcham was Bishop's Avenue or Gerrard's Cross, or perhaps both rolled into one. His mother had taken him there with his three brothers when he was five years old, and ever since it had remained a stretch of country with huge houses and tall, leaning trees. He had never been back, and when others spoke of a Mitcham in dreary rows of council houses, he concluded that the district, like Disraeli's England, was divided into two. So he continued to "come from Mitcham" to everyone except his mates in the Army.

Of all the unmarried Guardsmen in his unit he lived nearest to his home; across Chelsea Bridge, right in the main road at the end of the park and seventh on the left going towards Wandsworth. Yet he rarely went home. When he did the family were friendly, giving him birthday and Christmas presents or a meal, as the occasion demanded. His enlistment in the Guards had served as a resignation from the family unit. To his father it was an abdication from responsibility, both of supporting the home and of getting a steady job that would one day allow him to marry. To his mother it was the desertion of the son who had always been the least dependent on her. For Beeson himself it was another stage on the restless journey from job to job, an enforced halt this time, because he had contracted to stay seven years and hardly hated the life enough to desert. Dissatisfaction with life in the Guards was expressed in small bouts of absence without leave. These were always terminated by giving himself up, and he viewed the subsequent punishment with equanimity.

The Beesons lived in a house which was small, squalid and without bathroom or lavatory. The last was shared with three of the other houses pressed into a block of sixteen, grey bricks caked with the grime spewed from the adjacent power station and railways. When Laurie first saw the street it instantly reminded him of drawings by Sutherland and Piper of East End streets in the blitz. It had, in its dreary sameness, grubby street children and pathetic lace curtains, the quality of a nightmare. Its acceptance by Tom and his family was more reluctant than an outsider might have thought; for the Guardsman pictured himself living with Susan in a small, red-bricked house on the outskirts of London; in front of it a neat path, behind it a little garden, and on either side no house for at least five yards.

While still sure that Susan would come, Tom began to feel uncomfortable. His uniform made him conspicuous among the drably dressed people who leant against the display windows of Swan and Edgar. Piccadilly Circus in any case was no place for a lone Guardsman to be standing. He began to get irritated when men gave him sharp, inviting stares. They ought to have met elsewhere. Why was she so late? Did she not realise how embarrassing it was for him? When she finally rounded the corner from Regent Street, she was exactly half an hour late.

"Hullo," she said breathlessly.

"'Lo." His tone made it clear that her apology would have to precede his smile.

"Tom." She took his arm. "Tom, I've got a friend round the corner."

"'Oo?" He narrowed his eyes.

"Only a girl friend of mine. I had to bring her or else my father wouldn't let me come. I'll explain later. Come on. We can't keep her waiting."

"'Er waiting!" With a great show of reluctance he allowed himself to be led round the corner.

A short way up Regent Street a girl was waiting for them. A little older than Susan, she had long, dark hair and a Mediterranean face of coarse but compelling beauty. Unlike Susan, who wore the slacks and jumper that Tom had seen on their first meeting, she was smartly dressed in a long, black coat, high-heeled shoes and a jade green scarf. She smiled in a pleasant but doubtful way as the others approached, and shook hands gingerly with Tom when Susan introduced them.

"Daddy wouldn't let me come out alone after the other evening, so I had to say I was going out with Angela. Then he kept on talking for so long—and as we hadn't said we were going anywhere special, we just had to stay and be nice." She paused and Angela, carefully avoiding Tom's eyes, nodded half-heartedly. "Where shall we go?"

She addressed the question to Tom, but had to add another "Well?" before he answered: "Wherever you want."

They stood on the pavement getting colder, each waiting for the other to make a suggestion. Susan hoped that Angela would make some excuse and leave them, but felt that she could hardly suggest it after the girl had come all the way to the West End for her benefit. Angela herself wanted to leave them, mainly because she recoiled from Tom, but hesitated to let down Susan's parents. Tom became steadily more annoyed as the minutes went by. Finally his anger got the better of him.

"What *you* doing?" he asked Angela, speaking to her directly for the first time. "Once that's settled we know where to arrange to meet after."

"Angela's coming with us," said Susan quickly, hurt for her friend's sake and by this new aspect of Tom.

"Oh?" said Tom, surprised. He looked up and down the street as if seeking inspiration. "I got to be in early tonight," he announced sharply.

"Why?" asked Susan.

Angela spoke before he could answer. "I've just remembered that I really have something to do, Sue. Look, I'll meet you back here at ten. Is that all right?" She smiled at Susan and made as if to depart.

"Are you sure that's all right?" Susan asked her.

"Of course. See you later." She hurried off without saying anything to Tom.

They strolled back towards Piccadilly Circus, Tom watching the traffic, Susan occasionally glancing at him, but mostly pretending to study shop windows. Without a word they passed round one side of the Circus, across Piccadilly and down Lower Regent Street, each waiting for the other to speak.

"You shouldn't have spoken to Angela like that," Susan started, scolding gently. "If she hadn't come all the way up with me I couldn't have come. It's not fair on her." They crossed Pall Mall and went on down the steps to the Mall itself, but he made no attempt to answer or even acknowledge that she had spoken.

"Tom, it wasn't fair, was it?" Beneath her soft, persuasive tone she was beginning to get angry.

"Orright, it wasn't fair." He sulked openly now.

"Tom, there's no need to say it like that. Angela's a sweet girl and was only trying to help."

"'Ow should I say it then?"

She stopped still. "Tom, what's the matter with you tonight?"

"With me? I suppose you think I like 'anging round Piccadilly while all those bloody perverts like your friend Laurie stare at me. Bloody little——"

"You don't have to swear because you're angry."

"So my language ain't good enough now. First I don't know 'ow to speak to your 'oity-toity friends. Now you don't like my language." He stared at the ground. "Well, I shan't bloody well talk then."

Susan made no attempt to answer for a minute. Then her feeling of being committed overcame her more local anger. She had had the row with her parents and the argument with Angela. She had defended Tom and their friendship until the tears were postponed for privacy, but were there just the same. Now she was losing what she had fought for, feeling it slip away and making her struggle a waste. She was losing the first man who had ever wanted her for herself, and not for the pictures she would paint, the arty clothes she would grace or her views on Picasso, Braque and Francis Bacon.

They stopped by some railings in St. James's Park and gazed self-consciously at the thin stream of water. They were anxious to appear in harmony to others who might be passing, but conscious of the barrier between them and, in Tom's case, not eager to remove it unless pride were first assuaged. If she had turned and stalked away, he might have followed, for he, too, had committed himself, boasted of her to others, even shown her briefly to Bert. But when he felt her hand seize his arm, he sensed his victory and wanted it proclaimed.

"Tom." She spoke softly and kindly. "Tom, we mustn't quarrel like this. It's silly." She looked up at him to see if he was responding, but he continued to stare fixedly at the water. "Tom, this is only the start and we're already quarrelling like a couple of kids. It's so silly." She paused. "Don't you think so?"

Only a questioning raise of the eyebrows acknowledged that he was listening, but it was enough for her. "Tom, I'm sorry if I was late, but I really couldn't help it. It was all I could do to get hold of Angela and persuade her to come. Otherwise Daddy has refused to let me out. It's all terribly stupid. But they're like that. I'm sorry you had to wait, though. You do understand, don't you?"

He nodded.

"Say so, please, Tom."

"All right. I understand. But don't go leaving me waiting like that again."

For a moment anger blazed in her and she could hardly restrain her temper. But she let it cool before she answered. "We'll find some better place to meet." She tried a little laugh. "And I'll see that I'm always, always early." She looked up at him. "Look at me, Tom. That's better. Why so severe?"

"Nothing." His tone was still sulky.

Again she felt defeated. Suddenly she caught him by the shoulder and neck, pulled him forward and kissed him hard. He made no effort either to resist or return her feeling, and she let him go, hungry for his savage show of affection of the other night. Now she wanted to feel the tight grip of his huge hands and the fierce pressure of his lips, yearning the while for the smell of nicotine and maleness that he exuded.

Puzzled and unhappy she stared at the water, not sure how to arouse him from his sulking. For a moment she doubted her picture of a simple, unaffected youth and wondered if he, too, was not complicated in his own way. Her joy at meeting someone whose energy was not consumed by Art School cliques and groups, arguments and personalities, liaisons and teachers, was clouded momentarily by a picture of Tom as a neurotic misfit who had slunk into the Army. Although she knew nothing about him, he had stood for all that was uncomplicated and unsophisticated, all that was male as distinct from the men she met at school, who were only half men. Her anger changed to despair. She wanted to run home and cry at her father's side, silently admitting by her tears that her parents had been right. Then at last she turned and walked away from him, without a word or even a backward glance.

She walked back through St. James's Park, across the Mall and up the steps. At first she thought that he was following, and she listened for his heavy footsteps, irritated by the noise of cars and other people. At the Mall she looked right then left for traffic and managed, almost naturally, to glance over her shoulder. She saw no one behind her, but was not sure that she had covered the whole arc in so quick a look. At the top of the steps she stopped and turned to look back without pretence. There was no one to be seen on the far side of the road, and the emptiness was immediately reflected inside her. Bitterly she regretted leaving him. As long as she had stayed there was a chance of winning him over. Now she did not even know his proper address. She tried to see as far as the railings where they had stood, but the night was too dark.

She went on towards Lower Regent Street and started up it. At one of the steamship offices she stopped and looked in the window, studied without really seeing the details of the wonderful model ship that graced the window. Then impulsively she turned and ran back down the road, just conscious of people staring at her, but not caring. Back down the steps, back across the Mall, into the gardens and down the path. But the railings, when she reached them, were deserted. She scanned the paths, but there was no tall Guardsman's figure to be seen. From the little bridge that spanned the stream six paths branched, and she looked at them in turn as if to see which would beckon. Finally she chose the one that went in the direction of Victoria and ran along it, increasing her pace when two Guardsmen whistled and catcalled from a near-by path. At the road she stopped, out of breath and doubly despairing when she knew for certain that she had lost him.

She walked back slowly, skirting the gardens and going round by the Palace and down the Mall. This time she passed the steamship companies' offices without looking in the windows, hating herself for her impulsiveness, gradually seeing Tom again as the norm that she longed for and herself as the spoilt, neurotic member of the artistic clan. At Piccadilly Circus she stopped, then made her way to the Monseigneur News Theatre, automatically paying and entering, going to seek the comfort and anonymity of the darkness as a girl fifty years earlier might have sought the solitude of an empty church as a home for her despair. Sometimes she was conscious of the images on the screen and their meaning, but mostly she gave way to self-pity and self-hate. She was not religious in the sense that she believed and worshipped in the faith of her parents, but she called on God to help her, and more humbly to forgive her pride.

At five to ten she left the cinema and made her way to the meeting place in Regent Street, still empty but a little less despairing. As she reached the place where they had parted, she saw Angela in the distance, walking past the New Gallery towards her. Should she tell her what had happened? Should she, and so admit that her friend had been right after all?

"Susan!" Tom came out of a shop doorway and was beside her as he spoke.

Angela had nearly reached them and was waving gaily. "Susan, I'm sorry." That was all he said, or perhaps all that he had time to say before the other girl arrived.

"Enjoy yourselves?"

"Yes," answered Susan, nearly in tears. "Wonderfully. And you?"

[10]

In winter the front at Hove still displays charm and beauty. The Regency terraces and Brunswick Square, unlittered lawns and deserted promenades all regain the dignity which their architects once gave them. No one seems on pleasure bent. Braces and knobbly knees, swimming caps and scorched skin are remote indeed from the elderly residents in sensible tweeds and leather shoes. Behind the Regency façade lie the two towns, busy summer and winter with their own teeming inhabitants. Rarely does a bright winter's day bring them to the sea front. They are town not seaside dwellers, and only become aware of their littoral position during those same months that other town folk yearn for the sea, and sigh.

Laurie walked almost alone on the wide, pink promenade. He stepped carefully between the lines of the paving stones as he had when a child. "Fifty-five minutes to London" a large green notice had proclaimed at the station, long out of date in its estimate, but giving dormitory dwellers a feeling of living near the capital. To Laurie it might have said five hours, so cut off did he feel from London. The air was clear and he knew no one, and more important no one knew him. The scene of his shame was far behind, banished by the magic of the journey and the change it had entailed.

Undramatically he felt that he had eluded his pursuers and was safe. Even the sense of safety was exhilarating, for it carried with it a knowledge of temporary undefined duration.

When Laurie had been a child, he had heard grown-ups speak of Nazi persecution. "They're hunting the Jews," they had said, and he had translated the phrase into a visual equivalent. He had actually seen little men with beaked noses slinking close to buildings, spat at and kicked by everyone. He knew now how unnecessary the details had been. Nobody was actually chasing or spitting at him. But the possibility was almost as disturbing to his inner peace as the reality. This man and woman coming slowly towards him along the front, tightly wrapped in heavy coats, gloves and hats, were his potential pursuers. One word out of place, a foot amiss and they would become Eccles in their turn.

He turned to the railings and leant on them, looking out to sea. The waves were massive and pounding, dragging shoals of pebbles as they ebbed, then dashing them back on the beach. The wind was strong and carried with it sprays of spume and the tang of salt water. Even as he stood there, the sea's ponderous, dignified movements calmed him. Despite the display of fury at the edge and on the surface, the great mass hardly moved. It would be there hardly changed tomorrow and the next day, and the day after that. Summer would see its fringe peopled with shouting holiday-makers; winter would again bring more fury, but always the same ponderous mass, shifting hugely a few feet this way or that. So it was with his life. When the terror of the moment had ebbed, and even while it was still there, he would have to go on eating and sleeping. Food and a roof needed money. Money meant work and these basic needs would be the same during and after disgrace or prison. Yet as long as he was well and able to work, so long would there be hope of building a new life.

For a moment he became almost courageous. He would return to London, get a new job and start again. He would find a new flat, new club and new friends. There would be no more compromise or pretence. Everyone would be fully informed from the start. Postponed revelations with their consequent upheavals would be impossible. He started to walk again, close to the railings. As he passed a breakwater a huge wave broke over it and the spray was carried inland on the wind. He felt its biting freshness on his face and exulted. For a brief period he knew that everything except his actual physical life could be renewed, and the tingling of his skin under the cold salt spume underwrote that.

He stopped to clean his glasses and watch two small boys un-selfconsciously parading down the promenade. They were deep in conversation and Laurie envied their assurance and innocence. Then he turned back towards Brighton. Until then the sky had been grey and heavy, but as he started back the sun made a shy appearance, lighting as it did the gloomy yellow fronts of the Regency houses and the incongruous, aluminium lamp standards.

Then his new-found courage failed. It was true that he was free to start again, but it was also true that his nature would lead him, however he might struggle, down the very road whose end he had just reached. Even if he could mould or change this nature that was him, society's conventions would still defeat his endeavour. He might overcome his moral cowardice and forewarn those who accepted his friendship, but to what strange landlord, for example, could he explain himself? Yet if this one person was unaware of the truth, his security and peace would in time be threatened. How easy it must be, he thought, for those who can commend the questioning side of themselves to some unquestioning faith. For him such a solution was still beyond reach.

He walked on past the big hotels until he reached East Street. There he crossed the road and turned off the front, stopping before a modern bookshop on the left-hand side. He went in. He fingered the books idly, wondering perhaps if he ought to seek a job out of London.

"Can I help you?"

He let go the book and looked at the small, smiling girl who had addressed him. "No, thanks. I'm just browsing."

She seemed disappointed. "Certainly."

"Fact is," he said, partly to alleviate her disappointment and partly at the relief of meeting someone to talk to, "I'm on a bus-man's holiday. I'm a bookseller myself."

"Really?" she said, still smiling. She seemed about to follow up the conversation, then changed her mind and started to straighten some books. "It's cold today."

"Yes," he agreed and moved away to some other shelves.

The books were the same as those among which he worked, the same new novels, best-selling escape stories, bulging cookery books; even the same piles of those titles whose sale everyone had prophesied but nobody witnessed. He wondered whether his firm would give him a good reference. What, if anything, had Eccles already told them? Would he be satisfied by Laurie's leaving? Perhaps he was already sorry for his angry display of last night.

Laurie had wired the shop first thing that morning, wording the telegram to imply that someone else had sent it for him: "Kingston confined bed with 'flu," it had read. It had seemed then the obvious or perhaps the only course. Now he was not so sure. He would still have to go to the shop both to give notice and collect his cards. Or could he write and say that he was feeling generally run down and would like a seaside or country job? If Eccles had said nothing they would probably reply sympathetically, even perhaps offer him a few weeks' salary. He had worked for them for some time and was due to be given his own department. All this was now wasted. In one stupid lunch-time story he had thrown away six years of diligent, sober service. Momentarily he wished that Eccles had been run over on his way home on the previous night. What an intolerant, prejudiced bastard his friend was! He recalled now that he had twice changed his holiday dates to suit Eccles, and had also given him one of the most successful little watercolours that he had ever done.

Laurie moved round the shop, handling a book here, reading a blurb there, but all the impotent anger of the night before began to form again. Easygoing by nature, he began to hate Eccles and see in him all the forces of reaction and prejudice in his life. He closed a book with a snap and left the shop. He had to have a drink. Out in the street again his attention was distracted by a Guardsman, a smaller, more vital Beeson. Laurie watched him until their eyes met, then he hurried away, not looking back but absurdly, deeply frightened, waiting for the jeering shout as one waits for the child behind to fling a snowball.

He forgot about his drink and entered a snack bar, glancing round furtively as he went through the door. The long plastic counter was deserted. He studied the menu that was pinned high

on the pink wall facing. Why was pink so in vogue? Even public
lavatories were being tiled in pink, not to mention husky East End
youths who sported pink shirts and pink ties. Was the whole nation
becoming effeminate? He wanted to run after the Guardsman and
let his eyes feed on the rough khaki material, but he was being
asked what he wanted by a bored-looking man with a pink, rabbity
face. He ordered baked beans on toast and regretted not going to
a proper restaurant.

"Hullo!"

Laurie looked round. It was the girl from the bookshop. She
jumped on the high stool beside him, smiling as she had in the
shop. She wore an olive green coat and yellow scarf, and seemed
older now.

"Do you always eat here?" he asked.

"When funds are low," she replied. She ordered some sandwiches and a coffee. "Which bookshop do you work in?"

He told her and had one of those quick, incisive pictures of her
calling at the shop on her next visit to town, and being met with
curious, questioning looks when she mentioned his name.

"Do you like it?" she asked.

"Yes. I've been there ten years, except for the time I was in the
Forces."

"I've been here for nearly three years," she said.

They were silent for a while, then she asked: "Are you on a
special day off?"

"Not really," he said. I must not lie. I must not lie. "I felt awful
this morning, so I sent a wire to the shop and said I had a bilious
attack."

"How nice," she said. "I mean I wouldn't dare do a thing like
that."

"You would if you felt fed up enough." His voice carried a
strong sense of conviction, and he saw that he had disturbed her.

She busied herself with a sandwich for a little. "Are things as
difficult as all that?" she ventured.

"Yes." He wanted to go on, but had become aware that the
man with the pink, rabbity face was listening. He had seen the
face somewhere before. Was it at school? Or in the shop? Then
he remembered: it was a dentist in the Services who had refused

to fill a very painful tooth, and had offered him the alternative of taking it out or leaving him in pain. He could remember the brutal hardness behind the flabby, effeminate features, and he wondered whether this man could be similarly sadistic and unyielding.

"Are you going back to London after lunch?"

"Yes," he answered, "but not straight away. I want to go for a good long walk first and think things out." Confession was out of the question. She was a girl and a stranger, but he did want sympathy. "I've been badly let down—by a friend."

"Oh!"

They had finished eating and drinking. Unlike a restaurant, where they could have lingered, they felt a little silly staring at the plastic counter after the man had taken away their cups and plates. Laurie needed someone to bear part of his burden and she perhaps sensed his need, for she seemed disinclined to leave him. In answer to his questions she explained that she was the oldest of five children and had early been thrust into the role of deputy mother. It was she who had bathed the younger children, taken them for walks, escorted them to school and guarded them whenever the parents were away. Gradually she had ceased to play the role and had become it. Now the children had grown up and no longer needed her. Laurie sympathised perfunctorily and could think of no more questions, so they sat in silence.

The man behind the counter watched them openly and inquisitively. Outside it began to rain, large single drops at first, then a steady downpour. A young man came in, greeted the girl, then sat a few stools away from her and Laurie. He was thin and studious-looking, with a nervous twitching of the lips that made Laurie look away.

"What time do you start again?" Laurie asked the girl, conscious that three people were listening now.

"Two o' clock."

"Oh! A long time yet."

"Yes."

"Fancy a walk?"

"It's raining."

"Not much."

"All right." She did not sound very enthusiastic.

At once his desire for the walk was deflated. It did not occur to him from the look of her hair that it had recently been set. Inability to respond seemed the only reason, and with its realisation went his need to confide. He made no attempt to return to the subject of his unhappiness, but kept silence at bay by asking what books sold best in Brighton, and which authors she most enjoyed reading. It had stopped raining now.

They went down to the front and past the Palace Pier towards Black Rock. Here there were determined trippers clutching sticks of rock. They were killing time until the coach was ready to take them back to London, oblivious of the massive, calming beauty of the sea, except when spray damped the powder on their faces or fogged their glasses.

"How awful to be reduced to coming to Brighton by coach in the middle of winter," Laurie put in suddenly.

"Why?"

"Because coach trips only make sense for those sort of people when the sun's out, and they can sit on the beach and eat oranges."

"Perhaps they want to get away from London like you did." She paused. "We'd better turn back. It's quarter to two."

"We all seem to be running away all the time." He waited for her agreement but she stayed silent, looking out to sea. "Do you run away sometimes?"

"Yes," she agreed doubtfully.

"From yourself? I mean that's what people run away from really."

"No," she replied, puzzled. "It's my family I can't stand. They expect me to do everything, but nobody worries much about me."

The qualification of "much" sounded for Laurie the depth of her charity. "I haven't a real family, and precious few friends."

She laughed nervously. "It seems it's as bad if you haven't any family as if you have."

The Pier seemed quite deserted. It was beginning to rain again, light drizzle that penetrated everything. They walked more quickly, raising their voices a little when they spoke.

"If you suddenly learnt that a friend of yours was a thief, a sort of kleptomaniac—couldn't help doing it. Would you refuse to have anything more to do with him?"

They crossed the road and felt the disappearance of the wind as a blast of warmth as they turned into East Street. The girl looked suddenly worried, as if she had jumped to the conclusion that Laurie was the kleptomaniac and had been rejected because of it. "I would have to be sure it was kleptomania," she said.

They reached the shop. In the distance a clock could be heard striking two. The thin man, who had greeted the girl in the restaurant, was coming up the road. They stood there still not knowing each other's names.

"Can we meet again?" Laurie asked faintly, unused to the hackneyed connotation the words had for most people.

"When?" she asked confidently, as though on *terra firma* at last.

"Tonight," he said, "for supper."

"Impossible," she answered not unkindly. "I have to go home."

For a moment he was relieved. The invitation had been spontaneous, and even a moment later seemed fraught with the same responsibilities that might be involved in taking Susan home from the Club.

"What time does the shop close?"

"Half five." She paused. "I could manage some tea then."

"All right," he answered. He squeezed her hand in a rough, unpractised manner, and she smiled as she had when first offering to serve him in the shop. "Half past five then," he repeated, and gave the thin man, who had just reached them, quite a confident stare as he turned back towards the front.

[11]

"Susie, you're wanted on the phone."

"Yes, Mamma."

Susan put down her book and went into the hall. It was small, brown and dark. In one corner stood an oak table littered with unopened printed-rate letters, the local paper, an apple and the telephone. On a ledge below were the four telephone directories, out of order and not all facing the same way, and on top of them a scratched, leather notebook entitled "Messages". Susan picked up the phone.

"Hello. Susan here."

"Hello, Sue. This is Bernard. What about the dance tonight? Are you coming?"

"Dance? Oh yes." She paused. She had completely forgotten it, which was a shame. She would like to have gone, and Tom would have been as happy to see her tomorrow as today. He had said so. She was afraid that the others would think she no longer wanted them.

"Well?"

"I'm awfully sorry, Bernard, I can't make it."

"Oh!"

"I've got a date." She hoped that it was her mother whom she could hear beating a mixture in the kitchen and not the daily help.

"Who with?"

The pounding on the pudding bowl had stopped. "That would be telling." She was sure that her mother was listening.

"With that soldier boy?"

Supposing it was the daily help in the kitchen and her mother was listening on the upstairs telephone. She almost trembled at the thought of another row like last Saturday's. "Yes."

"Oh!" There was a pause and Susan tried hard to decide if there was in fact someone upstairs. "Who is he?"

"A friend of mine." Her mother came out of the kitchen into the hall. She was wearing an apron and carrying a rolling pin.

"Is that Bernard?" she asked Susan.

"Where'd you meet him?" Bernard questioned.

"Yes," said Susan to her mother.

"What do you mean 'yes', Sue?"

"I was talking to mother. In the Club."

"Ask him how his mother is." Susan's mother started back to the kitchen.

"She wants to know how your mother is."

"Very well. Can't you put your date off? We only have two dances a year."

"She's very well, Mamma," Susan called softly, testing what her mother could hear with the door open. There was no reply, so she called a bit louder.

"Good," shouted Susan's mother.

"No, I can't," said Susan into the telephone. The conversation was dangerous, but she was frightened to cut it off too suddenly. Bernard might say something to his mother which would be repeated to hers.

"Then bring him with you."

"That's impossible. He wouldn't fit. He'd be like a fish out of water."

"Who?" demanded Susan's mother, coming out of the kitchen. Susan put her hand over the phone. "No one you know, Mamma."

"We're a free enough crowd," said Bernard. "Mother has just said too free."

So *his* mother was listening. A later call between the two mothers would fill in the blanks. "All right, I'll come, Bernard."

"Alone?"

"Alone." She felt sad, haunted already by the complications. Some people lived a whole life without the complications that she met in a week.

"Where'll we meet?"

"The Club," she said wearily, and, having agreed a time, replaced the receiver.

Her mother came out of the kitchen holding a wooden mixing spoon. She was an enormous woman with a puffed, smiling face whose alternative expression was tearful. She bore most of humanity's burdens with ease, gave freely of her time to all and sundry, and devoted most of her brain power to finding eligible bachelors for Susan, and, more difficult, finding Susan when the eligible bachelors were eventually landed. Having spent years assuring her friends that an artistic streak in her family was coming out in little Susie, she revolted against all art from the day her only daughter showed the slightest interest in her fellow male students.

"Who wouldn't fit, Susie?"

"Oh, no one you know, dear."

"That soldier?" It was an accusation that carried with it the weight of two thousand years of being in opposition. This new danger had come from such an unexpected source. All the arguments against Susan's social intercourse with non-Jewish students were wasted. For nearly three years they had seemed effective,

though in fact they had acted as stimulants to *affaires* of which
Susan had soon tired. This soldier, Susan's aunt had assured them,
was a coarse, working-class *goy*, and so presented something more
dangerous and less easily understood.

"I told you and Daddy the other night I wasn't going to see
him any more. Isn't that good enough?" She went back to the
drawing-room without looking at her mother, who sighed loudly
and returned to the kitchen.

Susan sat in one of the green armchairs and picked up her book.
It was a soft green room, carpets, curtains and chairs roughly to
match. Two of the pale green walls held Susan's own paintings of
Surrey scenes; a third was disturbed by a Tristram Hillyer beach-
scape with its brilliant reds and stark outlines. She had bought it
at Sotheby's with the money earned from the sale of one of her
paintings to the aunt who had surprised her with Tom. Her father
never noticed it; her mother excused it to each new guest as a first
priority.

It had become a symbol of her emancipation from the simple
role of daughter of the family. It proclaimed that she had a taste of
her own and that she was young, modern, and rebellious. It was a
measure of her emancipation from the outlook of her mother, her
mother's friends and some of their daughters. She had chosen it
even as she would choose her husband. To her parents it was ugly
and beyond their minds and tastes. When the local rabbi came
to tea one Sunday and lavished praise upon it, their immediate
joy was diluted in the belief that he was being socially pleasant.
In any case he was also young and a little irresponsible. Susan's
mother had sighed when he was leaving. She had looked at her
daughter: what a fine pair they would make, and he so modern
and understanding.

An hour later Susan went to her bedroom to change. She could
not make up her mind which of the two green scarves best suited
her black dress, and while she dallied her father came in. Even as
she posed first with one, then with the other in front of the mirror,
she heard her mother come out of the kitchen. There was a brief,
muffled conversation in the hall, then her parents went into the
kitchen. She put the two scarves on her bed, shuffled them and
picked one with her eyes closed. She pulled on her coat, checked

the contents of her bag and started quietly down the stairs. She would leave without saying "good night". Trouble would break out the next morning, but that was better than a scolding and a row tonight. She opened the front door.

Her aunt stood there. "Hello, Susan. Mum in?"

Her father and mother came out as Susan was about to explain that her aunt would find them in the kitchen.

"Evening, Sue."

"Hello, Dad."

"Where are you going?"

Her aunt pushed past her and went into the kitchen with her mother. They left the door open.

"To a dance."

He was a thin, bald man who seemed to spend his life suffering silently. Even his smile was that of a martyr. He tolerated his wife, his work and the vagaries of his daughter, who meant much to him, even though she had to be seen mostly through the distorted vision of his wife. His face was lined and dark, and he always seemed in need of a shave. When thinking, he would push out one cheek with his tongue and look downwards. He acted as a medium for his wife's emotions towards others and was rarely deeply moved independently. But when his mother had died, he went away alone for three days, no one knew where.

"With who?"

"Bernard."

He sighed. "Enjoy yourself and don't be too late."

She kissed him happily and went to the door.

"You haven't said good night to mother."

"Good night, Mamma," Susan shouted, her hand on the door again.

Her mother came out of the kitchen, wiping her hands on a teacloth, while her aunt remained framed in the doorway. "Where you going?"

"To the dance with Bernard."

"With Bernard?"

Susan played with the handle of the Yale lock. "Yes." She was beginning to tense and found it difficult to answer in a friendly, casual way.

"I thought you had a date." Her mother continued wiping her dry hands, speaking the last word with obvious distaste.

Susan shook her head. Her father moved his weight from foot to foot. He sensed the coming storm, and waited for its fury without trying to avert or defeat it.

"You told Bernard you had a date. I heard you."

Susan remained silent. She stared at her shoes. She wanted to open the door, run away and never come back. She would throw herself on Tom's mercy, and his mercy would be escape through marriage.

"That soldier?" asked her mother in a querulous voice.

Susan shook her head again.

"Is that true, Susie?" her father asked, but so softly that only Susan appeared to hear.

Susan's mother turned to him. "Forbid her to meet that *goy* again! I won't have it! Oh, think, my daughter!" Her bosom was heaving and she screwed the teacloth into a tight knot.

"Sue, did you tell me the truth?"

"I'm going to a dance with Bernard."

"You know what you promised me Saturday?"

"I'm going to a dance with Bernard. How many times do I have to repeat it?" She opened the front door an inch. "Why don't you ring up Bernard's mother if you don't believe me?"

"Why did you say you had a date?" Her mother advanced a pace as she spat out the word "date".

Susan pulled the door back and hurried out, slamming it behind her. The night was fresh and cold, and she ran almost gaily, intoxicated with its tang of freedom. She did not look back, but she heard a door slam behind her and knew that they had checked to see if she had really gone. By the time that she reached the underground she would feel remorseful and angry again. For the moment her solitude and the clean, night air invigorated her. She had her youth. Freedom was always just around the corner. With a skip she started running once more.

[12]

Tom was waiting for her at the entrance to the Club. Not being a member, he could not enter until she arrived to sign him in. He greeted her with a smile as she came down the steps. She walked straight down and kissed him, holding him tightly despite the doorman's presence. He was surprised, for she usually discouraged such behaviour in public.

"What's up?" he asked, after she had signed him in and they had gone through to the bar.

"Why?" she countered, taking out a mirror from her handbag. "Don't I look all right?"

"You look terrific." He coloured and glanced round. "But you don't usually meet me like that. And you're toffed up a bit, too."

She paused. She had to break some news somehow, but hardly knew where to begin. She slid off the high stool and took his arm, pulling him off his seat and leading him to a quiet table in the corner.

"Tom, my people won't let me see you any more." She stared at his hands, white and strong. She imagined that his body was the same. She was so nearly his, so nearly and a Jewess. "Even tonight I've had to promise to meet Bernard here later and go to a dance with him."

"But you——"

"No, don't get angry, Tom. Tonight's nothing." She disregarded his further attempt to protest. "I just won't go when Bernard comes." She looked round her helplessly. There was too much noise and too many people, but she had started and must go on. "Tom, I've got to choose, them or you." Her voice dropped to a whisper as she lifted her eyes and met his. "I want you. If you'll have me." There were tears in her eyes.

"But what's bloody well wrong with me that we can't go together?"

A waitress hovered near. Please, please go away, Susan implored in her thoughts. We don't want anything to eat and we've got our drinks, and neither of us is even drinking. The waitress answered a call from another table.

"What's wrong——"

"Give me a cigarette, please, Tom."

He fumbled for a packet, left top battledress pocket, then right, then trouser pocket where he found them.

"I'm Jewish."

He looked at her in undisguised alarm and surprise. She took a cigarette, her hand trembling slightly. The wheel was still turning, but the ball had caught in a slot, and though it was too soon to read the number, it did not look like his.

"Hullo, Sue." It was Bernard.

"Hullo, Bernard." Social small-talk seemed ridiculous, but she had to know whether Tom's initial shock would be sustained before she burnt her boats completely. "You two have met before?"

"Hullo," said Bernard cheerfully.

"Yes," said Tom without enthusiasm. He wanted time to think. He had suddenly been put on a par with Susan. She was middle-class, educated, well-spoken and so above him. She was Jewish and so below. He was shaken; but what difference did it make? He searched for reasons to back his dismay. They were mean, they were flashy, they had funny customs, they . . .

"We'd better be going along, Sue," said Bernard.

"Susan can't go!" Tom became aggressive at once.

"I beg your pardon!"

"Susan's going dancing with me."

"But, Sue, you promised."

"Tom's right," she said with a flourish that seemed, at the moment, worth any price.

"But what'll your mother—my mother—what'll they say?" He was red in the face and angry. He knew that he had lost and this increased his annoyance.

"I'm sorry, Bernard, but you talked me into it on the phone. I told you straight away I had a date with Tom. You took advantage of my mother standing there." She excused herself half-heartedly. Tom was on her side: the boats could be burnt.

"Well," stammered Bernard, "you know your mother will be mad when she finds you're still going out with *him*." He looked at Susan as he spoke.

"Why?" put in Tom.

"Because you're not Jewish," said Bernard. The soldier had called forth his trump earlier than he had intended. He placed it firmly by adding: "And Susan is."

"So what?" demanded Tom. "I know that."

They were silent for a moment. "You're not coming, then, Sue?" Bernard asked sulkily.

"No," answered Susan. "Sorry."

Without a further word Bernard turned and crossed the room, disappearing through the door. They heard his steps on the stairs, then along the passage that crossed the ceiling. Neither of them spoke. Tom tried to remember what had really been wrong with a Jew who had once been in his company. Susan wondered whether she would be able to keep her hair appointment the following morning.

After a few seconds Tom gave up: even the man's face eluded him. He wondered what the boys would say at his marrying a Jew. Then he realised that they need never know: Susan didn't look Jewish; she didn't act it either. She was just like other girls, at least as far as he knew. Perhaps the Jews had special taboos about sex. That at least he would have to find out before he agreed to marriage.

Susan's thoughts, too, had wandered from hairdressers to marriage. She was in Tom's hands now: he might take advantage of the situation and refuse to marry her. He could demand her without marriage now, and despite her fears she relished the situation in a rebellious, challenging way.

"We'll 'ave to marry," said Tom finally, with the air of one who has considered a number of different courses and arrived at this particular one with the help of infallible logic.

"When?" asked Susan quickly; too quickly, she thought, but her eagerness coincided too nearly with Tom's thoughts for him to notice it.

"Soon as I can get permission from the C.O. Shouldn't take long. You're over twenty-one?"

"Just."

"We'll 'ave to get a room. Plenty goin' near where my people live."

For a moment the whole unknown background that surrounded Tom was illumined for her. She saw for a moment his mother, tall, suspicious, bearing a grudge against the girl who had taken her son away, and his father worried by so quick a marriage.

"What'll I do until then?" She felt as helpless as ever.

"Till then?" He realised for the first time how immediate was the problem. He had foreseen a few weeks' delay while the permission was obtained, his father's help in buying a ring sought and a room found. "Aren't you going home?"

"I can't—not if I'm going to marry you." It seemed absurd to talk of matters so momentous in the atmosphere of the Club. "Bernard'll tell them what happened."

"Is there—well, sort of anything different, I mean, if you're a Jew, when you marry?"

She was hurt by his tone. He would understand, though, later. She was sure of it. "No, Tom, none at all." She shook her head slowly from side to side as she spoke. His prejudice was shallow and natural, the prejudice of one who has never known a Jew personally.

He was relieved. "We'll 'ave to get you a room."

"Tonight?"

"Tonight?" He was shocked anew. "Haven't you any friend that could put you up?"

She shook her head.

"What about Laurie?"

She thought for a moment. "Yes, he might. He'd be safe, too." She smiled half-heartedly at a joke that she thought unfair.

"Oh, I'd stay along with you."

"Would you?" She was surprised and excited. This had not occurred to her.

"'Course. I don't 'ave to be in afore seven in the morning and it's not far to the barracks."

"We could try it anyway," she said. The idea was more than a solution: it would set an unbreakable seal on her decision.

"Wonder what time 'e gets in?" Tom had no doubts in the matter.

"He often comes here. Supposing we have a bite now, then come back. If he's not here we can go round to his house. You know the address, don't you?"

"Yes."

It was easier now, for they were discussing something in the immediate future. To Tom the way was clear. Susan, though, felt waves of fear and excitement. She wanted badly the conclusion that the plan entailed, wanted and was frightened by it; not only by the physical act itself but also by its consequences, and chief among these the possibility of her rejection. She might disappoint or fail him. They might be unsuited, and this revealed only too late. For a moment she bitterly regretted her inexperience as a result of spending nearly three years in an art school untempted.

He suggested their going again to the Jewish snack bar and she agreed. In the street they talked little. He tried to like the café and the people in it, but it was only the food he enjoyed. Susan found great difficulty in eating anything. The walk back to the Club was as difficult as the one to the café. She wanted to talk of their future together, but was afraid of arousing images that might upset his, and so lessen his determination to marry her. Tom was simply shy.

Back in the Club they secluded themselves in a corner and looked timidly at one another. Susan's confidence was increasing. He would look after her, protect and marry her. Tom was worried that she might change her mind. For a moment he even doubted the wisdom of spending the night with her. Better perhaps that they should be married first.

Slowly they started to talk about the other people round them, feeling their way towards each others' opinions, treading warily. At the slightest sign of real disagreement they drew back. Gradually they became warmer. Tom took Susan's hand unashamedly and at last she asked: "What'll your people say?"

"Don't know." It did not occur to him to be more encouraging.

"When will you tell them?"

"We'll go 'ome tomorrow."

First there was tonight, then tomorrow there would be another ordeal. For a moment it seemed almost too much and she was ready to back out, ready to face her mother, father and Bernard. The vacillation was short-lived. They would never understand her and she would only ever half-understand them. It was better to cut adrift now while there was a worthwhile issue.

"Perhaps Laurie's home by now," she said.

"Let's go."

They went by underground from Oxford Circus to Sloane Square. The platform and trains were almost empty. Susan envied the few people they did see. They obviously had so few cares. They looked a little sad, but London and the underground made people look sad. When the summer came again they would be off to the sea or the Continent, and there they would laugh and be happy, frolic like children and make easy, uncomplicated love. Susan glanced round the jolting carriage, her hand tight in Tom's. That woman there, clinging so tenaciously to her worn umbrella, and, two seats away, that man trying hard to roll a cigarette despite the swaying and pitching of the train. Their lives were simple. Even Tom's life was straightforward. Then at the next station the man stood up to leave the train, turning in the doorway and almost spitting a "Come on for gawd's sake" to the woman. They had not once spoken or looked at each other during the journey.

From Sloane Square they walked to Laurie's flat. In the darkness Susan found it easier to talk to Tom. They walked quickly, arm-in-arm, she conscious only of him and he quick to notice the approving stares of other Guardsmen whom they passed. Once Tom stopped to pat a large black dog who started to follow them and, absurdly, Susan's eyes filled with tears.

"Do you like children, Tom?" she asked softly as they walked on again.

"Yes. You?"

"Love them."

She wanted to expand the conversation to talk of *their* children, how many they would have and whether he preferred boys or girls, but she was still frightened of ruffling the harmony between them. When they reached Laurie's flat they were delighted to see a light coming from under the front door. They went down the steps and rang the bell.

Laurie opened the door to them. He was so relieved that it was not Eccles and some friends returned to attack him that his welcome was almost ridiculous. "What a grand surprise! Come in, Susan! Come in, Tom! This *is* a pleasure!"

They followed him into the living-room, surprised in their turn to see a small, smiling girl sitting in front of the electric fire. Laurie introduced the new-comers to her, then went to put the kettle on.

"This tea's rather cold," he explained when he came back, pointing to a pot and some cups on a tray. "I'll make you some more. You only just caught us, you know. Mary's last train leaves at eleven, so we'll have to go to the station soon."

"Have you far to go?" Susan asked the girl. She sat opposite her, still wearing her coat and gloves.

"Brighton."

"Oh!"

Mary's presence was not only a surprise to Susan and Tom, it was a complication in their plan. They could hardly discuss the possibility of staying the night in front of her; yet it would look rather ridiculous for them to wait outside while Laurie took Mary to the station, then call on him again when he had returned.

"Mary came up to see my pictures," explained Laurie, mainly to Tom, who had usurped his whole attention from the moment of entering the room.

Tom laughed loudly and Susan joined in. Mary sat quietly, holding her knees and blushing.

Laurie blundered on, determined to right matters by disregarding their innuendo. "She paints a little herself but doesn't get much chance. Has to look after the other children." Laurie was watching Tom. "Just lucky her mother came into the shop and she said she was going to meet me. So we came back here," he concluded lamely.

"You've been down to Brighton today?" asked Susan, trying hard to be pleasant and atone for her laughter.

"Yes," said Laurie.

"No bookshop?" asked Tom. He leant across and took Susan's hand. Laurie wondered whether he ought to be doing the same to Mary.

"I'll go and see if the kettle's boiling," he said as he stood up. "No, I took the day off, Tom," he added as he walked to the door.

When Laurie came back with the tea, the conversation jerked along in fits and starts like a car with water in the petrol tank. They talked of films they had seen, the Guards and the Jazz Club. To Susan's dismay, Tom related the incident of the boy with the hunched shoulders for Mary's benefit; she was surprised when

Laurie, far from seeming annoyed, appeared to listen eagerly to the story.

"Well," said Laurie at last, looking at Mary for the first time, "we must be going to the station. Sorry to push you two out." There was a general pause. "Or would you like to wait till I get back? I'll be back by quarter past."

"Yes," said Tom definitely.

"Thanks," said Susan.

Mary had hardly spoken. She stood up still smiling and offered Susan her hand. Susan took off her right glove and shook hands with the girl. "Sorry you've got to go so soon. Perhaps we'll meet again."

"Yes," said Mary. Then as she turned to shake hands with Tom, she added to Susan: "Are you two married?"

"Nearly," said Susan, smiling.

"Yep," said Tom.

"Nearly what?" repeated Laurie. He took no pains to hide his surprise or distress.

"Married," said Susan firmly.

"Congratulations," put in Mary. "Well, we must go. It's getting on. Bye-bye."

She went through the door and Laurie started to follow. For a second he nearly gave way to an impulse to order Susan and Tom out of the flat. Then he went after Mary, shouting over his shoulder: "Back soon."

[13]

Victoria station was ugly and unfriendly. There were few people about, but small waves were ejected from the underground at regular intervals, and these split into individuals and couples running to separate platforms. Whistles echoed hollowly. The train to Brighton was half full and Mary stood at the window of an empty compartment talking to Laurie.

"Six minutes to," he said, looking at the huge, dimly lit clock that seemed to float in space.

"Yes," she said.

He sought for something to take the edge off her disappointment. The evening had gone so well before Tom and Susan had arrived. Mary had become quite talkative and jolly, and in some indefinite, unspoken way, sympathetic. The others had fractured this contact at once. What had they meant: "nearly married"? Laurie could still hear the firm emphasis of Susan's "Married" in answer to his "Nearly what?"

"Will you be coming down to Brighton again soon?" asked Mary.

"Yes. Yes, of course." Laurie smiled. "What about Sunday? Can we meet then?" He hoped that she would say no. He did not want to get involved. He did not even want to meet her again. If she would only refuse this invitation, he would be vague about another. He would have atoned for the evening ending badly.

"Sunday?" Mary repeated. "Yes, that would be lovely. Will you come to lunch? If I offer to stay in Saturday night so Mum and Dad can go out they won't mind me being out Sunday." She grew more enthusiastic. "What train will you catch? I'll meet it."

The guard was blowing his whistle and an answering blast came from the front of the train.

"I'll be at Brighton station at twelve," Mary said, panic showing despite her smile and friendly wave. "Twelve at the station." The train jerked forward.

"All right," said Laurie. "Twelve on Sunday." He held out his hand and she seized it eagerly. For a few moments he walked awkwardly beside the moving carriage, then she let go his hand and he stopped.

"'Bye, Laurie."

"Good-bye."

He waved until the train was out of sight, then cursed the date as he started back towards the barrier. He resolved to write a letter excusing himself for being unable to keep it. In any case he had made up his mind to spend Sunday with Tom. They had still never been on their sketching expedition. He had not mentioned the idea to the Guardsman. In fact he soon convinced himself that the date with Mary followed the intention of making one with Tom. The announcement of the marriage was disturbing, of course. It may only have been a joke though, or a boast in front of Mary. Ahead of him leaving the station was a Guardsman. Laurie could not see his face or profile. But suddenly he had a vision of Tom's hands, strong and white, and he dallied with it until the hands seized him roughly and he knew that he would do everything in his power to prevent a marriage between Tom and Susan. By then he was already climbing the stairs of a number eleven bus.

When he reached the flat it was dark and he wondered whether they had gone after all. He opened the front door cautiously and quietly, then listened. From the living-room came the soft purr of murmurs and the pinched suction of kissing. He slammed the front door and started to whistle. He waited a moment for the light to go on in the living-room, but all remained dark and quiet. He knocked shyly.

"Come in," called Tom.

He went in, switching on the light as he entered. Tom sat in the big armchair. He had thrown off his battledress jacket and tie, and Laurie could see the smooth, white skin where his shirt hung limply open. Susan sat on his right knee, and her eyes, when she turned to smile at Laurie, were shining and intense. Tom had one hand inside her dress and Laurie waited impatiently for him to remove it.

Instead Tom said: "Don't mind?"

"'Course not," Laurie answered, smiling awkwardly.

"Come and sit on the other knee, love." The Guardsman indicated with his free hand.

"Tom!" Susan bent down and kissed him.

What a cheap tart she had become! Laurie was first shocked by his own thought, then triumphant with it. Wait till he told Tom the truth, reckoned up the number of art students' knees she had sat on, the countless boys—he almost shuddered—who had slipped their sweaty hands inside her dress and pressed . . .

"Laurie?"

"Yes, Susan."

"Can we stay here tonight?" She had said it exactly as she had told Tom she would.

"Here?"

"Yes."

"Where?"

"Anywhere. Laurie, you must help us. I can't go home. They've thrown me out for saying I was going to marry Tom. I'll have to roam the streets if I can't stay here."

"But Tom——"

Tom removed his hand and buttoned up his shirt. "She can't be left alone," he said; "'er condition!"

Laurie's relief, had he known that Tom was being purposely vague, would have been enormous. As it was the word "condition" conjured up a vision of women in pregnancy or periods. He was revolted and fascinated that something had already happened. Tom had done something to Susan. He was embarrassed and excited until suddenly he realised that Susan would have to have the bedroom, while he and Tom slept in the studio, and the excitement alone remained, mounting rapidly.

"Of course you can stay. Both of you. I'm only too pleased to help." He would have said more, but he hardly trusted his voice.

They petted each other and smiled, stopping to thank him and explain how he was fulfilling their confident expectations. They had known that if there was one person in the whole of London who would help them that night, that person was Laurie. Tom bit Susan's ear. "Yep," he said while he kissed her neck, "you're a sport, Laurie."

"I'll go and put some clean sheets on the bed for you," he said.

"Don't bother, Laurie. Tom, stop it. No, really, Laurie, don't bother."

Laurie smiled and left the room. He pulled the covers from his bed with gusto, fetched clean sheets and remade the bed. Then he went into the studio. He and Tom would use the divan in there; it would be more comfortable than the two armchairs in the living-room. It was a large divan and Tom could not possibly object. Besides, hadn't they been lauding him to the stars a few minutes earlier? He turned on the electric fire and cleared some canvases from the divan. Then he made it up with the sheets which he had taken from his own bed.

From the living-room came laughing and the sound of furniture being moved. He was irritated that they should fool around in his house. They might damage something. Still, as soon as the divan was ready he would suggest bed. From that moment forward the future was blank. He forced himself not to think of it. Time and again his brain dragged him to the moment when he and Tom would start undressing, and each time he called a halt, conscious of the large eyes, the strong, virile body and the huge, white hands, conscious too of a tingle of excitement that made him momentarily dizzy. As he went to leave the room, the sensation seized him anew, and the force of it made him pause and lean on the door lintel. Suddenly there was imposed on it the realisation that in the next room, not ten feet away, would be Susan—alone.

As he switched out the light, he heard a crash from the living-room. He rushed back. Tom and Susan, their arms linked, stood gazing at a pottery bowl that lay on the floor, smashed into a dozen small pieces. It had graced Laurie's mantelpiece ever since he had lived there. It was the first ornament that he had bought for his own home. He had loved it: from time to time picking it up and running his fingers round the cool, glazed surface; rejoicing his eyes again and again in the exciting red lines that pierced the brown glaze. It had become a mark of his taste and progress in climbing away from his family.

"We're awfully sorry, Laurie."

"Dunno 'ow it 'appened," put in Tom, raising his eye-brows as though genuinely puzzled. He squeezed Susan's waist.

"It's all right," said Laurie softly, near tears, and with a feeling of cold and heaviness in his stomach. "Wasn't worth much."

Susan reached out and took his arm. "We'll buy you another tomorrow. An even better one. We'll buy you a real Bernard Leach."

"It's all right," said Laurie. "I'd had it some time. Sort of had the value." Someone had created it, fashioned it, moulded it. Now its day was done. For a moment he forced his mind off the subject. "The beds are ready," he said. He stooped to pick up the bits.

"We don't know how to thank you, Laurie—and then we go and do this." She helped Laurie collect the pieces. They put them solemnly and carefully on the mantelpiece.

"Bed?" queried Tom.

Susan grinned, shyly now.

"I'll show you the way," said Laurie. He led them into the little hall, then threw open the door of his bedroom.

"There you are."

"You darling!" said Susan and kissed him on the cheek. Then she ran into the room and threw herself on the bed.

Tom guffawed. "You darling!" he said to Laurie and kissed him roughly and playfully on the forehead. "Night-night." He followed Susan into the room and closed the door behind him.

As Laurie heard the key turn in the lock, Susan shouted "Good night". He was unable to answer. He felt choked and helpless. Slowly he slouched into the living-room. Reaching for a pot of glue from behind the radio, he knelt on the floor and slowly, blinded by tears, started to fit together the jagged pieces of his brown glazed pottery bowl.

PART II

FLORENCE

[1]

The Arno was almost as brown as the buildings on either side of it. Laurie rested his arms on the embankment wall, pulling them away as the hot stone burnt his bare skin. Farther upstream towards the *Ponte Vecchio*, boys in brief trunks crouched under the mild waterfall, cool in the spray shaken from the sheet of water gushing over their glossy, black heads. Farther down, where the river erratically narrowed to a stream, smaller, naked children chased each other across the dried mud flats despite the heat, screaming and whistling incessantly. Laurie turned away from the river and wandered inland towards the church. He would like to see the Masaccio frescoes again; and this time without Norman's interest. Contemplation would be more rewarding than discussion.

The church, however, was shut and no one answered his ringing. A bunch of ragged children sat on the steps and watched him. They were tanned and dirty. They smiled sympathetically as Laurie gave the bell a last, long, irritated push, but moved away doubtfully as he came down the steps, almost as though he might hold them responsible for his failure to gain admission. He started after them to ask when the church would be open, but they broke into a run, shouting and jeering as they went. So he took the road that ran parallel to the Santa Maria del Carmine, and turned right deeper into the town.

Everywhere was bare dusty poverty. The buildings were old and dilapidated, cracked and unpainted. The streets were littered with orange peel and bits of paper. To Laurie it all had a strange, autumnal beauty, unmarked by a social realisation of its tragedy. The decrepit buildings, roads eccentrically cobbled and littered, old women draped in shawls and aprons, ragged children and evil-smelling garbage cans, these confirmed Florence as an unchanged city since the days of the Medici. But for that *Topolino* over there and the Lancia protruding round the next corner, this was in essence the same city that the Renaissance had known.

He leant against a wall and watched some children playing a highly complicated game of marbles. He was almost ashamed of his love for Florence as he saw it now, whatever it meant as such to its inhabitants. He thought of Wandsworth and the dingy street where Susan and Tom lived, and remembered their look of horror when he had described it, too romantically. But there he had needed a fog to touch up the atmosphere, softening here a streak of real ugliness, there a sordid patch; here in the harsh Italian sunlight it all seemed beautiful, even the garbage. A shout from one of the children, who had achieved some special success, woke him from his day-dreams. It was four o'clock. He must hurry back to the hotel. Norman Wayne would be awake within half an hour and there would be another row if he were still out.

He walked quickly and began to perspire. The holiday had been a failure. Without actually accusing Laurie of having persuaded him to leave the business in doubtful hands while they went away, Norman never allowed an hour to pass without worrying aloud about the shop. Were they taking money from the till? Did they deal with school orders as soon as received? Were they using the telephone for private calls? Alternatively he rubbed home the cost of the holiday until Laurie reacted perversely by trying to persuade Norman to eat in restaurants and stay in hotels far beyond their means.

When Laurie began to sulk, Norman changed embrocations. He spoke soothingly about the tremendous benefit of the holiday for Laurie and his painting. He showed an interest in masterpieces that was insincere to the point of being ridiculous. He asked questions that Bernard Berenson might have had trouble in answering, and he kept on asking them until Laurie sulked in a different way. Then he would roundly accuse Laurie of wasting his time staring at some pinched-faced urchin.

As Laurie entered the hall of the Albergo Leonardo, the porter beckoned him. "Signor Wayne has been asking for Signor Keengstone."

"*Grazie*," murmured Laurie and started to run up the stairs.

"Signor!" shouted the porter.

Laurie stopped at the first little landing and looked back.

"'e has gone out. He will meet you at Bucca Lape at ayt o'clock."

Laurie nodded and walked on. When they had parted it had been agreed that a cheap *trattoria* would have to suffice for the last few days. Having made his point and obtained Laurie's agreement, Norman immediately swung to the other extreme and proposed one of the most expensive restaurants in Florence.

Laurie changed quickly into his light glen check suit. It had been Norman's first present to him, a wonderful surprise and only three weeks after he had gone to work for the older man. How exciting it had seemed then! Norman had been so brilliant and sympathetic, had encouraged him to paint, had offered him a home, and had changed the offer to insistence by slow degrees, each degree punctuated by another suit, some shirts and finally a motor bike. He straightened his tie. Norman was still brilliant and even more encouraging. Yet somehow, somewhere, the gloss had become smeared, then chipped and was now routine in its ugliness and ugly in its routine. For a moment only, but quite clearly, he hated Norman Wayne.

He put on his dark glasses and went to the door. Suddenly he noticed for the first time that Norman had left a letter on the carved round table near the window. Laurie hurried across the large room. It was addressed to Norman's mother, round graceful letters completed by a curving line and two dots. Norman told his mother everything, even about Laurie. In that letter he would learn the truth. Was Norman enjoying himself? Was he really spending too much? He could steam the letter open and read it, then seal it up again. He looked out of the window across the Arno. It was cool in the room, but the sight of the brown buildings and muddy river brought back the mood of the afternoon. Florence was real, an echo from the past, not a strumpet town dolled up for tourists. He put down the letter and left the room quickly as if to allay another bout of temptation.

In the street he was met by the full force of the hot June afternoon. He walked slowly, stopping to look in the shop windows which were full of fascinating objects, almost all made by hand:

thick green leather purses and wallets, red leather-topped paper knives and appointment books. At Doney's he bought himself a *spremuta d'arancia*, sipping it slowly, tasting and savouring the orange. Once or twice the image of the letter to Norman's mother reasserted itself. He would go back and read it; find out what Norman really thought; crack the smooth shell that was all the world ever saw of the bookseller. Then a person or car caught his eye and he forgot the letter.

He left Doney's and wandered to the Galleria, the centre of the city. Like its counterparts in Rome and Milan, it was thronged during the early evening with people who slowly edged their way from one end to the other or sat at café tables sipping apéritifs. Near the centre, boys and men, acting furtively with their eyes, sold black market cigarettes. Farther down a crowd collected round a kiosk from which boomed an ugly voice full of football results. At the far, Arno end of the huge vaulted gallery was an enormous news stand. There were laid out magazines and newspapers in Italian, French, German and English. Beside the stand, leaning on a red bicycle with upswept handlebars, was a youth.

As Laurie moved away from the middle of the gallery the crowds lessened. He glanced in the shop windows, skirted the crowd collected round the kiosk, and called at the news stand. A picture of Picasso on the cover of a magazine caught his eye. He bought it, handing the old woman behind the counter a crumpled thousand-lire note. She gave him some change which he stuffed into his pocket. He opened the magazine and started to move forward again, the paper held in front of him. Below it just in front of him he saw a pair of feet in black cycling shoes and the wheels of a red bicycle. He lowered the paper.

The youth smiled at Laurie, frankly and provocatively. He looked about sixteen, tall, well-built and very conscious of his thick black hair and handsome olive face. He wore a pair of ultra brief shorts and a cherry and yellow woollen vest. Laurie smiled back shyly.

"*Americano?*" asked the boy.

"*Inglese,*" answered Laurie.

They both smiled, then the boy tried again. "*Fa caldo.* It's 'ot." He spoke English with a slight American accent.

"*Molto,*" agreed Laurie.

The boy moved a pace towards him, allowing the cycle to lean over with him. Then he adjusted himself so that his weight was balanced against it. "You tourist?"

"Yes," said Laurie. He looked round anxiously. Perhaps Norman was wandering through the Galleria. There was bound to be a scene if he saw him talking to some strange Italian youth. "Shall we have a drink?" He spoke slowly and distinctly.

Something was added to the boy's smile. For a moment it puzzled Laurie. Then he recognised it: it was a sign of connivance, the accepted counter to an opening gambit. He felt the same mixture of disgust and excitement that had possessed him when he had first asked Tom to have a drink. Only this seemed less sordid, either through the setting or lack of a fluent, common language. He had two hours to spare before meeting Norman at the Bucca Lape. He walked beside the boy, conscious of the other's well-developed thighs and smooth, tanned legs; eager yet apprehensive.

The boy took him to a bar behind the Piazza della Signoria. It was small and well stocked, and they leant on the counter near the entrance so that they could watch the boy's bicycle. He ordered another *spremuta* while the boy had a *Strega*. Laurie was not sure how to start the conversation. There was much to be said but little common tongue for saying anything. He wondered whether the barman understood English.

Then the boy spoke: "You English writer?"

"Good Lord, no!" answered Laurie, puzzled.

The boy smiled knowingly. "A lot English writers come Firenze."

Laurie felt a little out of his depth. He was not sure whether he was expected to answer on one level or both. So he answered naturally, but sought to give his own words the conspiratorial quality shown by the boy's.

"You stay long?"

"*Due settemane,*" answered Laurie. It was safer to pretend he would be there for some time. It might make the boy postpone any bad intention.

"Which *albergo?*"

"Leonardo." Now he was saying too much.

"You show me your room?" asked the boy. "Now?" He was

grinning all the while, showing off his white teeth and handsome charm. He looked round at his bicycle, and as he turned back his bare, tanned leg pressed against Laurie. Laurie glanced at the barman, a middle-aged Italian who looked thoroughly bored.

"*Va bene?*" asked the boy, eagerly pressing Laurie's leg again.

"*Va bene,*" said Laurie heavily, as if agreeing to some onerous duty.

The boy slid off his stool. "*Due mille lire,*" said the barman without looking at them.

"What!" said Laurie.

The boy left and hurried to his cycle. The barman repeated his demand. Suddenly all Laurie's fears came to the surface. The barman had overheard. There would be a scandal. Outside the boy was leaning on his bicycle, smiling. Laurie took out his money and counted two and a half thousand lire. The extra five hundred would satisfy him, he thought. He pushed it across the counter.

"*Grazie,*" said the barman, surprised.

Laurie joined the boy on the pavement. He was irritated now as well as frightened. How had he become involved so quickly? And why? Why not leave the boy now, arranging to meet him some other time? They walked for a few paces. Then the boy stopped.

"I forget my cigarettes," he said.

He gave Laurie the bicycle and ran back to the bar. Laurie waited. After a minute or two he began to get impatient. Supposing Norman should come upon him standing in the Piazza holding a red bicycle. He turned it round and went back to the bar. From the road he understood at once that the boy was arguing with the barman. Laurie moved back a pace, keeping out of sight, but watching. At last the barman went to the till, rang something up and took out a large note. He handed it to the boy, who eyed it, spat on the ground, then hurried out to rejoin Laurie.

[2]

The Bucca Lape was under the British Consulate. Laurie stood outside the large bookshop farther down the road on the other side. There was a fine display of art books, and usually he would have been engrossed in studying their covers. Now he was ill at ease. It was five minutes to eight and he did not want to arrive in the restaurant before Norman. If he did, Norman was sure to grumble at the position of whatever table he had chosen. Laurie felt hot and uncomfortable; he was perspiring freely, and was alternatively occupied by a sense of guilt and carefree abandon about the four and a half thousand lire with which he had parted so easily in the last two hours. As if to increase both feelings, he gave two hundred lire to a passing beggar who had not even approached him.

In the distance he saw Norman arrive from the direction of the Duomo, cross the street and disappear down the side of the British Consulate. He looked smart and cool in his biscuit-coloured tropical suit. He was pulling at his pipe and did not appear to see Laurie, who was still standing in front of the bookshop. It was very warm and there were few people about. Three boys stood arguing outside the English chemist's on the other side of the road. They wore black cotton smocks over their light jackets and short trousers. They were all good-looking and their smooth skins were tanned. Laurie hated them and their ensnaring beauty as suddenly as he hated Norman Wayne and his sleek, imperturbable smartness. He slouched on towards the restaurant.

The Bucca Lape was a basement. Coming down the stairs from the bright daylight it seemed dark and warm. On either side of the stone steps were the kitchens open for all to see, and the cooks, hot, sweaty and cheerful. The restaurant itself consisted of two arched tunnels, the ceiling and walls being completely covered with bright posters pasted higgledy-piggledy: "Come to England", "Fly B.E.A.", "Capri for the Perfect Holiday", "Bevete Cinzano", "Longines", "Lloyd-Triestino", "Dubo-Dubon-Dubonnet". At the far end in one corner sat Norman, his jacket draped carefully over the back of his chair.

"Hullo," said Laurie, sitting down.

"You look worn out," said Norman. He was smiling and obviously trying to be pleasant for the moment.

"Thought we were going to a *trattoria*."

"I waited until after four at the hotel."

Laurie stayed silent. Had this man brought him to that? Why

should he be spoken to like a paid servant? But his own vulner-
ability checked his anger. "I wanted to see the Masaccios again."

"I'd have come with you."

"The church was shut."

"So what did you do?"

"I tried to take a short cut back and lost my way." There was a
pause while they ordered *tagliatelle*, a steak and a *fiasco* of Chianti
Ruffino. "When I got back to the hotel you'd just gone out."

"I've seen enough of the Masaccios," said Norman, breaking a
slice of crisp bread with slow deliberation.

"I hadn't," said Laurie. "I wanted to contemplate."

"So did Huxley—his navel." Laurie was looking round the room.
"I'm not sure that art snobbery isn't as bad as sheer Philistinism,"
provoked Norman. "You once told me that Moore was inspired
by Masaccio, so I suppose that now everyone must worship his
frescoes whether they get anything out of them or not. Laurie,
you're not listening."

"I've heard it before." He turned back to the table but only
because the *tagliatelle* had arrived.

"So what?" Norman's anger forced its way to the surface. "You
don't expect me to find something new and exciting to say every
five minutes of the day after two years, do you? That's one of the
prices you pay. All you want to do is to ruin my holiday. It's costing
enough without that. You couldn't even get back to the hotel in
time when I'd specially asked you to."

"You probably went out early." Laurie was bored. He had
committed a greater crime than this and was too weary to bother
about such a triviality.

"Where would you be now if I hadn't rescued you from . . ."
He stopped, aware that his raised voice was attracting attention.

"I'm sorry," said Laurie, putting down his fork. "It's the heat or
something."

Norman went on eating.

"You used to be so tolerant and understanding." Laurie waited
for a reply. None came. "When you wanted me!"

The word "tolerant" struck a chord, though Laurie guessed that
the insult had found a deeper one whose answering echo would be
delayed but not unheard.

"It must be the heat," Norman agreed, obviously controlling his temper. "I went to see Catalini. It's a shame you weren't there. He's a most interesting chap." He paused for a moment while he ate, glancing at Laurie as if to discern how deep an impression he had made with the missed treat. "His knowledge of painting is fantastic. To hear him talking about the Fra Angelicos is like seeing them for the first time, one's vision incredibly enhanced by his explanations." He allowed Laurie to digest his second misfortune. "After a couple of those exquisite drinks he mixes—I can never remember what he calls them, can you?"

"No."

"Doesn't matter. Aren't these *tagliatelle* light? In a *trattoria* they would have been like rubber—he took me back to the San Marco in the Alfa. Of course, normally it's closed by six, but one glance at Catalini and the janitor opened up. It was like a revelation. Don't get me wrong, Laurie: your explanations helped me enormously. But Catalini's were like a revelation. In fact I'm sure that even you would have gained enormously from them."

"Yes."

To Laurie the meal seemed interminable. The ride back in the Alfa-Romeo, through streets that Norman and Laurie as strangers had never found, exhausted most of the main course. The Alfa itself spent the rest. A review by Catalini of the post-war Italian film industry carried Norman's monologue through to coffee and his final shot: if Laurie had been with him, he would have been able to accept Catalini's invitation to dinner instead of having had to rush back to the restaurant.

"You could have phoned to say you weren't coming."

"And left you to eat alone?" Norman called for the bill. "Anyway, I asked him to have lunch with us here tomorrow." Laurie nodded noncommittally. "You'll find him tremendously fascinating. He's picking us up in the Alfa at one."

The last sentence almost worried Laurie more than all the rest. In two years he had come to understand Norman's angry moods, jealousy and possessiveness. Norman continually needed human response. He was a good to brilliant talker if he had a sympathetic listener. When Laurie was feeling on top of the world, he succeeded in being that person. At other times he strove to provide the cues without sufficiently covering his boredom, or he purposely refused to help. In either case Norman became angry, remaining silent and sulking until a better audience was found. He lived on other people's expressions of understanding and sympathy, though the sympathy required was more that conveyed by the French *sympathie* than the English word's note of condolence. Deprived of this, he became like a baby robbed of its rattle, querulous and unpleasant, and at the same time a subject for an onlooker's amusement.

But the last sentence had introduced a new element, for if the words were slightly snobbish, the tone in which they were spoken was strongly so. For all his education and impeccable taste in clothes and furnishing, Norman had always been completely free of the taint of intellectual or social snobbery in its more superficial forms. Even the two famous authors whom he knew intimately by nickname were referred to by their surnames when talking to others about them. The unnecessary reference to being picked up in the Alfa was a new turn, and one more piece of the idol's shell chipped off.

"How much shall I leave?" Norman asked as he counted the change. "They've added on fifteen per cent already."

"A hundred'll do." This was another ritual, normally answered automatically, that tonight seemed redundant and irritating.

"Give me a couple of hundred," said Norman, folding his last hundred note into the bill. "I've nothing left until I go to Cook's tomorrow."

"Certainly," answered Laurie. His voice sounded funny. Casually he felt in his pocket. "Sorry, Norman, I can't. I've left the money in my jacket at the hotel."

"Sure?"

"Of course. Don't you trust me or something?"

"Don't be a fool."

"Then why did you say 'sure'?"

"Because you never use my name unless you're hiding something."

Laurie had no idea whether this was true or not. At the moment it was a bull's-eye. Unless he could replace the money he had spent, this conversation would make things ten times as bad. Now was the time to confess. Confess what? How stupid he had been not to have told Norman on arriving a story about being pickpocketed. His only chance was to evade producing the money this evening and sell something in the morning. He looked up and met Norman's gaze: it contained a mixture of triumph and regret. Norman always preferred to keep his psychological keys to Laurie's character to himself.

"We'd better go back to the hotel straight away," said Norman. "The girl who comes in to turn down the bed may find the money first." He stood up and walked towards the steps leading from the restaurant. Laurie followed.

They walked towards the Arno in silence. For a while Laurie toyed with the idea of saying that the money had in fact been stolen from the hotel, but finally he rejected the idea. Whatever happened no one else must suffer for his crime. Or was it a crime? Was it reasonable for him to behave like an ascetic just because Norman failed to represent the same emotional outlet to him as he presented to Norman. He was a normal, healthy human being with the usual appetites. He was entitled to satisfy them, the more especially since he was in a country whose laws did not object. Then, suddenly, in a simple and deceptively logical way, he saw the answer. He would offer to pay Norman the four thousand five hundred lire in its English equivalent once they were home. His dilemma almost vanished; it receded immediately to the position where it had become, and would remain, the focal point for Norman's jealousy and irritability. It might even, Laurie thought, stimulate Norman's interest in him which had recently been wearing very thin. But deep down he knew that he would never dare present such a proposition to Norman. He was about to add to himself that even Norman's jealousy would have little to feed on, since he knew neither the boy's name nor address, when he suddenly and delightedly remembered that he had arranged a further meeting for the following evening.

As they turned into the narrow riverside road running past the hotel, Norman turned to Laurie and spoke in a more friendly tone: "What shall we do tonight?"

"I don't mind." They were only fifty yards from the Leonardo now. If he could only think of some original, inexpensive way of spending the evening he might still postpone their entering it.

"Flicks?"

"Not unless you're very keen."

Norman shook his head. "No," he said, "we can do that in London."

"Look!" Laurie pointed to the centre of the river where a tanned Italian youth in black shorts and a scarlet tee-shirt was paddling a sleek canoe with the current. His progress was swift and effortless. Norman crossed the road to the parapet lining the river and Laurie followed. Other people had stopped to gaze at the swift, graceful passage of the skiff, but in a few seconds Laurie became bored and allowed his gaze to wander. It took in the brown, stuccoed buildings opposite, the dignified Ponte Vecchio and then, above and beyond, the Piazzale Michelangeli itself.

"Norman, what about getting the car and going up to the Piazzale? The view becomes quite terrific as it gets dark and we can sit out on the terrace of the café behind the 'David' and have a drink."

Norman turned from looking at the canoe which was fast disappearing. The people on the footbridge who had stopped to watch its progress continued their crossing of the Arno. "That's an idea. I'll slip up to the room and get my Leica."

"It'll be too dark by the time we get there."

"Not on your life! What's a really good camera for? You wait here. Shan't be a minute." Norman smiled, hurried across the road and disappeared into the hotel.

Laurie faced the river. He wondered whether Norman would remember the money again before they set off. There were a couple of hundred lire in small notes in the dashboard pocket of the car; that would buy them a drink or two. In the morning he would have to slip out early and sell something. It was a vain, minute hope and he knew it. It served, though, to stave off discovery until the actual moment arrived. The situation was fraught with difficulties enough without increasing them by repeated mental anticipation. Surely there was something saleable in his case!

It was getting dark. There were fewer people about now and the angry buzzing of the Vespas and Lambrettas had decreased to a faint hum, except when one of them darted along the water-front. Two boys chased each other along the mud flat across the

river, then ran into the ruins above. After a moment they could
be seen fighting and wrestling, framed in a ruined archway as in
a Cartier-Bresson photograph. It was already too dark to see their
faces, but Laurie guessed at their olive skins and beautiful features,
and envied their carefree play.

"Laurie!" He heard and did not hear.

"Laurie!" It was coming from above. He looked up. Norman
was leaning over the edge of a third-floor balcony. Even in the half
light he looked excitedly angry.

"Come up! Quickly!"

All thought of the afternoon, the money and the boy who had
had most of it vanished. Something had happened. Laurie waited
impatiently for a Lancia to drive past, then dashed into the hotel
and ran through the hall, up the stairs, and down a long corridor;
then up three stairs and down another corridor. The hotel consisted
of a number of houses joined together. He turned the corner of
the last corridor. Norman stood in the doorway.

"What's wrong?" asked Laurie.

"My Leica!"

"What——"

"It's gone!"

"Are you sure?"

"Absolutely. I've searched everywhere. I left it under the pillow
when I went out. The bed's been disarranged and then put straight.
You can see that. We'll get the manager."

Norman hurried out of the room and down the corridor.
Laurie followed. He felt exactly as he had when Eccles had arrived
so unexpectedly at the flat that evening. He could see quite, quite
clearly the expression on the porter's face when he had come down
the stairs with the boy. It had been a cross between a sneer and a
grin. He had regretted even then not having an extra thousand-lire
note on him. The situation had called for a tip.

[3]

Once or twice when Laurie had entered the narrow panelled hall
of the hotel there had been one or two English or Americans

standing about or talking to the porter who stood behind the little desk on the right. More often it was deserted and so confirmed Laurie's feeling that the hotel was almost empty, although a letter or guide book filled nearly every pigeon-hole behind the porter. Besides, they had been told by the manager that the place was fully booked until the end of September. Tonight this was confirmed. When Norman reached the bottom of the stairs, with Laurie close behind, the hall was full, mostly of English people who had just arrived.

Norman crossed the hall and tried to enter the manager's office, but it was full of people waiting to fill in arrival forms. He pushed his way out and struggled towards the counter at the porter's office, Laurie still following. A young American priest, whom Laurie had met in the hotel's gloomy bar the day before, seized him by the arm.

"Say, you and your partner seem in some hurry."

Laurie smiled, at the same time keeping an eye on Norman, who was now near the counter. "My friend's camera has been stolen from our bedroom."

"You don't say?" The priest glanced towards Norman, and Laurie, following his look, saw that the young porter who had watched him leave the hotel was still on duty. "Do you have a match?" the priest asked.

"Sorry." Norman was now at the counter. "Excuse me," said Laurie. "I must go. He may need me."

"Sure. Be seeing you."

Laurie smiled. "Yes, of course." He moved away and bumped into an angry-looking English spinster. "Sorry." He looked at Norman, then back at the priest who was still watching him. "Sometimes I wish I was a Catholic, too," he said. "It must be easier."

"You could be," called the American. Then Laurie heard Norman's voice, distinct above the general hubbub.

"Excuse me, porter. Excuse me, I said."

"One moment, sir. I must serve these people first." The young man was calm and smiling.

"This is important," shouted Norman. Laurie was next to him now. "My camera's been stolen from my room."

Conversation round the porter's desk died at once. Everybody looked at Norman, who had changed from an angry man trying to jump the queue to an Englishman cheated by foreigners. Worse, it had happened in the very hotel in which they were going to stay. The porter alone seemed unperturbed. He smiled pleasantly and knowingly.

"Meester Keengstone and his friend were there," he said simply.

"What are you talking about, you fool?" shouted Norman more loudly. "I'm Mr. Kingston's friend. Get me the manager."

By now the conversation was ebbing away in an ever-growing circle. Almost everyone in the lounge was listening. The porter tried to answer, but Norman refused to let him speak. He just shouted: "Get me the manager," punctuating it with "Did you ever see such a damned fool?" spoken either to Laurie or to the crowd around him. For the benefit of his fellow tourists he mentioned the make and price of the camera, where it had been hidden and the disarranged bed. He was perspiring freely and, on top of his genuine concern for the missing object, enjoying his anger. It had been pent up all evening.

The porter returned with the manager, a small, well-dressed man carrying an open fountain pen. The porter was talking rapidly, having lost his former composure. The manager, who did not appear to be listening, waved him back to the porter's desk.

"Are you the manager?" demanded Norman, still shouting.

"I am, sir. Will you please——"

"My camera's been stolen from my bedroom. It's a Leica."

"I know, sir. Would you please come to my office."

For a moment Laurie thought that Norman was going to refuse. There is nothing, his expression said, that cannot be said here in public. But after a beckoning glance to Laurie he followed the little man down the corridor. Laurie started to follow until suddenly he felt his elbow seized. He stopped and turned round. It was the priest.

"You come on out with me," he said quietly. "It'll be a lot easier that way—for both of you."

They made their way through the crowd and out into the street. The priest turned left and started towards the Ponte Vecchio with long, easy strides. Laurie walked a little behind him, finding it awkward to find a matching step. They came to the bridge and crossed it, neither talking nor looking into the windows of the tiny jewellery shops set into the sides. It was quite dark. Small groups of children collected in clusters, talking excitedly or playing games on chalked-out pitches. Their grandparents sat on stools in the doorways of the flats or shops, talking more quietly or contemplating the children with an amused, protective interest.

Laurie wondered what had happened to Norman. By now he would know all. He would have been extremely embarrassed. Martyr-like he would be packing to leave. They would probably have to journey well into the night, until their eyes were aching, as a penance and punishment. His sudden flight and failure to admit his part in the camera's disappearance would have added tenfold to Norman's anger. The priest slowed down as they started to climb the hill, and Laurie realized that his legs were aching. It was hard not to admire the boy; he had never once left him and had no pocket large enough to conceal Norman's camera, and yet he had managed to steal it.

"How—how did you know—you——"

"I was there when you went up with your young companion and there when you came down again." The priest smiled guilelessly at him.

"I see."

"These Italian kids are often not as innocent as they look."

"No." He wondered suddenly whether the priest had really understood. Ought he to call him Father, he asked himself. But he was so young, and Laurie was not a Catholic.

They had climbed quite a way towards the Piazzale Michelangelo. At a bend in the road the priest stopped by a wall and gazed out at the city that lay unfolded before them, vague shapes and twinkling lights, a blur of soft noise and the river shining.

"Why did you pull me out?" asked Laurie, more sharply than he intended.

"Your friend will find it easier that way. He doesn't know what happened."

"You don't know him! He'll be twice as bad because I deserted him."

The priest pursed his lips. "He has a right to be sore about it. Cameras don't grow on trees."

"That's not all," answered Laurie, looking down.

"I know," said the priest. "I guess the right and the wrong go back some way."

"It's probably all wrong from your point of view," said Laurie helplessly. "It's always the same."

"Giving in to temptation is wrong. Lying is wrong. Seducing children is wrong."

"He didn't need much seducing," retorted Laurie, colouring. So he did understand. "He was a crook in the first place."

"Guys like you started him in on it in the first place. You don't escape by being the second or twenty-second."

They leant on the wall and gazed out over the city. "Supposing you're born like me," asked Laurie, "what do you do?"

"Born?"

Laurie remained silent.

"Resist the temptation to sin," the priest said quietly. "Pray to your God for help. At least try." He smiled. "That's a big issue. In the smaller one, go back and tell your friend what happened, just as it happened. Don't make excuses. Just say you're really and deeply sorry. If you are sorry."

Laurie stayed silent. He realised that he had been hoping that the priest would offer to intercede for him. He knew that if he handled Norman wrongly at this juncture their relationship would be at an end. He would be without home or job. He needed help now, and all that the priest could do was to tell him to be honest. He knew that. He had known it for three years. But to know and to want were not to achieve.

The priest held out his hand. "I'm going on up to the Piazzale. Now, I think, is the moment for you to go down. If you want me I'm in Room 48. I hope it all figures out O.K."

Laurie shook his hand half-heartedly, then managed a smile as the priest strode up the hill. At the next corner the American looked back and waved, then was lost to sight. For a moment Laurie almost ran after him to beg for his intercession. But he knew it was hopeless. He must face Norman alone and at once. Slowly he made his way down past the Pitti Palace. It was closed and locked, but he thought of all the wonderful pictures inside. If he could only create one painting, just one painting, of a quarter the beauty of any of the Bellinis and Raphaels within; if he could only give others a tenth of the pleasure and experience that any one of these paintings had given him, then at least would the mess that was him and his life be justified. But even his magnificent idea of using the holiday as an inspiration to countless sketches and water-colours had come almost to nothing. Worse, it had come to spending precious hours with juvenile delinquents.

As he neared the hotel his pace slowed even more. He could see that the shutter to their balcony window was closed and the room in darkness. Norman must be downstairs waiting for him. He thought of wandering about the city until the early hours of the morning. At least Norman might become worried. Twenty minutes earlier he had left the priest; already he was prevaricating. He almost ran the last hundred yards.

The hotel entrance hall was deserted. A different porter stood behind the desk. Laurie walked straight through into the bar, expecting to see Norman there, but that too was empty. The manager's office was in darkness. He approached the porter.

"Is Mr. Wayne upstairs, do you happen to know?" He spoke calmly.

"He is out, sir."

"Thank you." Laurie felt relieved and disappointed. This was only postponement. He started up the stairs.

"Excuse me, sir."

"Yes."

The porter took a small piece of white paper from Laurie's pigeon-hole and unfolded it slowly. "A Signor Catalini phoned," he read. "He said Signor Wayne left his camera there. He will bring it in the morning."

"Thank you," said Laurie. "I'll tell him." He went on up the stairs.

PART III

SUSSEX

[1]

There were two rooms. The larger pieces of furniture were old-fashioned and badly worn. The lamps and ornaments, on the other hand, were aggressively modern: black paper shades and heart-shaped bits of pottery. Two threadbare rugs covered the linoleum. The living-room had heavy, brown curtains, while those in the bedroom sported an abstract pattern, and were bright and gay. The main room was large, and facing a built-in gas fire was a huge, sprawling couch, one arm disfigured by cigarette burns and the other leaning dangerously towards the floor. Laurie slept on it for the first few nights after his return from Italy.

It seemed strange to him that he derived warmth and satisfaction from Tom and Susan's sleeping on the far side of the brown door. Two years ago the same situation had driven him nearly mad with envy and frustration. Now the early-morning sight of Tom wandering into the kitchenette, wearing only woollen vest and pants, excited him without arousing either. Even on the second morning, as he lay listening to Tom washing, he was still pleasantly surprised at the way they had received him. They had simply assumed that he would stay with them until he had settled matters with Norman and found a place of his own.

When he returned from his flat-hunting on the second afternoon, Tom was already home. He had changed little since Laurie had first met him at Marble Arch two years earlier. He seemed softer now, but Laurie knew that the change lay as much in his conception of Tom as in the effect that Susan had had on him. Only his hands seemed the same, rough and strong.

"'lo, Laurie. Want some tea? I just made it."

"Thanks," replied Laurie. "I'm worn out with wandering around."

"Find anything?"

"I'm afraid not. Look, I'll move on tomorrow. Go home or something."

"What the bloody 'ell for? You're awright here, aren't you?" He handed Laurie a chipped pottery cup, brimful of tea. "Sue won't be in till late. They've a flap on at 'er office, 'appens too bloody often for my liking, but it's a good job and she likes it. Advertising."

"Yes, she told me."

"We can go out for a bite if you're not doing anything. There's a café down near Mum's place that's awright." He laughed. "Even Sue'll come there with me."

Laurie found the conversation awkward. This was a new stage in the relationship with Tom. In the first year or so after Susan and Tom had married, he had seen them fairly often. They had treated him with amused contempt, teased him about Norman Wayne and visits to Brighton to see Mary. Then one day when he had been with Norman, they had all four met at the Club. Norman had disapproved of Tom and silently discouraged Laurie's visits to Wandsworth, putting obstacles in his way whenever possible. In the six months before the Italian trip he had only come to the Wandsworth flat twice, and each time Tom had been on duty. Without Tom, Susan had treated Laurie sympathetically, but still with an air of amusement, as if contemplating a mild though pleasant freak. Now all this was changed. Laurie was a friend who had once helped them, and in turn needed help. That was all, and they were ready to give it without qualification.

"I think I'll put on 'civvies'," said Tom after a long pause. "Makes a break. Sue likes me in uniform."

Half an hour later they went out together. Despite the discouragement of the day's home-hunting, Laurie felt delighted by the prospect of an evening with Tom. For the first time since Norman had driven him to the station in Florence, he was momentarily on top of the world. As they avoided some children playing on the pavement of the narrow street, he thought quite calmly of Norman's return at midnight four nights earlier. He recalled the hard, unusual way in which he had given Laurie orders to pack, the packing in complete silence and the drive to the station. He had known Norman in every stage of anger, but never before had he seen him so cold and hard and silent. Then they turned into the main road, Tom started to talk of a sergeant who was getting him down, and Laurie forgot Norman and the scene of their parting. That was something to face when Norman returned from Italy.

Tom's café proved better than Laurie had anticipated. They had steak, fried egg and chips, and ate it in silence, not like the Frenchmen to whom food is more important than chatter, but because Laurie was unable to strike the right note and Tom was unafraid of silence. The Guardsman was well known there, and Laurie detected a note of warning in the way he had been formally introduced to the waitress as a "friend of the wife's". When she had taken their order and disappeared into the back room, he confided to Laurie that she was the "boss's daughter", as if the bookseller would more easily approve of her as such. When she was clearing away the empty plates at the end of the meal, Tom patted her play-fully on the behind, but avoided Laurie's eyes afterwards. Laurie suddenly wondered whether either Susan or Tom was happy.

After the meal they went to a near-by pub and started to drink steadily. Tom asked Laurie about Italy and the bookseller obliged. Finally he felt the barrier drop between them, and without embarrassment he told Tom the whole story of the boy and the subsequent row with Norman Wayne.

"Feel like that myself sometimes," said Tom. He was sprawled awkwardly across a slightly rickety chair at one end of a long deserted bar. Laurie sat close to him on a similar chair and they looked for all the world like a couple of tipsy passengers on a bus. The barman, fat and wearing a waistcoat without jacket, was talk-ing in a murmuring undertone to a middle-aged woman who was clutching her handbag. Other people came in from time to time, and the barman only left the woman long enough to serve them.

Laurie did not answer. He was not sure what Tom had meant, though he was fairly sure that what he considered the logical interpretation of the remark was the wrong one. Besides, he had had a great deal to drink and was a little frightened of himself. He hoped that Susan would be home before them.

"Sue," went on Tom, waving his hands about and watching the woman who leaned ever closer to the barman, "we get on awright. Only not for long. She talks about things I don't know

about. Then she says I won't try and learn. We make it up in bed."
He took another swig of beer. "It's like always being on your best
behaviour. Not swearing, not whistling, not putting your hands in
your pockets. Not eating cheese off a knife." He drained his glass.
"Sometimes I want a girl like Jean at the café. Boss's daughter. Like
you and Norman." He staggered up to the bar and ordered two
more pints.

Tom was not drunk, just friendly and easy, and Laurie was
warming to his warmth. He felt that Susan ought to be more
understanding. He would be if he lived with Tom. Further, he
would try to entertain the Guardsman instead of berating him
for his ignorance. Tom would be nice to live with, too; easy and
friendly like tonight. It was just a question of treating him right.
He smiled at Tom as the Guardsman handed him another glass
and Tom smiled back. What pals they were becoming! Perhaps the
row with Norman had been a blessing in disguise.

They went out into the darkness together, arm in arm, neither
of them embarrassed. They staggered a little, pausing to comment
on a girl's legs or a shop window display. Laurie was alternately
prey to fear and excitement. Suddenly Tom pointed to a youth
who watched them from the other side of the road and said:
"Fancy 'im?"

Laurie blushed and laughed. Tom squeezed his arm and laughed
with him. They staggered along and soon arrived home. Tom
dropped on to the huge couch and pulled Laurie down beside him.
The room was barely lit, a dull glow coming from under the black
shade on the lamp in the corner. Tom closed his eyes and put his
arm round Laurie's shoulders, and they sat there in silence, Laurie
more conscious than ever before of the Guardsman's physical
presence, of his muscular thigh, and of his own hand squeezed
between them.

Now there was no doubt. He was poised on the brink of his fulfilment. This was the moment he had waited for ever since that day
when he had first seen Beeson at Marble Arch. This represented
the immersion of everything that was Laurence Kingston into
someone who would complete the man that alone he could not
achieve. This was different from the sordid incident in Florence a
week earlier and would make Tom his for ever. Susan would have to

pay the price for failing to make her husband happy. As in a trance he watched his hand move to Tom's leg, settle there and feel its strength. Even as he watched, even as the thought of Susan entered and left his brain, they heard her quick footsteps on the stairs; the door opened and she was there. Neither of them had moved.

[2]

Susan paused, but, however briefly, it was long enough for Laurie to become aware of it. Then she smiled, shut the door behind her and threw her bag on the table. Going to the mirror over the fireplace, she touched her hair, patting it superfluously. It was close cut, in urchin crop style. Laurie carefully shifted his hand from Tom's knee, but when he tried to move away altogether, the Guardsman's arm held him tight. Susan came across and kissed Tom on the lips and he responded lightly.

"You two've been drinking," she said in mock disgust.

"I'll say," said Tom thickly. "Got to do summat when the wife's always out."

Laurie searched for something to say. Tom's challenging tone and Susan's pause at the door had produced a tension that might snap unpleasantly. He had already noticed something more positive than boredom unrelieved by early passion, not uncommon after two years of marriage. The baser side of him might welcome differences between them, but not in the form of a row in his presence. Besides, Susan was no rival to his feelings for Tom. Laurie felt that there was room for them both.

"Someone has to earn the necessary for you to go drinking."

Laurie was shocked by the bitterness of her tone. It was so unexpected after the easy banter of her first remark. She stood with her back to the table, leaning on it, yet alert. She was opening and closing her left hand in a deliberate way, opening it slowly and shutting it with a snap. She looked frail in the half light.

Tom removed his arm from Laurie's neck. "I suppose you think I like spending my evenings alone, eh? All the other blokes go around with their missis. If they was to see me they'd bloody well think I didn't have one."

"There's no need to swear because you've been drinking."

Laurie stood up a little shakily. He was not sure what he was going to say or do. He hoped vaguely that the movement would act as a curtain to their quarrel. They both watched him, momentarily distracted, then Susan, apparently deciding that he was going to do nothing, returned to the attack: "I never once saw my father drunk——"

"I'll swear in my own 'ome if I want to," Tom put in, as if he had not heard her last remark. Laurie stood stupidly, looking from one to the other. He took off his glasses and rubbed his eyes. "Why don't you go back to your bloody father?" the Guardsman added, as if her remark had only just caught up with him. He stood up and lurched across the room, then went into the lavatory, slamming the door behind him.

Susan went back to the mirror and played at straightening her hair. It was a round mirror framed in dark oak, arches of curved pattern dividing the inner ring of the frame from the outer. Laurie stood watching her. He thought of the *Arnolfini* portrait, of the marriage sealed by the artist's picture and of the scenes from the life of Christ surrounding *that* mirror. He thought of marriage, an unknown land that would remain for ever unknown. His negative attitude in standing by was perhaps no more than an unconscious revenge: let them have their marriages and all that go with them.

"Sue, this is all my fault." He felt and sounded awkward. "I should have stopped him."

From the lavatory came the sound of Tom being sick. Laurie's idyll dissolved into something messy and sordid, the momentary disillusion ricochetting off Tom on to Susan. If she had not arrived his dream would have come true by now. He would have found himself at last, known that timeless moment of peace whose memory would have lasted for ever.

Susan swung round and for a moment Laurie thought that she was going to agree with him. But she shook her head sadly. "This isn't the first time, Laurie; or the tenth or the twentieth. We can't even put an end to it—the marriage, I mean. When we're together it's like—we're poison to one another. But we can't stand being apart. When Tom was away on manoeuvres I was—oh, it sounds silly, like a Hollywood 'B' picture or a novelette—but I was lost.

We need each other, except when we've got each other. You see, we sort of love and hate each other all at the same time."

"Was it always like that?" asked Laurie, embarrassed by her confidences.

"Not at first. We had to fight then. There was my family, and his family hated me. Once they knew I was really married my family stopped fighting. I've never seen them since." She moved a pace towards Laurie and added quietly: "I'd like to. I don't know why. I suppose it's silly to quarrel. They were right and so was I. I'm not happy in the ordinary sense of the term——"

"Who is?"

"—but I wouldn't give Tom up."

"And Tom? Are you sure of him?" He could only have asked the question with the help of alcohol.

"Not really." She moved back to the mirror and looked at herself carefully. "It would be the end if he left me. I could never face them at home." She spoke very quietly. "Some nights when I come back and he's not here, I think he'll never come."

The drink and her confidence increased Laurie's boldness. "Aren't you going to have children?"

"Tom says we should wait till he's out of the Army."

"Why?"

"In case he's moved around."

There was the sound of water flushing in the toilet and Tom came out. He was paler than usual and his large eyes were bloodshot. He smiled at Laurie sheepishly, then went up to Susan and took her by the waist. "Be an angel?"

"What do you want?" Her voice was choked.

"Make us some coffee." He turned her to him and kissed her savagely and briskly. Laurie straightened the cushions on the couch and started to make his bed from the pile of folded sheets and blankets beside the leaning arm. He busied himself without turning round until he heard Susan cross the room and go out to the little kitchen. Then Tom was beside him.

"You all right?" asked Laurie.

"Will be after the coffee," the Guardsman answered. "She's a good kid really." He helped Laurie straighten the second blanket. "You warm enough? Bloody draughty place this." He tucked the end in carefully. "Only she can't forget she comes from the upper class. Wants to change me all the time."

Laurie sat on the bed. "You're not sorry you married her?"

"The other chaps think she's tops."

"And you?"

Tom moved into the same position in front of the mirror that Susan had taken up a few minutes earlier. "Blimey, I look white."

"You always do," said Laurie with a laugh. He crossed his feet. "You wouldn't leave her?"

Tom stared at him as if his eyes would unravel some additional meaning in the question. "For who?"

"For anyone," answered Laurie, staring straight back at him.

"I'd be a laughing stock with me mates after all I've said about 'er."

Laurie smiled, then muttered: "No Englishman ever admitted joining the Army to defend his country."

"What do yer mean?"

Laurie pulled the top sheet over the blankets and disregarded the question. "Don't you want children?"

"Kids? S'ppose so. Only not while I'm in the Army."

"Why not?"

"Get moved around for one thing."

"They'd go with you."

"Mightn't be right."

"Taking them around?"

Tom sat on the bed. "No. It's all a bit mixed up, Susan being different."

"Jewish?"

"Different class, sort of."

"She's happy here. Why shouldn't her children be?"

"Is she?" The Guardsman looked surprised. It was a question he had not faced before.

"Of course. Why do you think she stays?"

"She can't go 'ome. They quarrelled something awful." He paused to remember. "I went up there with 'er one night. She thought if they met me they might soften." He looked at Laurie, his large eyes opening slightly. "They went on as if I wasn't there. Kept talking of that *goy*. When Sue got upset they begged me to

leave 'er alone." He stopped again and looked towards the kitchenette where Susan could be heard putting cups and saucers on a
tray. "'er ol' man took me in another room. Nice house they've
got. He offered me money to leave her alone." He lowered his
voice. "She doesn't know about that."

"How did you answer him?"

Tom laughed roughly. "I told 'im where he could put his money.
Then we went." He ran his tongue slowly round his lips. "I think
they were a bit afraid of me." He grinned and looked at Laurie. "I
think you used to be, too."

"I still am," said Laurie, smiling.

"Like hell!" The Guardsman turned towards the kitchen door.
"Come on, Sue girl." He studied his shoes. "Are you really?"

"What?"

"Afraid of me?"

"Yes."

"Why?"

"It's all mixed up with a lot of things. You're something I'd like
to be, I suppose. The things I'm not. I'm not those things because
I'm frightened of them—boxing, shall we say? And as you represent them, I'm frightened of you."

"You worry about things too much."

"I suppose so," said Laurie. It was clear that Tom had not
followed him. "We both seem to have sobered up."

Tom did not answer. Susan called for help and he stood up. As
he started across the floor, Laurie also moved towards the kitchen,
and they collided. Their bodies touched. Quietly, strongly, Tom
caught hold of Laurie's head. Stooping down he kissed Laurie
hard on the lips. Laurie caught the Guardsman feverishly round
the waist. As quietly and firmly Tom disentangled himself.

He patted Laurie on the shoulder. "You poor kid," he said. He
crossed the room and disappeared into the kitchen.

Laurie stood for a moment, then rushed to the lavatory, where
he was violently sick. When he came back into the room, the
others were drinking coffee. They were both friendly and normal
towards him. They discussed Italy.

[3]

Laurie went to see Norman next day, travelling by underground. He sat there, jolted and shaken by the train's noisy progress, and lived the scene of his collision with Tom over and over again. He felt anew the ridiculous kiss, and almost glanced in embarrassment at the sheepish-looking women opposite, so real was his re-creation of the moment. He tried to imitate the exact tone of voice that had spoken the words "You poor kid". The endless shades of affection and understanding to which he matched the three words provided him with that rarest of homosexual experiences: love returned. It had been too spontaneous to be false. Seen through the prism of his own feelings and needs, only love showed. He had no need of pity now.

He knew with an instinct born of many disappointments that the moment and the words belonging to it were the apex. For a second his love and Tom's pity had become one. It could never again have the same spontaneity whatever opportunities offered. He wondered if there was a way of finding an equivalent in paint for that knowledge. He began to form a vision of the grey Wandsworth street peopled by figures who cried out for love and compassion: "You poor kid." His vision contained dreary, grey houses, grubby children playing in the gutter and a plot empty of everything save bomb rubble, derived from the studies of Sutherland, Moore and Piper, as well as from the actual street where Tom and Susan lived.

The train stopped and he stepped on to the platform. At the bus stop outside the station, two of Norman Wayne's customers said "Good morning" to him, and he suddenly felt nervous. He not only had to face Norman but some of the staff as well. Then he remembered that he still had a key to the house and decided to let himself in; he could then ring up Norman, who would already be at the shop. He no longer felt envious of the suburban middle-class as he surveyed their orderly rows of houses from the upper deck of a bus. He had his own inner sense of security now. The only doubt came from Tom's more usual, matter-of-fact attitude that morning. But then Susan had been there.

Susan, surprisingly, had talked of the night before as soon as Tom had left for barracks. In a business-like, friendly manner she had told him to be wary of Tom. The Guardsman had little measure of his own emotions. On a subsequent occasion his behaviour of the night before might appear to him in a very different light. She was only mentioning this because she liked Laurie, and of course Tom liked Laurie; and she wanted it to stay that way. Laurie was too much taken aback to find out what she included in Tom's "behaviour of the night before".

Then abruptly she had shifted the searchlight to herself. "Things are getting a little difficult, Laurie. Tom's drinking a lot—and he carries on with other girls. Not serious, but——" Susan spoke in a quiet, casual way without any of the intensity of the night before. "I suppose our marriage isn't a great success, but few are. But the sex side of things works well and still means a great deal to us. And I could never go home again, so the marriage *must* last." She paused. "I look to you, Laurie, to help; you're our oldest friend."

As Laurie started to walk up the road to the house which had been his home for two years, he wondered why she had considered it necessary to run the whole gamut from "hands off" to "please help". It would have been simpler to ask him to move out. In any case he would go as soon as he had settled matters with Norman. He could hardly go on sleeping in the next room to them after last night.

The house was not empty when he arrived. Laurie learnt this too late and cursed himself for not having rung the bell first. He thought of letting himself out again when he heard steps on the landing.

"Who's there?" It was not Norman's voice.

"Laurie. Laurence Kingston."

"Oh, hullo, Laurie." It was the senior assistant from Norman's shop. Tall and thin, he descended the stairs slowly, as if making a stage entry. "Are you——" He took the pipe out of his mouth and waved it towards Laurie. "Are you still one of us?"

"No," replied Laurie. He was embarrassed and not sure what to say.

"Mr. Wayne told us you had a sort of nervous breakdown and were staying with friends."

"Oh?" Laurie wondered how much he was supposed to know of Norman's movements. "Where is he now?"

"At the shop. He sent me for his brief case: he left it behind this morning. You coming down to the shop?"

"No," answered Laurie, "but tell him I'm back, will you?"

"Are you better?"

"Partly." Laurie wished he would go. "Excuse me, I must make a call." He went towards the cream-coloured telephone on the table by the staircase.

"Oh, of course."

Laurie started to dial a number.

"See you later."

Laurie nodded in reply. As soon as the front door had closed, he replaced the receiver, wondering whose number he had rung and what had happened to his painting of the telephone.

He went into the drawing-room and sat down. The room was charming and superficially artistic. Each wall and its nearby furniture made up a page out of "Perfect Homes"; it even looked as though it had been put together in monthly instalments as the magazine came out. All the walls except the one facing the window were covered with a neutral wallpaper; the exception had a grey and cerise pattern that echoed the colour of the carpet. A guitar hung on one side of the fireplace and an arty bookshelf on the other. The lamps were awkward and modern, and the suite, not unattractive with its curves and stillborn wings, was grey. Two *chianti* bottles in straw jackets hung below one another by the door.

It was at that moment that he became conscious of a thought that had long lain maturing within him: the room exactly expressed its owner's personality. He recalled his first meeting with Norman and the strong, polished impression that the older man had made. The room had had a similar impact on him; its unreality only became apparent as time went by. It seemed in retrospect that his admiration for Norman had changed to contempt in a moment. In fact, long hours spent together had slowly corroded the first impression until the second was revealed. Underneath the veneer there was only the Norman who had shown such childish alternations of jealousy and anger that night in the Bucca Lape.

He remained quite still when he heard the car draw up outside. He nearly reached for a magazine, but knew that Norman would see through such a pose at once. "Put it away, dearie, it doesn't hide your nervousness," he would say, and then launch into a long lecture on Laurie's ingratitude as shown in his appalling behaviour in Florence. He heard the key turn in the lock and the door slam. The last of his defiance vanished. Even a *chi-chi* drawing-room was a palace of security compared to no home at all.

"Laurie?"

"I'm in here."

It was not until later that he diagnosed the curious expression on Norman's face as one of acute embarrassment. He had never seen it before. They shook hands formally and Norman sat in the grey chair opposite him. It had the air of an interview for a job.

"You back all right?"

"Yes, thanks," said Laurie.

"I sort of expected to find you here."

"I thought it better to stay with friends."

Norman looked at the window so intently that Laurie half expected him to comment on how well the curtains had been cleaned in their absence. Instead he quietly asked: "Will you come back?"

The question was rather unexpected: its form completely so. Norman might perhaps have asked him if *he* wanted to come back, the stronger to make the lesson of what he had lost. But this was an appeal couched in the form of an invitation, and its power made the scales of Norman's superficiality, jealousy and childishness dissolve as easily as scum before a detergent. But he was still conscious that if this was Norman's better side, it was only part of the whole; his immediate object achieved, one of the other parts might, unconsciously perhaps, oust this one.

"I think it's better if I don't, Norman."

The answer seemed to have been expected, for Norman followed it quickly with: "What will you do, then?"

"I'll get another job and some sort of flat again. I've still got the premium from the sale of the other one," Laurie half smiled. "Thanks to your insistence." He nearly added a word about a premonition, but he was too near tears for that type of levity.

"I think you're making a mistake. Let's be frank, Laurie. In one sense it makes little difference to me. I'm over the 'rave' stage where you're concerned. But we've got a lot in common and we get on well in the shop. We can offer each other companionship, and if we each look elsewhere for partners, there's no reason why it shouldn't work very nicely."

"Until you meet someone you want as a companion instead." Laurie was surprised at his own hardness, but he knew now the danger of Norman's becoming reasonable and logical, as he called it.

"That's not likely while you're living with me. For a long time now I've been coming to the conclusion that the only really satis-factory solution for people like us is to divorce sex and friendship. To say it like that sounds sordid. But if the way we're born demands certain adjustments to life, we must accept the sordid as one of them." Norman's voice became richer in tone as he warmed to his subject. "It was Gide, Laurie, who so rightly said 'I did not choose to be born as I am.' You've just got to accept and meet the situation accordingly. Right?"

"Yes." Laurie agreed, as always. Norman was not right; in fact, he was quite wrong. Sex divorced from love was extremely sordid. Anything sordid was unpleasant and to be avoided. Yet his convic-tion of this was no match for one of Norman's broadsides. They no longer impelled him to mental surrender, but he still lacked the courage to fire back. The most he could manage was to water down his "Yes" with an "I suppose so."

"There's no supposing, Laurie, it's a fact. Right. Once grant this and the rest seems clear enough to me. We both need com-panionship and we both need sex. We also need companions who will understand and permit our sex—with other people. You and I fulfil all these qualifications. We like each other very much, are not shocked by each other's sex life——"

The telephone provided the interruption that even Laurie would have needed to make. It was inconceivable that the man who had uttered the last phrase was the same who had packed him off home like a naughty child so very recently. He must not allow Norman to go on, gradually dragging Laurie with him, until the moment that he would agree to return. He was a free agent, an adult and not entirely devoid of intelligence. Why was he so afraid of speaking his mind at moments like these? What had he to lose now that he no longer wanted to return?

Norman came back. "That was Nigel. He wants us to go round to dinner on Friday and tell him all about Italy. I said we'd love to."

"Thank you, Norman, but I think it's better if I don't return." It sounded so stilted as to be artificial, and yet it was exactly what he felt. "No, please don't interrupt for a moment. I'm very grateful for all you've done for me: introducing me to people, taking me everywhere, holidays. But I want to branch out on my own. I'm tired, quite honestly, of being your friend instead of a person in my own right. That's how everyone knows me. I'm just part of your props, like your car and your house." Norman looked genuinely pained and Laurie glanced down as he continued. "It's not that I haven't enjoyed the two years together. I have. But I want something more, even if I have to give up other things for it." It still sounded false, and he wanted to get up and go. He had had his say, yet Norman still sat there as if expecting something really important.

"That's what you wanted to say?"

"Yes."

"But, Laurie, such independence is a myth. We're always dependent. Sartre's 'Hell is other people' *is* true. You'll be dependent on your new employer, your new landlord, your new friends. You'll have to shape your cloth to their cut or lose that suit too." He paused, pleased with the effect. "As a matter of fact I have news for you which will give you a whole new field—independence of me—while you're still living here. I'll tell you about it in a moment." He looked round the room. "How will you feel living in a couple of measly old rooms after this? And you, artistic and responsive to the contemporary idiom. Will you enjoy——"

"But it will be my own, Norman."

"And then what? Does a chair become more comfortable because it belongs to you? Will your water taste better than my 1947 Burgundy? No, Laurie, and you know it. The truth is you're hurt. I stupidly and unreasonably lost my temper in Florence and wounded your pride. Your claim to independence seems to stitch up the wound. Time, and my sincere regret for behaving like that, will do it anyway, and at much less cost."

"Oh, I'm not worried about that any more."

"Yes, you are, Laurie. You were insulted. I took advantage of my money and treated you like a servant. It was unforgivable, but I'm only human. I'm genuinely sorry it happened, and the measure of my regret is shown by the way I've been working in the last twenty-four hours to get you what you've wanted for so long. That's what I was coming to."

"No, Norman." He did not want to hear the offer, whatever it was, until Norman had accepted his decision as irrevocable. "I'd like to be alone again, for a time at least. At some time in the future we might try again. But not just yet."

Norman sighed and stood up. He walked to the window and stood gazing out. "Then all I do ask is that you don't go setting yourself up in a big way. Take a room for a few weeks. Get a job if you like, or stay working with us. There's plenty of room for you with all this new school business coming in. In a month or so you'll find that you've probably changed your mind. I know what I'm talking about, Laurie." He turned back and smiled. "Anyway, we're good friends again."

"Yes," agreed Laurie, smiling grimly.

"I must get back to the shop, Laurie. You can collect your things whenever you like, and then let me have your key. Take a few days more, then ring me on Sunday and let me know whether you want the job back."

"I don't——"

"Oh, there's dinner with Nigel on Friday. Will you meet me here or at the shop?"

"Here."

"About six?"

"Yes."

"Well, cheero." Norman strolled to the door.

"Norman, what were you going to tell me?"

"What? Oh, I almost forgot. I've got you the job as a part-time art teacher you wanted so much. I'll give you all the details on Friday."

[4]

Laurie went to an office in Oxford Street which claimed to have hundreds of furnished and unfurnished rooms on its books. At the corner of North Audley Street he stopped to buy some bananas from a barrow. A man in front of him was complaining loudly about the misleading price signs. He turned to Laurie as though for support. It was Eccles.

"Hello. It's you!" He half turned back to the barrow boy. "It's all right for people like you and me." He glanced at Laurie. "But for people who come up from the country, it's a disgrace."

"We've all got ter make a livin', sir," said the barrow boy.

"Where are you now?" Eccles asked Laurie as he accepted and paid for his bag of fruit.

"At Wayne's," answered Laurie. "Half a pound, please," he added to the fruitseller, pointing at the bananas.

"All lovely bananas. Two-and-four a pound." He weighed them, anxiously scanning the street at the same time.

"Are you better?" asked Eccles, narrowing his eyes slightly.

"Some oranges for a summer cold?" asked the barrow boy.

"I'm keeping well," replied Laurie, and to the fruitseller: "No, thank you."

"You better watch out otherwise," said Eccles. "Your type's had its day." Then he made off without a word of parting, neither angry nor pleasant.

Laurie was made uncomfortable by the last remark. He hated people who threw off equivocal remarks which were meant to sound ominous. He had an almost superstitious belief that they portended trouble when addressed to him personally, and had he been a Catholic, he would have crossed himself at that moment. Vaguely discomfited he continued on his way down Oxford Street until he reached the letting office.

It was a small room on the fourth floor. Behind two of the four desks sat girls, one a violent blonde with thick lips, the other non-descript. The blonde was giving a dissertation on contemporary young men when Laurie entered, and she continued without pausing. There was a filing cabinet in one corner and on it a number of chipped, unwashed cups and saucers. Beside them was a carelessly opened packet of tea and a tiny puddle of milk. The room smelt of gas although there was no ring to be seen.

The blonde stopped at last. "Yes, dearie?"

Laurie outlined his need, paid a guinea and was given a bunch of cards to work through. The blonde resumed her monologue. The nondescript made entries in a register and, presumably, listened to her friend. At last Laurie found a bed-sitting-room in Bayswater that looked promising.

"And I say if he takes you, he takes you. Not to go runnin' after every bit of you-know-what the moment it raises an eyelid at 'im." She paused.

"Yes, dearie?"

"This looks interesting," said Laurie.

"Does it, dearie? Well, you go along and see." She took the card from him. "Mrs. Murphy. Irish she'll be. Then you come back and let us know or ring us up." She gave him back the card. "I mean they'd make an awful fuss if we started chasing after other boys when they'd bought the tickets to go in." The voice followed Laurie down the stairs and almost into the street.

Mrs. Murphy may once have been Irish, but no trace of it was left. If, on the other hand, she had married an Irishman, this was not for the moment clear. A tiny man, whose breath came in wheezes, sat by a fire in the nearly darkened room as Laurie exchanged formalities with Mrs. Murphy. He sat silent, staring through the fire, not even turning round to mutter an occasional "Yes" to Mrs. Murphy whenever she sought his support. He agreed with her that it was a clean house and a decent house, and that no one made any noise or brought in women after nine o'clock. He only looked at Laurie as the prospective tenant followed Mrs. Murphy out of the room. His eyes were sunk deep into pockets of flesh.

They climbed to the second floor. The staircase was clean, but the carpet was worn and dreary, and the walls were plastered chocolate brown. The room, however, was almost a delight. It was large and had a large window that gave out on to a Carel Weight scene: a square seen through a trellis of tree branches, iron railings, a woman hurrying across the road and a little girl leaning on a bicycle. The room was papered with an inoffensive, stone-

coloured paper and the furniture was not too solid. Laurie paid
a week's money in advance and undertook to see that no women
stayed after nine in the evening. He had a room of his own again,
and if it fell short of his old basement flat, he would have plenty of
time to search for another, once he had found a job.

He was so pleased with finding a reasonable room quickly that
he decided to hurry back to the flat and offer to take them out to
dinner. Susan had mentioned that they both hoped to finish work
early and go to the cinema. Well, they would all eat out first and
then he would take them wherever they wanted to go. He rang
the office in Oxford Street to tell them that he had taken the room,
then caught the bus to Wandsworth.

It was ten past five when he reached the flat and he guessed that
neither of them would yet be home. Tom's raised voice faulted his
guess even before he could put his key in the door. He hesitated,
wondering whether it would be better to wait until they calmed
down before he went in.

"Don't be bloody silly!" It was Tom's voice, clear and angry.
Although Laurie felt awkward standing on the stairs, in case someone came up, he was frightened to enter the flat.

"I suppose if you take one of yer la-di-da girl friends by the arm,
you're a bloody lesbian, then." Only the Guardsman's words were
intelligible; Susan's came through the wooden door like a duck's
quacks. Then their voices died and Laurie went in. He felt that his
good news and invitation might restore peace.

Susan sat on the couch, crying. Tom stood over her, his thumbs
tugging at the khaki braces, looking half ridiculous, half aggressive. His right boot lay on the floor next to him; he still wore the
left. They both looked round sulkily as Laurie came in, but quickly
faced each other again, as if vigilance was imperative. Laurie tried
to smile or make a laughing greeting, but their looks were too
sullen.

"I've found a room," he said after a pause, almost apologetically.

"Good," said Tom without taking his eyes off Susan.

Susan started to cry out loud.

"Oh, shut up, for God's sake!" The Guardsman lunged at her
shoulder. His gesture seemed compounded of anger and compassion.

"I've seen Norman, too," said Laurie a little more brightly. "He was quite decent. Wanted me to go back. But of course I wouldn't."

Susan stopped crying. "Where's the room?"

"Bayswater. I thought we'd celebrate. The three of us. Go out and have something to eat, then a flick."

They both looked at him now, and he hoped that gratitude for his little plan would swamp their other feelings. "I'm not allowed to come," said Tom. He bent down and started to unlace the other boot.

"What do you mean?" asked Laurie.

"Don't, please, please don't start all that again, Tom."

"Who started it in the first place?"

"You did, by saying that you were going out alone on the one night I had free this week."

"Oh, I thought you were going to the pictures together," put in Laurie.

"Who said so?" Tom demanded of Susan.

"I told Laurie I thought we might."

"I suppose you'll have to sit between us," said Tom, kicking his boot towards the wall.

Susan stood up and grabbed him, burying her head in his shirt and shaking with sobs. Tom smiled, not unkindly, over her head. "All right, all right. We'll be ready in half an hour, Laurie. We could do with a bit of celebratin'."

Over dinner in a small Soho restaurant Tom and Susan were embarrassed with each other. Laurie tried to make conversation, treading carefully in case he reminded them in any way of the quarrel. He gave them unnecessary details of Norman's home and of his own new room. He told them about Mrs. Murphy and the strange little man staring into the fire.

"Will you go there tonight?" asked Susan, "or spend a last night with us?"

Laurie was stirring his coffee, his mind suddenly on his ominous meeting with Eccles.

"You can stay as many nights as you like," said Tom, slightly aggressively.

"I didn't say he couldn't. Only he wouldn't want to," answered Susan too snappily.

Laurie wanted to drink again to the success of his new career, but their wine glasses stood empty. One witty or interesting remark might ride them over this hurdle, probably the last. In five minutes dinner would be over and they would be hurrying to the cinema.

"You don't have to push 'im out after the way he's been decent to us," said Tom.

Laurie thought of telling them about his meeting with Eccles. Tom, at least, would have been amused. But he was too late. Before either of them had fully realised what was happening, Susan had stood up and rushed out of the restaurant wildly enough to have attracted the attention of the few other diners.

"We been workin' up to this for a long time," said Tom sulkily, "Let's go to the flicks, for flippin' hell's sake."

[5]

Laurie changed from train to bus at Lewes. It was a cold night, windows steaming over on the inside and white breath spiralling from pedestrians on the outside. A layer of fog, draped like a coverlet over the valleys, was suddenly lit by the headlights, white and insubstantial. The passengers grumbled about the weather to the conductor; a farmer predicted a change of Government to his companion.

The bus stopped outside a village school. The conductor's smile and the stares of the other passengers momentarily peopled the street for Laurie. Then they were gone, reduced to a whine in the distance; and he was alone, looking to left and right, worried at leaving the single street lamp that stretched out its arm from the school wall.

The prospect of talking to a group of strangers on art appreciation had seemed a little daunting even from the distance of his new room, gas fire blazing and a beer to hand. Now it was ominously so, and added to it were the passing fears, as insubstantial as the fog, that this was the wrong village, the wrong night, the wrong time. In the friendly letter the group's secretary had assured him that the bus would be met. Surely there were so few buses that all locals knew their times of arrival.

A boy approached on a bicycle. He stared at Laurie, free-wheeling as he did so. It was a good, hard country stare that took in Laurie's face and raincoat, books and folio of reproductions. The boy's pointed head wheeled slowly as he went by, watching distrustfully. Then he swung round and came back.

"Want someone?"

"Mr. Rogers, please. I believe he lives in the White Cottage."

"That's it." The boy sat astride the crossbar and jerked his head in the direction of a small white cottage, twenty yards beyond the school. It was set back among the trees.

"Thank you," said Laurie. His feet were beginning to feel damp, and he wondered whether there was a hole in his shoe or if his feet were just cold. He wanted to look while under the lamp, but the boy was watching him. "Goodnight," he added, and started towards the cottage. The boy did not answer, but stood there watching, never for a second taking his eyes off the stranger.

Laurie fumbled with the latch of the gate, and each glance increased his nervousness when it revealed the boy still standing astride his bicycle. At last the gate opened and he stumbled in. He almost tripped on one of the loose bricks that lined the front path, then found the knocker and rapped it loudly. The door opened and a huge, smiling man stood there.

"Mr. Kingston?"

Laurie nodded.

"Come in, come in. It's a beastly night, isn't it? Hello, Tom." He was waving to the boy, of whom he had caught sight as Laurie went past him. "Another Tom," he added, closing the door. "Bates's son. Take your coat off. I'll take it. Here's Jean. Mr. Kingston, our new lecturer, Jean, and this, Mr. Kingston, is Gwen and Martin. Gwen's twelve and Martin's fifteen. Shake hands, children. Now you come in by the fire. I'll take those books." He paused. "Or would you like a wash?"

He nodded towards a little door under the stairs. Mrs. Rogers disappeared into a room at the back of the hall, and Laurie went into the tiny cloakroom. There was a small handbasin and lavatory, and everything was spotlessly clean and smelt of lavender. One of the two guest towels had been used by someone who had left grimy fingerprints, and Laurie wondered whether it was the boy or the girl. Then he came back into the hall where Mr. Rogers was waiting for him.

He pushed Laurie into the sitting-room, a long low room with oak beams breaking the ceiling into sections, and a roaring log fire half-way down one wall. The children stood at a respectful distance while Laurie was ushered into an armchair by the fire. Mr. Rogers busied himself piling Laurie's books on a small table at one end of the room, then came and sat opposite Laurie, beaming all the time.

"Run along and tell Mummy we're ready to eat," he told the boy. "We're glad you could come to tea, Mr. Kingston; it gives us a chance to get to know one another. You'll find us a friendly group, though we don't know much, you know. You'll have to put that to rights."

"Are these the first lectures you've had on art appreciation?" asked Laurie.

"No, we've had others. John Everard. Know him?"

"No, I don't."

"Tea's up," called Mrs. Rogers, putting her head round the door.

Mr. Rogers led the way to the kitchen, followed by Laurie and Gwen. Martin was already sitting at the enamel-top table. At the five places were plates of sausages and mash. Mrs. Rogers sat down and started to pour the tea, while Laurie was put at the head of the table opposite her. The ceiling was low and again broken by beams, while the walls were distempered white, with the cupboards a brassy red.

"Do it all myself," said Mr. Rogers, watching Laurie's gaze. "Not what you call painting."

"Oh, it looks jolly good," said Laurie weakly. The kitchen was warm and his glasses had steamed up. He started to clean them.

"Do start," said Mrs. Rogers with a nervous laugh. She handed him a cup of tea.

"We don't stand on ceremony," said Mr. Rogers.

"You come by car?" Martin asked in a loud, adolescent voice.

"No, bus."

"He wouldn't be lecturing if he could afford a car," put in Mr. Rogers, smiling. "We run a little pre-war baby Austin, but even that eats up more than I can afford."

"Can't you wangle it on this income tax racket, then?" suggested
Laurie.

"I wouldn't know how to and if I did I wouldn't. Help yourself
to bread. Wangling isn't in my line. The State educates my kids
and someone's got to pay for that, which means everyone. If I
shirk someone else has to pay more, don't they?"

"Yes," agreed Laurie. He felt uncomfortable at once, though there
had been neither snub nor superiority in the tone of Mr. Rogers's
answer. He realised at once that he had slipped so completely
into the morality and outlook of Norman and his friends that Mr.
Rogers's attitude seemed reactionary, almost Victorian. The scene,
in fact, was almost Victorian in its Christmas-card jollity: the range
with the kettle steaming, Mrs. Rogers echoing everything with a
happy, nervous laugh, the children eating hungrily and intently,
and Mr. Rogers stating an unfashionable piece of honesty quite
unselfconsciously.

"We'll pull through, though," added Mr. Rogers after a pause,
"though once or twice I told Jean we mightn't have the cash to
license it for a quarter. We've always managed it somehow, though."
He pushed away his empty plate and replaced it with his side plate,
heaping it with bread and jam. "These Phaidon books any good,
Mr. Kingston? Jean gave me one for Christmas on Bellini, and Gwen
and Martin Michelangelo, or however you say it, on my birthday."

"Oh, they're excellent," answered Laurie, pleased at the change
of subject. "In fact, I never quite know how they do it for the
money."

"Didn't they used to be half a guinea before the war?" asked Mr.
Rogers. "I bought one soon after we were married."

"I think so," said Laurie.

"Mr. Kingston wouldn't remember much about before the war,"
put in Mrs. Rogers.

"Cigarettes a shilling for twenty and whisky a shilling a nip is
what someone says at this stage," countered Laurie, smiling.

"I wouldn't know," said Mr. Rogers. "I don't drink."

"Or smoke," added Martin for him.

Victorian, thought Laurie, was the wrong label. A Victorian
would have said that smugly or primly. Mr. Rogers was simply
commenting on a state of fact, not passing an implied moral

censure. There was something unselfconsciously good about the whole atmosphere. He wondered if they were religious.

"Are you staying the night?" asked Mrs. Rogers, breaking into Laurie's thoughts.

"I hadn't considered it," he replied. "I mean, thank you."

"Didn't I mention it in my letter? I meant to. It'll mean doubling up with young Martin here, but you're very welcome and it'll save you a wretched journey. He and Gwen have got separate rooms at the back."

"But won't it be a bother?"

"A bother?" cut in Mrs. Rogers. "Gracious no! Why, we keep open house here. Three of Tom's relations were here only Sunday night. It's no trouble to us, I can assure you." She laughed. "We're up a bit early, of course. Tom has to be at work by eight."

"Do stay!" It was Gwen. She had not spoken before, and Laurie looked at her for the first time, turning away from Martin, who had been attacking a piece of crumbling Madeira cake. He was a good-looking boy, resembling his father so that even at fifteen it was clear that the fresh, impish expression would one day harden into the bluff squareness of Mr. Rogers's face. He had tousled fair hair and his hands, surprisingly, were spotlessly clean. Beside his broad shoulders his sister seemed frail and delicate, but she too had a healthy colour.

"All right," he said, smiling at them all in turn. "I'll stay." He felt as though he had committed himself to something more serious than a mere domestic matter.

[6]

The schoolroom was small and the desks minute. Laurie wondered about the age of his pupils, and whether the antiquated stove provided more warmth for the daytime infants than for the motley collection of middle-aged people who filled the back two rows. They were mostly women in brown coats, and they looked unfriendly even before he had said good evening. What could they want to know about European painting and sculpture? Why was *he* trying to supply whatever the answer? A ghastly painting of the

Virgin and Child hung on the cream-painted brick wall opposite, and led him to wonder again about the religious affiliations of Mr. and Mrs. Rogers. Nearly two thousand years of Christianity had if nothing else succeeded in arousing such a thought whenever good people were encountered.

Mr. and Mrs. Rogers knew and exchanged greetings with everyone present. Of one they asked news of a son, of the next a cow that was calfing. A messenger at his old bookshop had invited Laurie to his wedding several years earlier. The service in the church had been passable, but the meal in a small café had been agony. Everyone had talked of the Arsenal or the bridegroom's wedding-night intentions with a knowing leer, though without a drop of alcohol. He had felt uncomfortable throughout. Now in this brown and cream schoolroom, miserable from cold and fear, he was as much out of it as he had been at that wedding.

Mr. Rogers rescued him. He made an amusing speech introducing the new lecturer. "I'd call it the Horrible Pictures Group," he started, "since Mr. Kingston is going to talk about this modern stuff. Still, he's going to try to hang 'em the right way up." Each remark was greeted with genuine enjoyment, not just a polite audience-to-chairman titter. Mr. Rogers hoped that their new tutor would not work them too hard and prophesied a stay-away strike if he did. Then he sat down at the left end of the arc of chairs, leaving Laurie facing the twenty-odd expressionless faces. After a brief, passing desire to plead a headache or fainting fit, he started. Within five minutes it would have been difficult to stop him.

He warmed quickly to his subject. He asked them to accept the fact that until now they had looked at pictures as they had looked at anything else; this was wrong. He hoped to show that to appreciate pictures in the fullest sense needed a special technique of looking. With this at their fingertips they would tread more surely even in the fields of modern painting, of which they were frightened, he gathered. He paused for answering smiles, but none appeared. With this technique at their fingertips they would be horrified at the monstrosity of the Virgin and Child behind them. Nearly everyone looked round, but only Mr. Rogers relaxed his expression. "It's a failure," thought Laurie, and used all five of his funny stories that he had meant to ration out at one per week.

After the lecture Mr. Rogers congratulated him. "You've assessed our needs exactly," he said. "Even Jean could follow your explanations and she's not really interested in painting. She likes music. In fact, I think they all enjoyed it."

The class stood around in groups. As he gathered up his reproductions and books, Laurie heard scraps of favourable comments. He was surprised and deeply pleased. In ninety minutes he really seemed to have aroused their interest in painting. He felt a glow of satisfaction, and with it came a determination to take even more trouble with the preparation of the following week's lecture. He had assumed in a facile way that his not inconsiderable knowledge of art was sufficient in itself. He was beginning to perceive that the attack of a lecturer had to be carefully planned if the defence put up by the listeners, in the form of apathy, prejudices and tiredness after a day's work, was to be overcome.

Mr. Rogers led him back to the cottage, and half the class, it seemed, followed. Gwen and Martin had cleared away the tea things and laid plates of sandwiches and biscuits. The kettle was boiling. Laurie's protest that all this must be a great expense was dismissed by Mr. Rogers with "Gives us a chance to talk over what you've been telling us. Wouldn't be stretching my nine pounds three and six a week far if I couldn't give a few friends a cup of tea and a sandwich," he added. Laurie remembered a shin bruise that he had once acquired under the table from Norman for daring to hint, with others present, that the bookseller earned over two thousand pounds a year.

They all stood round the fire drinking and eating, while the children passed sandwiches and Mrs. Rogers refilled cups as they were emptied. A busy little woman in thick stockings gushed her thanks over Laurie until he became quite embarrassed and moved to a tall, spindly girl who had been to the Sistine Chapel. One member of the class had actually seen Picasso—from a distance. Gradually the room emptied until only Mr. and Mrs. Rogers and Martin were left. Gwen must have gone to bed earlier, Laurie realised; the boy seemed to be watching him curiously.

"Tom, you'll rake a pair of pyjamas out for Mr. Kingston," said Mrs. Rogers, piling up the cups and plates on a tray.

"Don't bother. I never wear them," replied Laurie too quickly.

"Thank you all the same." His answer seemed in no way to disconcert them, though if Martin's was a double bed, it might have done.

Gwen was shouting from upstairs meanwhile, and for a moment the noise puzzled all of them. Mrs. Rogers opened the door and called out to her, receiving in reply the angry information that no one had come up to say good night. They called their greetings from the bottom of the stairs, Laurie included, and then Mr. Rogers went up to his daughter.

"I hope you won't find Martin too restless," said Mrs. Rogers as they came back to the fire. "Whenever I come in to wake him, the covers are all over the place."

"They're not!" denied Martin.

"I'm a sound sleeper," said Laurie, smiling. So it was a double bed. He had refused pyjamas and had to share a bed with this well-built, impish boy. Martin looked older than fifteen, too; seventeen perhaps, or he would do in a dark suit. Mr. Rogers came down, and as he came into the room his eyes met Laurie's and he smiled. Instantly Laurie recoiled from his own thoughts. It was not only, he mused, that they were such a likeable family; there was some quality of natural goodness that transformed such thoughts from the unsocial to the outrageous.

"What are these modern artists really getting at?" asked Mrs. Rogers seriously as she sat down.

"Mr. Kingston'll be answering that during the course," Mr. Rogers put in quickly.

"I will and I won't," said Laurie slowly. "It's a big question. For one thing they're not all getting at the same thing or for the same reasons. Some are exploring new channels, feeling the old dried up. Others have something to say and feel they've got to shock to be heard. You see, our senses are so sated with run-of-the-mill stuff."

"It's not much good shocking people if they can't understand you when you've got their attention," replied Mr. Rogers.

They were silent for a moment, each considering their own arguments. "Were you in the Forces?" asked Martin. He was leaning on the mantelpiece, his chin supported by his hand.

"Yes," said Laurie.

"Did you paint there?"

"A bit."

"What? Guns, bombs, planes?"

"People mostly." I would like to paint you, just as you stand, sweater breaking over your behind like a spent wave, rolled at the front like an unbroken one; cocky, masculine, assertive.

"Other chaps with you?"

"Perhaps Mr. Kingston would like to go to bed. You must be tired after your journey and all that talking," Mrs. Rogers added directly to Laurie.

"Whenever you go."

"We don't keep late hours," said Mr. Rogers. "I have to be away early and Martin, too. His school's a long way off."

"What are you going to be?" Laurie asked the boy. The question sounded hackneyed and routine, but he was really interested.

"I'd like to go in for forestry." Martin straightened himself, then flexed his arm muscles. "Open air, sort of."

Mrs. Rogers stood up. "Well, you take Mr. Kingston up, Martin. We'll damp the fires——"

"And lock the doors," said Laurie, smiling.

"We don't bother about that, do we Tom? Everyone round here knows everyone else. Well, I hope you sleep well, Mr. Kingston. Martin'll show you where everything is. Good night."

He followed the boy out of the room and up the stairs, watching the rim of the sweater dancing to left, to right, as each foot mounted the matted steps. He followed Martin into the bedroom, a crowded room with sloping ceilings, beams and a large double bed. The walls were pasted with pictures of racing cars cut from magazines and newspapers. The floor was covered with green lino, softened by worn rugs on either side of the bed. On a chest of drawers were three silver cups. When Martin saw Laurie looking at them, he grinned and threw himself on the bed, his head in his arms, the sweater rucking to his thin waist.

"It's quite comfy," he said, head still buried. "I'll show you the bathroom." He jumped up and led Laurie out of the room to a primitive bathroom and lavatory. "Plenty of hot water," said Martin. "Mum always says she wonders how I'd know that." He left Laurie there wondering which towel he should use. Laurie washed slowly and carefully. As he dried himself he examined the cracked mirror and glossy walls, both flecked with spots of tooth paste, the geyser and the high, old-fashioned bathtub. He was thinking of the next half-hour. It was a test. He must see it as a test. If there was anything decent left in him now was the moment to discover it to himself. Otherwise he might as well go back to Norman and Norman's sort of life. But there was the sweater, first breaking over tight, hard buttocks, then dancing on them, finally rucking to show the small waist.

He dried his face, studying it in the mirror. There was something unpleasant, weak and yielding about its expression. It was so easy to excuse one's weaknesses, wallow in a welter of self-pity, and come up with justifications for every back-sliding. He noted that his eyes were bloodshot, and round his mouth there were a few pimples. These people had not only been very charming and hospitable to him; there was something good and clean about them, something uninhibited in a nice way. It needed someone as low as himself to answer this with thoughts of crude, uncontrolled sexuality. For this there could be no justification whatsoever. Those bloodshot eyes and pimple-studded cheeks meant nothing to Martin; he was a normal, ordinary boy. He could offer the boy nothing, except perhaps dubious self-justification at an enormous price; and the payer receiving nothing but corruption for his money. Laurie folded the towel carefully. The mental image of himself as a cor-rupter coincided exactly with the face in the mirror.

He went back to the bedroom. Martin was pulling the sweater over his neck, his hands almost hitting the paper shade round the lamp. Laurie closed the door and busied himself with undressing, starting with his shoes and socks, then tie and jacket.

"How do you get to school?" he asked Martin.

"By bike," answered the boy, smiling. He took off his shirt and threw it on a chair next to the chest of drawers. His skin was white and smooth. He started to unbutton his trousers.

"Take you long?" Laurie took off his own trousers and folded them carefully.

"'Bout half to three-quarters of an hour," replied the boy. "Depends on the wind." His trousers had fallen about his ankles and he pushed his pants after them, kicking them off. He stooped and picked them up, the light playing momentarily down his spine. Mr. and Mrs. Rogers were coming upstairs, talking quietly. Martin reached for his pyjamas under the pillow.

Laurie tried to look and tried not to look. He had seen the light on the boy's spine and the muscles to each side of it; was aware, it seemed for ever, of the boy's smooth, strong thighs. Then the pyjamas were on and his agony over.

"Gosh, the sheets are cold," said Martin, nestling down into them. "You'll be sorry you don't wear pyjamas." He was staring at Laurie's nudity with frank curiosity.

Laurie switched out the light, felt his way to the bed and stumbled in. "It's not too bad," he said. "Soon warms up. 'Specially with two people in it." That was what Norman always said, though he meant something else.

Suddenly Laurie's consciousness of the boy's physical presence overwhelmed him in a wave of crazy desire. He felt hot and excited all at once. He wanted to seize the boy, feel the rippling muscles that the light had lapped and stroke the smooth, strong thighs. Then he heard Mr. Rogers call "good night" and he answered in unison with Martin, and knew that the test was over and he had come through unscathed. The Rogerses' hospitality would not be traduced.

Laurie lay on his back, his hands behind his head. "Have you got plenty of friends round here?" he asked.

"There's Tooley," the boy answered. "He's my special mate." He was silent for a moment. "He's left school now, so we don't see so much of each other. 'Course there's the chaps at school." He paused, then added: "They're all right."

"Do you go to the cinema much?" The test was over, but he wanted to keep them awake just a little longer.

"No. Too far. All right if we all go in Dad's car."

They were silent for a minute, then Martin said: "We'd better go to sleep. Mum wakes us early." He paused again. "Good night."

"Good night, Martin," said Laurie, savouring the boy's name. "Sleep well."

The boy mumbled something in reply, then was silent. For the first time Laurie heard noises outside. A car went past, and what he took to be a frog croaked. From the next room he could hear the

Rogerses talking in undertones. Then he became aware that the boy was breathing regularly. He must be asleep, Laurie thought, and allowed his mind to wander dangerously down all the paths that passing the test had blocked. His variations on the theme were many and unsubtle. His arms were getting tired and he raised his head, freeing them.

At that moment Martin stretched and turned. It was too dark to see anything. The boy's arm came to rest on Laurie's open, outstretched hand. Slowly, trembling the while, he closed his hand, feeling more and more the young muscles in his grip. This is madness, he kept repeating to himself, madness, madness, madness. He felt a wave of fever masking his thoughts and senses. He was holding Martin's arm tightly now and he could feel the even jumping of the boy's heartbeats. He started to move his other hand.

"Let go!" said Martin quietly, his voice even and matter of fact.

"Why?" Laurie was pleading already.

"You'd only be ashamed in the morning," replied the boy softly. Without waiting he pulled his arm free, moved farther to his own side of the bed and, turning over, appeared to have fallen asleep at once.

[7]

Laurie stared gloomily at the square. It was not proving as easy to obtain a job as he had thought, and he was frightened that he would soon have to start using his savings. These in turn constituted his passport to an unfurnished flat. He would not be paid for his lectures until the whole course was finished and even then it would not amount to a great deal. He really ought to be preparing his next week's lecture now.

He turned away from the window and picked a piece of typing paper from the table near the door. In future he would return home after the lecture, whatever the travelling difficulties. He could never again face Martin alone, even though the boy had been as natural in the morning as during the previous evening. Was he acting, as he laughed and teased Gwen over the breakfast table? Did the whole incident really mean so little to him? And how was he so certain of Laurie's shame on the next day? He had felt the shame just the same, a deep shame full of remorse. Nor had the resolutions, made as he lay there wide awake, in any way lessened. He looked at the blank piece of paper and stopped his thoughts long enough to write "Berenson" at the top. Then he put it aside and went out of the room, downstairs.

He telephoned Norman from the phone in the hall, putting his sixpence noisily in the white cup that stood for the purpose. The little man would be listening in any case, and Mrs. Murphy, usually in the kitchen below, would be straining her ears. A key sounded in the lock, the front door opened and a smart, spectacled girl came in. She had the room next to Laurie's and smiled pleasantly whenever they met. She had a soft, timid voice that contrasted with her smart appearance and air of efficiency. It reminded him of Mary. In a way he had treated her badly, using her when he needed sympathy, then writing less often, at last not answering her letters at all. This turning friends on and off was unlike him. He would write to her that day. But what for? Norman's voice interrupted his argument.

"Very well, thank you," he said in answer to Norman's question. "Except——"

"Except?" Norman repeated. He sounded impatient.

"I haven't found a job yet." He could hear Mrs. Murphy in the sitting-room. She must have been sitting over the fire with her husband. She had come over to the door now.

"You mean you want to come back here?"

"No."

"Then what?"

"I wondered if you knew anybody needing someone." He was no longer shy of asking. This was the outcome of his new relationship with Norman: they were simply friends, at least as far as Laurie was concerned.

"I can't talk now, Laurie, I'm busy. Will you be in the Club tonight? Where are you living, anyway?"

Laurie told him.

"Shall I come and see you there?"

"Yes, by all means."

"It won't be before half past six."

"That's fine. Will you stay for a bite?"

"Bite? No. No thanks, Laurie, I've already arranged to meet someone later. See you at half past six." He repeated the address and rang off.

Laurie went out and bought a bottle of Tio Pepe before returning to his room. It was Norman's favourite apéritif. Then he went on preparing his lecture. He began to wonder how far his deviation added to his feeling for painting in studying a Michelangelo male figure, when he heard his name being called. He had reached the point through Berenson's theory of tactile values and was enjoying it to the exclusion of all else. Mrs. Murphy shouted his name again. He stood up. The piece of typing paper was covered with scribblings: names, dates, schools, styles, influences. He opened the door.

"Yes, Mrs. Murphy?"

"There's someone to see you."

He knew at once that it was not Norman. Firstly it was only a quarter to six. Then she would have called that there was "a gentleman" to see him. He had lived in digs before and knew the social gradings. He could think, though, of no one else who knew his address.

He ran down the stairs, amused at his continued irritation at the worn stair carpet. It annoyed him more than any other aspect of the building's decay. He tried to remember whether the stair carpet at home had been worn when he was a child, but could not. Instead he recalled that it was over a year since he had been home, and arrived at the bottom to find Tom, in uniform, waiting for him. Mrs. Murphy's round, slightly puffed face expressed disapproval and curiosity.

"Hullo, Tom."

"'lo."

"Come on up. Thank you, Mrs. Murphy." He led the way. "I thought it was Norman at first. He's coming to see me."

They were walking side by side, Tom looking round him, Laurie conscious again of the stair carpet. It was funny how easily he had come to accept not going home. He hardly even thought of them, yet he had been closely attached to his mother until she married again. Then came his period in the Services, new friends, new values and the understanding that the new marriage came first. Outwardly, the relationship between himself and his mother had changed slowly; deeper, it had snapped even before he went into the Forces. He knew that now, and no longer even cared. Only it had something to do with a worn stair carpet, or why did he start to worry about it again during the last few days, and always prompted by the stairs.

"Come in, Tom."

Tom followed him into the room, looking round as he went. "Not so nice as your other place," he commented as he sprawled in the sole armchair.

Laurie nodded, studying the hands, large and white and strong, as they kneaded the arms of the chair. "Beggars can't be choosers," he said, "but I'll soon find something better."

"'ave I interrupted you?"

"No, Tom."

The Guardsman nodded. He pulled up his left trouser leg and scratched the white skin thoughtfully. "I never seen Sue since that night," he said at last in a throaty voice.

"You haven't been back to the flat?" Laurie felt excited at once.

"I 'ave, but she hasn't. Not a word."

"Where is she, then?"

"What I came to ask you."

"I've not heard a word from her."

"Would you phone 'er parents for me?"

"Me?"

"Yep. Easier'n for me."

"All right," agreed Laurie.

"Now?"

They went downstairs. Tom gave Laurie a slip of paper with the number on it, then went to stare out of the narrow, oblong window by the front door. Laurie dialled the number slowly. If she had gone home, then this was the end between them. The end for them, but for him it was perhaps the beginning. The number started to ring. He looked at Tom, who stood in an unconsciously graceful yet provocative attitude, just as he had that far-off night at Marble Arch. Laurie had waited a long time, but his waiting was nearly finished now; he felt sure of it.

"Hullo?" It was a slow, woman's voice.

"Can I speak to Susan, please?"

"She's restin'. Who is it?"

"Laurence Kingston, a friend of hers."

"She's restin'."

"Could she call me back when she gets up?"

"I'll tell her you phoned."

"Would you give her my new number, please?" He looked at the phone, then repeated it slowly twice.

"Kingston. I'll tell her you phoned. Good-bye." The receiver was replaced.

"She's at home all right," said Laurie to Tom's back.

The Guardsman turned round. "Is she phoning back?"

"I don't think so," said Laurie. "Her mother didn't even bother to repeat the number."

"Then I'll go round." Tom put his hand on the front door and opened it. Then he stopped. "I left my titfa upstairs. I'll come and get it."

He bounded up the stairs two at a time. Laurie followed breathlessly. In the room the Guardsman paused for a moment. "Thanks for helping, Laurie." He joined Laurie by the window as he spoke. "You're a sort of general 'elp where we're concerned. And I suppose you've troubles of your own." He patted Laurie on the shoulder, then turned to leave.

"Let me know what happens," said Laurie, still looking out of the window. He closed his eyes to see whether he had managed completely to develop the image of Tom standing in front of the little, oblong window in the hall, right hand on hip, left leg straight and body slightly bending to the right. He had, even to the feel of the scrubbed neck below the close-cropped hair: the theory of tactile values in action.

"O.K. Be seein' yer."

"Cheerio."

He heard the footsteps dying on the stairs, the faint slam of the front door, then saw the khaki figure bobbing across the square. At the far side Tom turned, scanning the tall houses. He saw Laurie and waved. Laurie waved back and watched until the Guardsman had disappeared into the twilight. Then quite savagely he kicked the skirting board, afterwards observing the dent he had made with a quiet joy. He returned to Michelangelo.

Half an hour later Mrs. Murphy brought him back to the present by announcing that there was a gentleman to see him. Only this time she brought Norman up the stairs with her, so that they caught Laurie by surprise and without even the cork removed from the Tio Pepe bottle. It was obvious by the way that she lingered that Mrs. Murphy regarded the immaculately dressed bookseller with more approval than the uniformed Guardsman. Only Laurie's second, carefully enunciated "Thank you, Mrs. Murphy," finally persuaded her to go.

"Not a bad room," said Laurie, nodding to Norman to take the only armchair. Norman grunted in reply. "I shall only stay here until I find a flat, of course, but it's large and the view's nice. Sort of Carel Weightish."

"I think I've got you a job," said Norman.

"Where?" Laurie poured him a sherry without asking.

"Not too much, Laurie, please. I've got a heavy evening in front of me. Where you were before."

Laurie put down the bottle. "But, Norman, you know what happened with Eccles."

"Yes, but I met old Moore. Asked me how you were getting on. I said wonderfully, only business wasn't quite good enough for me to keep you and my manager."

"Yes, but Eccles——"

"To hell with Eccles, Laurie. What are you always so frightened about? Did Eccles tell them anything before? So, why should he now? Why do you for ever build hurdles that aren't there? If you stand up to Eccles, you've got nothing to worry about. Moore thinks the world of you, and I wouldn't be a bit surprised if the old boy's not 'queer' himself."

"But he's married."

"So what? Well, it's up to you. I've done my bit." He finished his sherry. "I said you'd go along in the morning if you wanted the job. You must make your own decision." He stood up.

"Thank you, Norman. You're in a dreadful hurry."

"I've got a date. Not what you think. So long, Laurie, and good luck." He went to the door and opened it. "Somewhere along the line I seem to have messed things up between us, I'm afraid. I'm not really sure quite where. And it's a bloody shame." He went out without looking back or closing the door. Laurie had never heard him swear like that before, and he knew Norman meant what he said, and was right.

[8]

"It's no good you sitting there every meal sulking, my girl, believe me." Susan's mother turned to her father: "Isn't that so?"

The bald little man at the head of the table nodded. Susan remained silent, as she had for most of the time since her return home. She had explained things to her father in his office, where she had gone to seek him out. Apart from wondering every so often what Mum would say, he had listened sympathetically, a vague smile on his face expressing either contentment at his daughter's impending return or mild cynicism at the failure of the marriage exactly as Mum had foretold.

"You don't eat anything," said Susan's mother, but the girl continued to stare at her plate, from time to time pushing a piece of meat from one side to the other. "Perhaps you need a holiday. We'll go to Bournemouth. It's nice there just now."

"No, thank you," said Susan quietly.

"All right, so we won't go to Bournemouth. But cheer up!" She forked half of a large roast potato. "Who's Kingston, a Mr. Kingston?"

Susan looked up. Her glance took in the patterned wallpaper, the sideboard with its photographs and her mother's large, inquiring expression. "A painter I know."

"He rang while you were sleeping."

"Did he leave a message?" She tried to keep eagerness out of her voice, but Laurie was a link, and a strong one at that.

"No."

"Didn't he leave his phone number?"

"Maybe, only I didn't quite get it."

"Well, why didn't you ask him to repeat it?" She was angry now.

"Sue!" It was her father warning her.

Susan's mother put down her knife and fork with a gesture of satisfaction that may have included the unnoted telephone number as well as her own excellent cooking. As soon as the others had finished, she gathered the plates and disappeared into the kitchen. They could hear her moving about noisily, and she soon reappeared with clean plates and an apple pie. Susan and her father had meanwhile sat in silence, staring at the table.

"Did he say he'd ring back?" asked Susan as soon as they were all served.

"Who?"

"Laurie."

"Laurie?"

"Mr. Kingston then."

"No. Who is he?"

"A friend of mine."

"A Jewish boy?"

"What's that got to do with it?" She was almost shouting now.

"Sue, please." The little man caressed his dark chin and looked appealingly with his eyes.

"I'm not a prisoner," started Sue, when the door bell rang.

"Who is it?" asked Susan's mother.

Susan started to move but her father stood up first. Glancing at his wife to check that his action was in order, and receiving a glance of permission, he went to the front door.

"It's Tom!" shouted Susan. She stood up and reached the dining-room door at the same moment as the Guardsman. She held him very tight, shaking slightly. Behind them stood her father, patient and again smiling. Susan's mother sat at the table, massive and angry, waiting for the incredible scene to sort itself out. When it failed to achieve this of its own accord, she rose portentously to her feet.

"Mr. Beeson, get out of my house!"

"Mother!" Susan let go of Tom.

"Look 'ere," Tom said. "There's no need for all this. Sue and me quarrelled. We were both silly, me mostly. If you 'adn't thrown us out two year ago it wouldn't 'ave all got serious like this."

"Get out!" screamed Susan's mother, her face red and puffed, her bosom heaving.

"If he goes, I go."

"Then go, both of you. You're no daughter of mine."

For a second Susan thought that her father was going to intervene. She stood quite still watching him. Then, when he continued to stare at Tom's boots, she walked past her husband and father, took her coat from the hall cupboard and went to the front door.

"Come on, Tom," she called quietly. "Good night, Dad. Thanks for your help." She followed Tom through the door into the street, not once looking at her mother, who still stood by her chair, scarlet in the face and holding a spoon on which was perched a piece of apple pie.

In the street Susan started to cry. She walked close to Tom, their arms linked, her hand firm in his. It had all happened so quickly. She was not even sure that Tom had come to fetch her. She only knew that he thought their quarrel silly and the fault mainly his. But she cried just the same, until at last he looked down and softly asked her to take it easy. She withdrew her arm from his, found a handkerchief and wiped her eyes.

"We'll 'ave kids," he said, "if that's what you want." He said it kindly, looking straight ahead of him from under his peaked cap, heedless that they were at the mouth of an underground station as he spoke. Nor did he notice that she was crying again as he went to buy the tickets. He only noticed her going into the "Ladies" as he turned away from the hatch, otherwise he might have thought that she had run away. When she came out she was smiling shyly and looking more composed.

In the train they sat next to each other on a long seat facing inwards. They could see each other's reflection in the window, and they kept smiling and winking. Farther down the carriage, facing them, sat a Guardsman from a different battalion, and he watched them intently as if quite unobserved. His staring gave an added intensity to their little game, and Susan began to wish that they were going home, and not to the Club.

She leant over and shouted in his ear. "Have you missed me?"

"'Course." He blushed and answered without turning, but winked at her in the window.

"Very much?"

He smiled in agreement. She took off his cap, stroked his hair, then put it on again. He glanced at the other Guardsman, then straightened it.

They left the train at Piccadilly Circus and walked to the Club. In Great Windmill Street they met two other Guardsmen from Tom's unit, one of whom was Bert. Susan vaguely remembered him from their brief meeting two years earlier. They talked for a few minutes, then Tom suggested that they accompanied him and Susan to the Club for a drink. They agreed, and Susan was sorry: she wanted badly to be alone with Tom.

Everybody in the Club stared at the unusual party as they entered, and watched them as they stood at the bar round Susan. Conversation was difficult: Susan resented Tom's friends at this moment; the two Guardsmen were shy in new surroundings and Tom could think of nothing to say. He glanced round the room, tried a little gossip about the way people dressed or talked, and lapsed into silence after receiving the polite laughter of his companions. After the second beer Bert told Susan about his life in the merchant navy before joining the Guards. One drink later the other Guardsman, whose name was Phil—"bloody silly name, but I didn't ask for it"—described the life of a pit boy. Tom occasionally interrupted their tales of woe with an "It's no worse than marriage", and accompanied the remark with a wink at Susan. Then Laurie arrived.

He felt out of it at once. He was mystified when Tom called "Phil" a bloody silly name, and everyone laughed; and their barrack-room jokes seemed dull. He started to tell Susan of an art exhibition that he had seen the day before, enthusing at length about a Hitchens landscape. Bert, Phil and Tom discussed a corporal whose guts they hated. Susan asked Laurie whether he would start painting again now that he lived alone. Bert and Phil left; they possibly had a date. Laurie started to describe his lecturing, warming to the subject even as something inside warmed to the memory of Martin. He talked of his approach and then of Berenson.

"Can it, Laurie," Tom interrupted suddenly. "That's enough for one evening."

"You be quiet," said Susan. "We've heard all about your friends' lives, let Laurie tell his."

"We've had enough about painting for one evening, for God's sake, Sue. You two've been at it 'ammer and tongs since Laurie came. Let's 'ave another drink."

Laurie ordered another round. The gruffness in Tom's voice excited him. He wanted it addressed to him, to crush him; and yet he was afraid of crossing Tom.

"Go on, Laurie," said Sue evenly after Tom had paid for the drinks. "Why hasn't the theory general validity?"

"Because it only applies to figure painting."

Laurie watched Tom closely the while. When the Guardsman turned away he watched his brown, calculating eyes and remembered their expression the night that Tom had kissed him. When the Guardsman glanced his way, he looked down at the hand that gripped the counter rail, white and strong. Laurie watched, too, as Tom caught the eye of the girl behind the bar and winked at her. He saw him raise his eyebrows in the direction of Susan and paint an imaginary brow on the top of his forehead. Susan turned when she followed Laurie's stare and was in time to catch Tom laying his arm on the barmaid's hand. The girl laughed and drew it away, but when her eyes met Susan's she stopped laughing abruptly.

"Let's go home," proposed Susan coldly.

"One more drink first," said Tom. He ordered them without asking the others.

Susan pushed hers away, but Laurie quietly put it back in front of her as Tom turned to pay, shaking his head in warning. Then he raised his glass. "Happy days to you both," he said, smiling.

"Good old Laurie!" said Tom, grinning.

Susan drank in silence.

[9]

Laurie walked slowly from the bus stop to the shop. He was early. He had been early, too, on the previous day when he had arrived for his interview with Moore. He had felt embarrassed, but the interview had proceeded smoothly, and he had started work at once. His enthusiasm had not been checked until nearly lunchtime, when one of the assistants had explained that Eccles was away with a slight attack of influenza. He had already begun to hope that Eccles had left altogether.

He had also hoped that he might have a few days without him, but this was similarly darkened when he reached the shop that morning. He saw him from the other side of the road, noted with distaste the confident round face. He had not really considered what attitude to adopt, blindly following Norman's theory of meeting problems only when they arose. The sight of Eccles, though, made him sure that his return was a mistake. Eccles, at best, would give him nasty looks every time a young man came into the shop, or indulge in innuendos in front of the other staff. At worst, he might even go to Moore and register a protest. He started across the road.

"Hallo, Laurie." Eccles showed no surprise, so Laurie guessed that he had already heard of his return from one of the others waiting for the shop to be opened. He smiled nervously in answer.

"Are you quite better?" Eccles inquired loudly but pleasantly.

"I don't know what you mean," answered Laurie, indignant at once. He glanced at the others, two men and three girls. They were half-heartedly watching a pavement toyseller unpacking his goods.

"I thought you retired from the old firm to avoid a nervous breakdown."

"Oh," said Laurie. The others were watching him now. "Yes. I see what you mean. Completely better, thanks. I'd almost forgotten it, it seems so long ago."

"Did you have a nervous breakdown?" one of the girls asked.

"Sort of," Laurie answered.

"It's a wonder we don't all get them, working here," put in an elderly man. "I spent half an hour showing cookery books to a woman yesterday, and at the end of it all she said she'd better go home and discuss it with her husband."

The others laughed politely. An alarm bell started ringing and they all looked in the direction of a clothes shop which was just being unbolted.

"But yours was brought on by shock, wasn't it?" Eccles asked Laurie casually. Before he could obtain an answer, the manager arrived and started to unlock the main door.

There was plenty to do that morning: unpacking, sorting, dusting, repairing jackets and selling books, and it was not until lunchtime that Eccles spoke to him again. Meanwhile Laurie had decided to thrash it out with him: if he was going to behave as he had earlier that morning, Laurie might as well leave at once. He would apply a yardstick to which he had started to resort more and more: what would Mr. Rogers have done in the same situation?

"Coming to lunch?"

Laurie felt a little cheated. He had already decided that he would ask Eccles that question, adding that he welcomed the chance for a frank talk. He made up his mind to regain the initiative, having in his mind Martin's soft, certain reply. If a mere boy could show such simple courage, how easy it should be for him.

"Yes," Laurie replied. "I wanted to speak to you anyway." His own words frightened him, but at least he had said them. Eccles did not reply but followed him out of the shop and into the busy street. They had to wait awhile before the lights changed and they could cross Oxford Street.

"What did you want to speak to me about?" asked Eccles as they reached the far kerb.

This was not how Laurie had pictured the scene. The end of lunch was his chosen moment for gently broaching the subject, not while they were pushing their way along a crowded pavement. He glanced at his companion: there was no particular expression on the chubby face.

"Why not drop all these hints?" demanded Laurie quickly. "Either go to Moore and tell him you won't work with me or stop it. Then we'll know where we stand." They were twice separated while he made his statement. "I don't mind which, but I'm not going on working here with you making sly remarks every five minutes." Laurie forced himself to look at Eccles as they turned into a quieter street.

Eccles suddenly stopped. "What the hell are you gassing about?"

"You know," said Laurie, stopped, turning back to him.

They both started walking again. "I bloody well don't," replied Eccles. "Hints?" He wrinkled his nose. "I'm as pleased to see you back as anyone."

They reached the café and climbed the stairs. Laurie felt that he had spoken, and lost. If he wanted to continue the conversation, he would have to bring up the incident of the cigarette case and the Guardsman. Well, at least he had spoken, and it might have taught Eccles to be more considerate in future. So they talked of awkward customers and the possible retirement of the manager.

He tried to recall Eccles's expressions and voice during the rest of the meal, as the bus carried him once more to his lecture that night. There had been nothing to indicate how Eccles felt: they had talked as noncommittally as in the old days before Laurie had met Tom. Naturally he still distrusted Eccles, but he was not sure whether the distrust came from the other's manner or was of a more instinctive, personal nature.

The Rogerses seemed even more friendly and hospitable than on his first visit. Any fears that Martin might have spoken to his father about the incident in the bedroom were dispelled almost as soon as he entered the cottage. The boy himself was completely natural and friendly, and Laurie's previous resolve not to stay the night melted before the subject was broached. Besides, old Moore had been pleased to hear about the lecturing and had stressed that by leaving early on the day of the lecture and coming in later next morning, Laurie was to guard against unnecessary strain.

Gwen was in bed with a cold, so while Mrs. Rogers prepared tea and Mr. Rogers stoked the boiler, Martin took Laurie up to see her. She looked quite cheerful propped up in bed and told Laurie of a visit that afternoon from two girls at her school. "They gave me those flowers," she said, pointing to a bunch of anemones in a jam jar by the bed. "Muriel's father's taking her to London on Saturday. Mum says I can go if I'm better in time."

"I hope you are," said Laurie.

"Won't you sit down?" asked the girl in an off-hand, grown-up manner.

Laurie sat on a white chair wedged between a chest of drawers and the wall behind the bed, while Martin stood in the doorway, his arm resting on the low door frame, his head on his arm. Then Mrs. Rogers called him and he hurried downstairs, waving to the other two as he went.

"He likes you," said Gwen suddenly.

"Oh, and don't you?" Laurie countered, blushing.

"He didn't like the man who came before you. He used to dribble."

"And I don't," said Laurie, still uncertain how to treat the turn of the conversation.

"He likes you special," said Gwen, folding and unfolding the edge of the top sheet. "He said so."

"Oh," said Laurie.

"We talked about you after you'd gone last week."

Mr. Rogers called him from downstairs.

"I must go," said Laurie. "I'll see you in the morning and I hope you'll be better by then."

"I like you too," said Gwen, looking straight at him.

Impulsively he kissed the girl on the forehead, then joined the others in the hot, steamy kitchen.

Gwen was still awake when they came back from the lecture, so they all went up to say good night to her again. She was a little feverish, and her eyes were strangely intense and adult. She took her mother's hand and held it tightly, while the four of them watched without speaking. Then they went down to the sitting-room, where Martin sat on the arm of the couch in front of the fire, and Laurie and Tom Rogers faced each other in the big armchairs.

"I don't think it's much, is it?"

"Gwen?"

"Yes."

"No, just a touch of 'flu," replied Mrs. Rogers. "I thought it best not to invite the class back, though, in case she was asleep. The noise might have kept her awake with all of us here." She laughed nervously. "Though we'll never eat all those sandwiches, just the four of us."

They were silent for a while, each staring at the fire.

"Why don't you bring some of your own paintings, Mr. Kingston?" Martin asked. "I bet they're smashing."

Laurie started. He had been thinking of Eccles and the harm that he might cause. "My paintings?" He faced the boy, who was still sitting astride the armchair. "They're not very good."

"Why do you paint, then?" asked the boy.

"I enjoy it," answered Laurie, "and it gives me a chance to express myself." He scraped his lower lip with his teeth. How shocked they would be if they knew how desperately he wanted the boy. If Tom represented the stronger, coarser qualities that he lacked, Martin stood for the youth, beauty and suppleness which were so quickly passing. Even two years ago a boy like Martin would have meant little to him. Now he felt almost as strongly aroused as when he was with Tom. "It's easier to fight loneliness," he added hurriedly after a long pause. "I mean reading or music helps to do that, but not so well in my case. And loneliness is everybody's greatest problem, loneliness and the inability to reach just one other person." He sighed. "If they're not the same thing, that is."

"Loneliness?" echoed Mr. Rogers.

"Yes," said Laurie.

"But if you've friends and relations, and———"

"They all add up to nothing. How do you know what's going on in their minds, even perhaps at the very moment they're talking to you? How do you know their innermost thoughts and desires? Can you really ever know what even one person thinks of you?"

"Just a second, Mr. Kingston. That's a tall order. We all feel different things at different times 'bout the same person. But I don't get your loneliness business at all. I'm not lonely. Are you, Jean?"

"No." She laughed nervously. "We'd better not get involved in a long debate at this time of night." She laughed again.

"It's early, Mum," said Martin, looking sharply at her. Until then he had kept his eyes on Laurie ever since they had all come into the room.

"Don't you get the feeling of being alone in the world, tied to people and places by strands so thin and feeble that the tiniest puff of wind can break them?" He was almost echoing Norman's tone of voice. "Supposing you pinched a few pounds from your firm and were caught. Who would want to know you after that? Wouldn't you feel lonely?"

Mr. Rogers laughed. "Jean and the kids wouldn't cut adrift of me for that."

"Are you sure?"

"'Course I am."

"Why, it's only natural," added Jean.

"Besides, that just wouldn't arise. The 'me' who hasn't this problem of loneliness that you talk about is the same 'me' who wouldn't pinch the money."

They were quiet for a little. Martin shifted his position on the arm, swinging his leg over so that he was sitting sideways, his feet just touching the floor. A log slipped on the fire and a splinter of wood fell, sizzling, on the hearth. Mr. Rogers picked it up with a pair of tongs and put it back on the fire. A slow-moving, noisy vehicle, perhaps a tractor, crawled past the house and on down the hill.

"Anyone like some cocoa?" asked Mrs. Rogers.

They all said "Yes", Laurie last. "I hope I haven't offended you," he added.

"Offended us? Good Lord no! It's always interesting to hear someone else's point of view. No, we're not offended, are we, Jean?"

"No," she said, and laughed again as she went to the door.

"Did you sleep all right or did that rascal keep you awake?" asked Mr. Rogers.

Only for a second did Laurie wonder whether there was an ulterior meaning behind the question. Then he knew that if Mr. Rogers had meant something else he would have said it. "I slept very well, thanks."

"So did I," said Martin, "so you must be a quiet sleeper too."

Laurie laughed, waiting for Mr. Rogers to rebuke his son for almost being rude, then knowing that such a natural retort would never be checked here. Instead they started talking about some of the points that he had raised during the lecture, and the subject lasted until they had finished their cocoa and were preparing to go to bed. As before, Martin and Laurie went up first, Mr. and Mrs. Rogers staying to attend to the lights and fires.

In the small bedroom they undressed together, Martin no longer curious, Laurie excited. He found it impossible to keep his eyes off the boy, noting again the easy grace of his movements and the light on his spine as he bent to pick up his trousers. In vain he sought for something to say. Martin pulled on his pyjamas, tucked the jacket in the trousers and jumped into bed.

"Gosh, it's cold," he said, burying himself in the sheets.

Laurie stood for a moment naked, waiting for the boy's head to reappear from between the sheets, hoping for some show of curiosity. He glanced down at his body. His belly was becoming slightly rounded and the protruding hip bones were almost lost in the surrounding flesh. His legs were white and had sparse hairs starting below his thighs. There was something graceless and awkward about his body.

"Hurry," called the boy without taking his head from the covers. "You'll get frozen stiff."

"Coming," answered Laurie. He turned out the light and jumped into bed. The sheets were cold and he felt a warmth emanating from the young body beside him. But he was in control of himself now.

"Are you lonely sometimes?" asked the boy, at last lying back on the pillow.

"Yes," replied Laurie quietly.

The boy thought for a minute. "It's like people and their Christmas cards," he said at last.

"I don't quite——"

"They put them all over their living-rooms. When people come, they see how many friends they've got. They should put them in their bedrooms."

"Surely they only do that to brighten their living-rooms," said Laurie.

"Oh," answered Martin doubtfully.

They lay there without talking, and as last time Laurie wondered whether Martin had perhaps fallen asleep. "Are you still awake?" he whispered.

"Yes."

"Do you get lonely?"

"No," said the boy, at once and with certainty. "There's always Dad and Mum and Gwen. Have you got a family?"

"Yes, but I don't see them much. I haven't seen them at all this year. My mother married again." He wondered why he was telling the boy this.

He heard the boy's hand moving before he felt it. Then it had brushed against his own, seized it and stayed firmly on it. "You'll be all right," said Martin softly. "I like you. So do Dad and Mum and Gwen."

Then the hand was withdrawn. Laurie waited for the boy to continue, but a minute or two later he heard deep, regular breathing and knew that this time the boy was really asleep.

[10]

The following Sunday Laurie went home. He was not sure what had made him decide to go, and having given his mother no warning of his intention, he was a little anxious about his reception. She opened the door, kissed him and behaved exactly as if there had not been a year's interruption to his visits. She even assumed that he would be staying to lunch and muttered as much, hurrying off to the kitchen to put some extra potatoes in the oven.

He went into the living-room and was surprised not to find his stepfather there. Perhaps George was still in bed, though it was already a quarter to twelve. Laurie was amazed to find that he could no longer muster feelings of dislike for either of them. He tried hard to stir them up against his mother, who had not even bothered to trace him during the last fourteen months. But he could feel nothing except a mild indifference coupled with a wish that his home could mean something more to him. Life seemed so much more settled for those to whom it did.

His mother came back and sat on a hard chair by the window. She had taken off her apron and tidied her hair. She was shorter than Laurie, eager-looking and smiling. "Life is hard but I manage well enough," her expression seemed to say, and Laurie suddenly realised that she too had her problems, as if such a thought had never occurred to him before.

"You still living with Mr. Wayne?" she asked, scrutinising him carefully.

"No," answered Laurie. "I left him when I got back from Italy." He paused as if expecting her to follow up the point, but she remained silent, studying him. "I'm in a room in Bayswater for the moment."

"Want to come home?"

"And George?" For a moment he half hoped that George was dead or had left her, but when the smile remained he knew that it was a vain hope.

"He never minded you."

It was true, of course. Laurie had objected to his stepfather, disagreed and even quarrelled with him, but George had never so much as hinted that he should leave home. That had been his own doing, an impulsive decision about which he had started to waver from the moment it had been announced until the hour of his departure.

"Would you like a cup of tea now?" asked his mother.

"Yes," he said, and smiled shyly as she passed him going to the door.

He had never even considered the possibility of coming back home to live. But why not? His fierce attachment to his mother had long since attenuated to a point where her affection for George would rouse little jealousy. It would cost him less. It might even give him the fairly stable background that he badly wanted. But when his mother came back, he told her instead all about the Rogerses and his lectures, of their hospitality and his class, the journey and the return to his former job.

Then he heard George standing outside the house talking to a neighbour, laughing loudly and swearing. "Would you like me to come back?"

"What a silly question, Laurie!" She had also heard George and pulled the curtain back to watch him. "George is here. I must go and serve the lunch." She straightened the cloth on the table by the wall, laid another place, then went out to the kitchen.

As inconsequentially as he had decided to come home, he now wanted to go. Indeed if George had not been standing outside the door, he might have gone. As it was, he waited, wondering again whether it would work if he came home to live. He was older now and more settled. He had begun to realise what living with other people involved, and he knew that he was willing to make a number of sacrifices for the companionship that it brought. Loneliness was a greater burden than dependence. He was not quite sure, though, whether living at home would banish its spectre.

"Why, if it isn't young Laurie! And where have you been hiding yourself away, lad?" They shook hands. "Your mother's been jolly worried about you, you know, though when I rang the shop they always told me you was well."

"Rang Wayne's?" asked Laurie, puzzled. "Nobody told me you had phoned."

"I spoke to Mr. Wayne himself all but once. He was polite

enough. Why didn't you come back and see your mother, eh? You didn't quarrel, at least not that I know of."

"I don't know," replied Laurie weakly. Now that he was back, he was no longer sure that he had ever known. It seemed ridiculous that he could have anything against this bluff, friendly man, and surely if his mother loved George and was well looked after, that was sufficient.

George put his head round the door and called to see if lunch was ready. Laurie's simple reply seemed to disconcert him more than if he had said "To keep away from you." His mother called that lunch would be another ten minutes, some of which he could occupy washing his hands instead of rushing out as soon as she brought in the meal.

"Want a wash?" George asked Laurie.

"No, thanks."

"I'll have to have one in a minute. This damn, watery beer goes through you like a dose of salts."

"Mother wants me to come back here to live," said Laurie, as much to change the conversation as to discover George's reaction. Laurie could be quite crude in his own way and enjoyed drinking beer, but there was something in George's crudity that irritated him.

"You're not staying on with Wayne, then?"

"I've left him already."

"Got a job?"

"Yes."

"What you hesitating for? Your room's still free, you know, lad, and home's always home."

His mother came in to check that the men had washed. George kissed her and left the room. They could hear him plodding upstairs, walking overhead, then shutting the bathroom door. Laurie stood up and looked out of the window. The road was deserted save for a child who walked painstakingly between the cracks on the nearside pavement. He was a boy of about thirteen and had clearly been crying. Laurie wondered whether he had done something seriously wrong and had been sent out instead of being given lunch. By the time that the boy had turned the corner in the road, his mother had left the room. Then George came back.

"That's better," he said, rubbing his hands together. "Did you get a holiday this year?"

"Yes," answered Laurie, "in Italy."

"I was there in the war. Naples, Genoa, Leghorn." He dropped his voice a little. "Had some good times, too. Some of that I-talian stuff is pretty hot, eh, Laurie? How did you do?"

"Very well, thank you," Laurie replied and saw for a moment quite vividly the smooth tanned legs of the boy, as he had seen them first from under the magazine. He could no longer visualise the boy's features, but as he remembered his eyes, the child who had been crying came round the corner at the end of the road. George stood beside Laurie, peering out.

"The Matthews kid. His father died last night. Hard luck on the boy and he's taken it badly. He'll soon get over it, though. Another week or two, you know, and he'll have forgotten it except for odd moments or over a pint when he grows up."

"For some people it's never forgotten," said Laurie dreamily, watching the boy closely, comparing him with Martin Rogers. "Never."

"I'll go and see if your mother wants some help," said George, and left the room.

They came back with the lunch as Laurie was thinking that his mother was no longer Mrs. Kingston. She had another name now and it symbolised the gap between them. He would never really feel at home here, he thought. It was not only that he had so little in common with them; it was that he had no strong feeling of love which often swamps the gaps of culture, education or interests. The smell of the Sunday joint, being waited on and his mother's approving smile discharged a wave of nostalgia that was soon dispelled by the boredom and lack of mutual interests. He hardly remembered one of the relations or friends of whom they spoke, and he had been talking about Florence for some minutes before he realised that his enthusiasm was not being communicated.

He had planned to stay all day as this was his first visit for so long. But at three o'clock he announced that he had a teatime appointment and would soon have to be going. The loneliness of a cinema seat seemed preferable to staying.

"Will you be along next Sunday, Laurie?" his mother asked.

"I'll let you know in the week," he replied. "I'll drop you a postcard on Wednesday."

"And what about coming back to live?" There was a slight eagerness in her voice.

"I don't know," answered Laurie. "At the moment I just don't know." In fact he was quite sure, but did not want to witness the disappointment on his mother's face when he said "no". It would be easier to add it to the same postcard that excused him from lunch next Sunday.

"Nice date this afternoon?" asked George cheerfully. "Who is she?"

"That would be telling," said Laurie. He stood up and shook hands with George. He wondered whether Susan and Tom would be home. Then he kissed his mother lightly on the cheek, thanked her for lunch and left. It was only when the bus started to move that he remembered meaning to ask whether he had ever had an accident through a faulty stair carpet. Now he would probably never know.

[11]

Susan moved slowly about the rooms, dusting the flat top of a table here, the seat of a chair there. Tom had been on guard all night and would probably not be back until half past ten or eleven, having breakfasted at the barracks. It was ten o'clock now, so she had plenty of time. She was not, however, working slowly and erratically because of this: the reason lay deeper. Although her relationship with Tom had seemed unremarkable since her return, a vague sense of unease remained. Even in bed she had the feeling that they slept together because she was there and not because he really wanted her any more.

He was like he had been on the night of the quarrel in St. James's Park, only more pleasant on the surface. Nothing that she did seemed to reach him. She had cooked him special meals, bought him a new tie, been careful not to cross or correct him. Throughout he remained pleasant, but cold. She wondered whether he had found someone else, this time of more than the usual, passing interest. She felt afraid and alone, and knew for a moment, as the negative of a print, the intensity of joy that had surged through her when he had come to her mother's house and rescued her.

The bell rang. It was only just after ten and Tom always let himself in with his own key. Her uneasy feeling increased and she waited for a second ring. When it came she thought it too short and delicate for Tom. There was no one else whom it could be except Laurie, and Laurie had told her that he was going home for lunch that day.

It was Bernard, smiling but apprehensive.

"How did you know I was here?" Susan asked. Tom must have had an accident. But why send Bernard? And how did he come to know?

"Aren't you going to ask me in, Susan?"

She held open the door and he came in. He looked round dubiously, then selected the sofa that had once been Laurie's bed, and sat down. He put his hands on his knees and leant forward. "Your Dad sent me. He wanted to know how you were. Your Mum doesn't know."

"How did you get my address?" asked Susan, relieved and annoyed at the same time.

"You gave it to him when you went to see him at the office."

So Bernard knew that story. Probably her mother's whole, huge circle of acquaintances knew it. She could picture the excited phone calls of triumph after she had had the news that Susan would be returning home. "Tell him I'm very well, thanks."

"Are you really?" Bernard looked earnest.

"That's what I said."

"You don't look it."

"I've only just got up and I slept late. I don't expect visitors at this hour."

"Your husband out?" He looked down at his hands as he spoke.

"He's on guard, but he'll be home soon."

They were silent. She wanted to say something that would make up for her sharp answers and sharper tone. Bernard had done her no harm. In fact he had come out early on a Sunday just to inquire whether she was all right. But she could think of nothing to say, and her shabby treatment of a few years back prevented her talking openly. It occurred to her that he might once have been fond of her, though at the time she had not been aware of it. She used to reckon that he simply wanted a partner and she had served. Now she was not so sure.

She leant over and patted his hand. "Thanks for coming, Bernard, but I'm quite O.K. Tom and I have our differences like anybody else, but that's soon over and Daddy has nothing to worry about. Tell him I'll phone him next week." She took her hand away and started towards the door, then hesitated. "Would you like a cup of tea or coffee?"

"Please, Susan. I seem to have had breakfast very early this morning."

"How did you get here?"

"My Dad's car."

"Tea or coffee?"

"Whichever's easiest."

"It makes no difference to me."

"I don't mind, Susan."

Then she started to laugh, at first quietly like a giggle, then almost hysterically. Bernard smiled in sympathy, then gradually started to laugh with her, at last standing up and holding his side. All tension had gone and they abandoned themselves completely to their mood of hilarity. They faced each other, Susan crying now, and laughed in gusts. Every time one of them stopped the other would break out until they were both shrieking again, Bernard only a little less wildly than Susan. Neither of them heard Tom come in or was aware of him until he stood next to them, shouting: "What the 'ell!" For a moment they both stopped, then Susan started again. After a few moments Tom smiled weakly and tapped his head to Bernard to indicate that she must be mad.

"Well, I must be off," said Bernard.

"'Bye," said Tom.

"What about tea or coffee?" Susan asked and straightway burst out laughing again.

Tom led Bernard to the door and opened it for him. He waved to Susan as he went, but she was still doubled up with hysterical laughter, and could only manage a weak, baby's wave. Tom slammed the door behind Bernard.

"What's 'e want?"

"Came to see how I was," Susan answered, still chuckling.

"When did he come?"

"A few minutes ago."

"I bet!"

"Tom, what do you mean?" She was serious at last, but laughter or tears were near.

"How did he know where we was?"

"Were."

"Eh?"

"My father gave him our address. He was a bit worried about me and sent Bernard to find out how I was."

"And 'ow were you?" Tom took off his battledress jacket and threw it on the couch.

"Would you like me to bring you a cup of tea in bed? You'll feel better after a morning's sleep, and we can have a late lunch."

"I feel fine now, thanks."

"Aren't you going to get some sleep?"

"Later. You seem to forget the way that little bugger behaved towards us once in the Club. I'm not 'aving him in my house, that understood?"

Susan started to cry. Tom left the room and went into the bathroom, slamming the door behind him. This was what she had once wanted, this brute, unthinking man whose strength and forthrightness she had so envied. Now she only wanted to find a way of reaching him, show him how miserable she was and how happy he could still make her. The truth was that he no longer wanted her. That was it. That was what she would have to face. Whether there was someone else she did not know; either way he had had enough of her.

He was a long time in the bathroom, so after a while she went into the kitchen and made some tea. It only took a few minutes, as the water in the kettle was still hot from her breakfast. She buttered some rolls that she had bought the day before and spread them with black-currant jam. Then she brought the tray into the living-room and sat on the couch to wait. So little seemed to stand between them, and so much. A smile and a kiss and her nightmare would be over. But she was terrified that she could no longer stimulate either.

She crossed to the mirror and studied her face.

Then she fetched her bag, applied some lipstick and removed the traces of her tears. She combed her hair carefully and brushed the odd specks of dandruff from her black jumper. Why did she no longer attract him? What would she do if in fact this were true? She knew now that she could not go home again. She could never face her mother if the marriage really were at an end. Still, she had a good job and would soon find a room. But the sudden feeling of security brought with it a paradoxical wave of depression. Then Tom came out.

"I've made some tea and rolls," she said, smiling at him.

"I've had breakfast," he replied without looking at her. He stroked his newly-shaven chin in the mirror, then stopped abruptly. "But I could do with a cuppa just the same."

She poured out two cups, and he came over to take one without speaking. "Did you get the best shifts?" she asked sympathetically.

"Yes," he replied. He took a buttered roll and sat on a chair by the table. He opened the roll and dunked the half without jam in the tea.

"Laurie dropped in last night," she said, stirring her tea absent-mindedly.

"What did *he* want?"

"Just to know how we were."

"Bert's asked me to go and have lunch with him. 'Is folks is down from Manchester."

She waited until her first anger subsided. "I've got lunch for us here."

"You'll have to eat for both of us then." He smiled grimly.

"Tom, what is the matter with you? Or me for that matter? Or both of us?"

"Nothing I know of. These rolls are good."

"Well, it's not like you to go out to lunch on your own on a Sunday."

"I'm going with Bert and his folks."

"Nor do you usually go out with Bert and his folks."

He drained the cup noisily. "Any more char? It's not like you to have your father checkin' up every five minutes on whether I'm treating you proper."

"I couldn't stop him." She tempered her voice and herself, then felt it to be useless. "Tom, have you had enough of—well, the marriage?"

"If that's what you think."

"I'm asking you what you think."

He looked at her as he might have looked at a complete stranger. He drank his second cup of tea quickly and collected the crumbs that he had made. Leaning back he dropped them into his mouth and chewed slowly. Then he stood up and went towards the bedroom, stopping at the door. "Yes," he said softly, "I've 'ad just about enough."

Susan started to cry and was still crying when he came out and passed through the living-room. She heard his footsteps descending the staircase and the front door slam. Then it was silent and she was quite alone.

[12]

Laurie stood back and surveyed the painting. Then he took it off the easel and held it in front of the mirror. The resemblance to Tom was amazing. He had caught the large calculating eyes, the solemn-stupid expression, the white skin; the hands were even better than the face. They folded in each other on the Guardsman's lap, powerful, protecting and starkly white. He stood the canvas on the bed against the wall and stepped back across the room to look at it. It was a tremendous success. Standing on a chair he reached up and yanked one of Mrs. Murphy's pictures off the rail. Then he fixed his portrait on the outside of the frame, stood away and surveyed it again. He was delighted, the more so as it had been done from a photograph that he had surreptitiously borrowed when living with Tom and Susan.

Impatiently he knocked up a wooden trellis frame to protect the still-wet canvas and wrapped it carefully in brown paper. Before tying it he undid the paper, took one last look, then sealed it. He changed into a suit, gave his shoes a quick polish and put on his coat. It was already eight o'clock and getting chilly. He hoped that Susan and Tom would still be at home, and foresaw their unexpected pleasure when they were shown the painting.

The first bus seemed to crawl and when he had to change to another, the wait was interminable. He kept the painting on his knees, almost sorry that he had tied it so carefully. He would like to have had another look. He was puzzled that he had not thought of the idea before, and wondered whether he could do a similar portrait of Martin. At least he would like to try, and would broach the subject to Mr. Rogers the next day. He remembered then that he had done no preparation for his next lecture. Every moment since his return from lunch with his mother on the Sunday had been devoted to the portrait of Tom. No matter, he would discuss portrait painting with them. He left the bus in high spirits.

Susan took a long time to answer the door, and he began to think that they were out. Then he saw a light come on under the door. For a moment she stared at him almost without recognition. She looked pale and tired, and only just managed a smile as she waved him in.

"Hullo, Susan. Tom in?"

"No." Her voice was low.

"I've brought you a surprise, a wonderful surprise."

Her "thank you" was perfunctory, and she asked him to sit down, speaking in the same low, lifeless voice. He put the painting on the couch, sat down beside it and started unravelling the string. With a smile on his face he tore off the brown paper, revealed the picture and stood it against the back of the couch. Susan started forward, then relaxed.

"He's been with you, then?" she asked.

"No," replied Laurie, puzzled. "Do you like it?"

"Yes. When did you do it?"

"Started Sunday, finished tonight. I did it from a photograph, plus knowing Tom well." He was disappointed at her lack of enthusiasm. If it was not, perhaps, quite the Tom that she saw, he had at least expected some favourable criticism from a former art student.

"Tom's gone."

"Where?" He guessed that she referred to a posting.

"Left me. No one else knows."

"But why?" He let go of the painting.

"It seems he's had enough of me."

"But, Susan, that's impossible."

"He's done it just the same."

"For good?"

"I presume so." It was as much as her pride could stand. With a little sniffle she stood up and went over to the portrait. She picked it up and turned it to the light, studying it carefully.

"Watch out, it's still wet," called Laurie.

"It's very good, Laurie," she said at last, "very, very good. I'm not sure the expression is quite right. You've given him a slightly, well, stupid look—Tom never has that. Strong—silent, perhaps, not stupid though. But it's much the best painting you've ever done."

"And the first for some time."

"One day, not now, I'd like to buy it from you." She laughed. "If I can afford your price, that is. But not now, anyway."

"I'm awfully sorry about all this," Laurie started. He knew that she really thought the portrait good, so he hastened to turn his attention to her problem. In any case he was not sure what to do with the picture, not sure whether he had painted it for himself or for them. He wanted it, but he also wanted them to have it, not as a purchase but as a gift from him.

"Perhaps it'll all blow over. Like last time," he said at last.

"I don't think so, Laurie." She thought for a moment, then brightened. "Would you like some coffee?"

"Please."

He followed her into the kitchen and watched her make the coffee. She seemed more at ease and thanked him quite gaily for bringing the portrait so soon after finishing it. Then quite simply she told how Tom had left on the Sunday morning without even a real quarrel. After lunch she had gone to the cinema to take her mind off the matter. When she returned about a quarter to seven, she found that Tom had come back, collected all his clothes and left again, leaving the front-door key on the table under the mirror. There had been no note.

"Of course," she concluded, as she carried the tray into the living-room, "if I'd been here I might have persuaded him not to leave. But 'ifs' don't get you very far, and anyway it's no use him staying here while he feels like that."

"Is there someone else?" asked Laurie timidly.

"I don't think so. He was always running after someone, but I don't think there's anything serious. No, he's just fed up with me, whether I like it or not. It might have been different if we'd had children, but we didn't. Of course, I made his life a misery by trying to make him lead my life. So he said. Oh, if only he'd give me another chance. I wouldn't make the same mistakes twice. Piece of cake?"

"Please."

He was sorry for her. He thought of offering to see Tom in order to intercede on her behalf, but knew that she would never allow that. Perhaps Tom would come to see him. Ever since the humiliating night when they had first stayed in his basement flat he had hoped that the marriage would founder, and simultaneously despised himself for the hope. Now that it had happened and he could see how unhappy Susan had become, he was not so pleased. His day-dreams had always involved Susan returning happily home, while he moved in to share a flat with Tom.

"What are you going to do?" asked Laurie.

"I shall go on living here for the moment," Susan answered. "I've got a good job. If Tom doesn't come back I'll move farther afield. It was only so that he was near the barracks that we lived here once I started working."

"You wouldn't go home?"

"No," she replied quite definitely. "I wouldn't."

She asked him if he was going on painting, and he told her about Martin. When he had explained the circumstances, she could see no reason why Mr. Rogers would object to his painting the portrait, always provided the boy agreed. Children could be funny about such things. Perhaps he would be so pleased with the result that he would offer it to the next year's Academy. They laughed over this, and Susan went on to explain that her work and looking after the flat had robbed her of the inspiration and time for painting. Now she would take it up again.

"We could go sketching on Sundays," said Laurie enthusiastically. "What a long time ago it seems since I wouldn't let you come with Tom and me. We never went after all." He knew at once that he had led the conversation into a wrong channel. He rose to his feet, picking up the portrait at the same time. "Well, I must be off, Susan. You know my phone number. Please phone me or come round if there's anything I can do."

"Thank you, Laurie." She watched him wrap the portrait. "Don't forget," she said, "I'm going to buy that from you one day. When it's all blown over."

They shook hands and she accompanied him to the street. It was a black night and he stood there for a minute getting used to the darkness. Then he turned and smiled at her. She opened her lips to speak, then changed her mind. She came forward a pace, put her hand on his shoulder, and smiled. "We've both sort of lost someone we loved," she said awkwardly. Then she went back into the house before he could answer, closing the door softly behind her.

[13]

Laurie pushed away the easel and closed one eye. He put down his palette, stuck the brush in one corner and wiped his fingers on a paint rag. He went to the window and closed the curtains slightly, adjusting it until he had screened sufficient light for his purpose. Then he drew the wooden chair up to the easel and settled down again. He brushed a couple of strokes on the canvas then stopped, smiling.

"Try and relax," he said. "You're tensing. Let yourself go. That's better."

Martin relaxed his body and expression. He was leaning on the mantelpiece, legs crossed, three-quarter profile to Laurie who sat four or five feet away. He grinned whenever Laurie spoke, but tended to become taut as soon as Laurie started to paint. Otherwise he posed well, neither fidgeting nor changing his position unless Laurie requested it. Even when the others came in to speak to them he remained still.

"Do you want another rest?"

"Not unless you do," Martin replied.

They had been working since a quarter to ten and it was nearly noon. At eleven o'clock Mrs. Rogers had brought them some Bovril, and they had adjourned for five minutes. Although he had devoted most of his time to the body and pose, Laurie was satisfied with the result so far. He was painting more fluently than usual and felt sure that the face, whose outline he had just completed, would present no greater problem than had the easy twist of the body.

During tea before the last lecture he had told them of his success in painting Tom. Timidly he had broached the subject of doing a portrait of Martin for next spring's Academy. He had hurriedly explained that he could probably do it from photographs. But Mrs. Rogers had at once suggested Martin's sitting for him, the boy had spontaneously expressed his willingness and Laurie had seized the opportunity. He had come down the previous evening and spent it making sketches of the boy as they had all sat in the living-room talking. Now he had the whole of Sunday to get a basis for the portrait on canvas. He hoped that by working on it at home during the evenings, he would finish it with only two or three more sittings.

"Not had enough yet?" asked Mr. Rogers, coming into the room with a bowl of rust-coloured chrysanthemums.

Laurie put down his palette. "Yes," he agreed with a sigh. "That'll do till after lunch."

"May I look?" asked Martin.

"Not really," said Mr. Rogers with a chuckle.

"If you want to," said Laurie.

The boy came across to the easel and studied the picture. His eyes dropped from the face down the white sweater to the tight jeans, then back to the face. He looked puzzled and disappointed. "You haven't filled in the face," he said doubtfully.

"Not yet," answered Laurie, "but I think I've got the body, especially the twist." He turned his own body in imitation. "That's what I was most anxious about."

"Does that matter?" asked the boy.

"I told you not to look at it, my lad," put in Mr. Rogers, using his handkerchief to wipe away a water stain made by the bottom of the vase.

"Very much," said Laurie. "I want to try and express some of the ease and grace you show when you're standing about."

The boy blushed. "Will you start on the face after lunch?"

"Yes," said Laurie, wiping his brushes.

Mr. Rogers went out. Laurie felt awkward. Somehow he had disappointed the boy. He gathered up the palette and brushes and went up to the bathroom. When he came down again, Martin was still staring at the painting, and he wondered for a moment whether the boy felt a desire to destroy it. He did not turn as Laurie came in and continued looking at the painting when spoken to.

"Why did you want to paint me?"

"I like you. I thought you'd make a good subject and I wanted to do someone in the prime of youth." His words and tone sounded silly and awkward. He wished that one of the others would come in. He could hear them in the kitchen, setting the table, moving saucepans and laughing or talking. Somehow he had exposed the boy, or perhaps himself, and this had obviously worried Martin. He went to the door and closed it quietly. Then he stood by the boy and put his hand on the wide shoulder.

"What's wrong, Martin?"

"Nothing, I don't think." The boy looked at him at last.

"Would you like to drop the whole thing?"

"Yes, if you don't mind."

Laurie was instantly disappointed. He had only made the suggestion to help in unearthing the boy's sudden change of mood. The painting was going to be a success and now it was to stop. He tried to decide whether it was better to argue or wait till after lunch to see if the boy changed his mind. Of course, he should never have let Martin look at it. Yet he had always considered that a curious tradition.

"What'll you do with the canvas?" Martin asked. He looked steadily at Laurie, but seemed embarrassed.

"Paint it over and use it for something else."

"Now?"

Gwen came noisily into the room. She studied the canvas from the door, then came closer, peering at it over the top of imaginary glasses. She was also in jeans and her sweater was yellow. They looked more alike than usual.

"It's smashing!" she said.

"You don't mean it!" said Martin sharply.

"I do," she said hotly. "That's just how you stand. And you're always slippery like that in bathing trunks. It's exactly you."

"It's not," said Martin, raising his voice. He was blushing again now.

"It is and I like it," the girl shouted.

"Mr. Kingston's going to smudge it all over in a minute."

"Why?"

"'Cause he is."

"I wasn't speaking to you. You're not going to smudge it over, are you, Mr. Kingston?"

The door opened and Mr. Rogers came in, closely followed by his wife. "Here, here, what are you two quarrelling about?"

"Martin says Mr. Kingston's going to smudge all over the painting and destroy it."

"Are you?" Mr. Rogers asked Laurie.

"Yes," Martin chipped in.

"But why?"

"Martin says he'd rather I didn't go on with it."

"What's up?" Mr. Rogers asked his son.

Martin looked at his father angrily. Tears were forming in his eyes. Suddenly he tipped up the easel and kicked the canvas as it lay on the floor. Then pushing his way past his father and mother, he ran out of the room. They heard him cross the kitchen, open the back door and go out. Laurie picked up the canvas, set up the easel and fixed the painting in place, dusting the corners where it had become dirty. Mrs. Rogers went out, taking the reluctant Gwen with her.

"What brought this on?" Mr. Rogers asked.

"I've no idea," answered Laurie. "He was a bit disappointed when he saw I'd worked all the time on the body. Then he seemed to get really angry at the idea. I suppose I should have warned him that I wanted to get over the hurdle of his stance while I'm actually here. It's easier to work on the face at home."

"It's unlike him. I'll have a word with him when he cools down. Anyway, shall I put the easel and painting in our bedroom and we'll see which way the wind blows at lunch?"

"By all means," said Laurie. "I'd like to go on with it, but I don't want to upset the kid."

Gwen came back when she heard her father go upstairs. Shyly she helped straighten the chairs. She told Laurie that lunch was nearly ready and asked him whether he wanted a wash. He thanked her and said he did, and when he stooped to replace the tubes of paint in his box, she went down on her knees to help him. She was clearly sorry about her brother's behaviour, but was not sure how to atone for it.

They started lunch without Martin. As always the red and white kitchen was warm and steamy. Mr. Rogers carved carefully and his wife heaped the plates with potatoes and sprouts. She put one plate in the oven, but nothing was said about Martin's absence. Laurie was sorry, but still puzzled at what had happened; it marred the contrast he had wanted between this and last Sunday's lunch.

Martin came in as they were finishing their first helpings. His face was red and he was out of breath. "Sorry I'm late, Mum, Dad," he said, sitting down.

Mrs. Rogers fetched his plate from the oven and put it in front of him. "Thanks, Mum. Gosh, I'm hungry." He attacked his food even more enthusiastically than usual.

"I suppose you've missed not seeing the Sunday papers?" Mr. Rogers asked Laurie.

Laurie nodded.

"We don't take them," went on Mr. Rogers. "I don't know why, except it's good to have one day's rest from our bright, peaceful world. That's what Jean and I say, anyway. Ostriches, I suppose." He held out his empty plate to his wife. "Not too much, dear. But I guessed you read them. You mention them so often."

"I don't always read them on a Sunday," said Laurie.

"What's the good of reading them any other day?" asked Gwen.

"I'm mainly interested in the book and art reviews," Laurie replied, "and they're as interesting on Wednesday as Sunday."

"Do they write about your paintings?" asked Martin. He was speaking with his mouth full. His tone was half-sarcastic, half-admiring, but he looked down as he spoke.

"No," said Laurie, "I've never had a one-man show. A review of a mixed show once described one of my paintings as competent."

"That a compliment?" asked Mr. Rogers.

"To some people," Laurie replied.

"Can I have some more, Mum?" Martin asked, looking up at her. "I met Jim Young. They were up half the night with that cow that's calving. I'm going down with him to have a look at her after lunch." He snatched a glance at Laurie and blushed when their eyes met. "I'll be back for tea, 'cause Jim's going to the flicks in Lewes."

Martin remained silent for the rest of the meal. As soon as he had finished his own sweet he asked if he could leave the table, and hurried from the room without looking at Laurie. Mr. Rogers launched a conversation about the possibilities of a contemporary artist living by painting alone. Laurie was surprised, though, that even when Gwen left to go to see her friend Muriel and Mrs. Rogers was doing the washing-up, no further reference was made to Martin's behaviour.

Laurie had also expected Mr. Rogers to suggest a walk after lunch, but it transpired that he and Mrs. Rogers were going to see a friend about acquiring timber for a new garden shed. They had arranged it earlier, thinking that it would leave Laurie and Martin to go on with the portrait in peace.

"You can come with us," Mr. Rogers said, "but I expect you'd rather take a walk with your sketch book."

Again Laurie searched for a note of disapproval in Mr. Rogers's voice that might show sympathy with his son's unexplained mood, but the suggestion was put forward in a friendly manner. "Yes. Good idea," agreed Laurie.

He collected his sketch pad and pencil, put on a green gaberdine windbreaker that he had with him, and left the house before them. He wandered down the road in the direction the bus took after he had left it. The leaves were falling and lay in red-brown shoals round the trees. The air was fresh and the sun had long lost its summer strength. The road was deserted of cars and people. At a junction Laurie turned left into a narrow lane and started to climb, passing a large, deserted farmhouse on his right.

Near the top of the hill a young farmer in a flat cap and dark suit, whose trousers were too short, bade him good afternoon. Otherwise he saw no one. He was walking quickly, hardly bothering to worry whether there was anything worth sketching, and when he reached the brow of the hill where the lane swung left, he felt sweat break on his upper lip and body like patches of a rash. He paused for a moment, warm and clammy. Then he went on down the hill.

Half-way down, in a small opening that led to a field, two boys sat on a tree trunk with their backs to the road, smoking. One of them was Martin. Laurie stopped when he saw them and they turned round. Martin smiled at once. "Hullo," he called. "Having a look round?"

"Yes," said Laurie. He approached them diffidently, walking between two deep-dug cart-tracks.

"This is Jim," said Martin, taking a pull at his cigarette.

"'lo," said the greasy-haired youth. He had dark, murderous eyes and the air of a gipsy.

"Hullo," said Laurie.

They were silent for a moment, but there was no longer any sign of embarrassment in the way that Martin looked at Laurie. Then Jim stood up. "I must be off. Going to the flicks," he added to Laurie by way of explanation. Both boys giggled. "Be seein' yer."

"Good-bye," said Laurie, not sure that he wanted to be left with Martin at the moment.

"Cheers," said Martin.

They watched Jim walk to the road and turn right up the hill. Once or twice they caught a glimpse of him through the hedge as he neared the brow, then his footsteps died away and it was quiet everywhere.

"He's going to his girl," said Martin admiringly as he pulled at his cigarette.

Laurie recoiled from the boy's new-found hardness. He seemed so sure of himself now. "I'd better push on," Laurie started. "I'd like to do some sketching while the light's still good."

Martin said nothing for a moment, and Laurie thought that he was perhaps trying to think up some sarcastic remark. But the boy threw away the stub of his cigarette, and twisting his heel in the mud, stared at the marks made as though they were an oracle. "Did you smudge it?" he asked quietly.

"Not yet," answered Laurie. He had started to move away,

but stopped now. In a second the boy was beside him. He felt the roughness of Martin's sweater as the boy put his arm round Laurie's neck. Martin had to reach up slightly as he was a little shorter than Laurie, and the curious sight they must have made on the fringe of a muddy field almost made the older man laugh.

"Do you want to go on with it?" Martin asked, his voice barely audible.

"If you want me to," answered Laurie. He stroked the boy's head with his right hand, conscious of the compromising, nearly ridiculous scene, but glad of it.

"'Course I do. What do you think?" The boy let go of him. "Come on! I'll race you back to the cottage. We'll start before the others come in. One, two, three, go!" He started off at a goodly pace, Laurie behind him, happier than he had been for years.

[14]

When Laurie reached his room it was already after eight o'clock. He had spent the last hour examining a dilapidated mews flat by torchlight. It belonged to an aunt or great-aunt, he was not sure which, of Eccles. A long lease on it was for sale and the rent was small. It was in a very neglected state, having been unoccupied for years, but this encouraged Laurie, because it would enable him to start from scratch and create a home that would reflect his taste and personality. He had only postponed his final decision in the matter because the offer had come through Eccles. Was there a catch in it? Was it being done for the aunt or for Laurie? Eccles had been increasingly friendly during the last few weeks, but it was a friendship that Laurie still distrusted. Norman would have spouted a theory about Eccles's own sex feelings becoming more secure. The need to gain security by railing against inverts had decreased. Perhaps on this occasion Norman would have been right, for Eccles was to be married at Easter. Anyway, he would tell Norman the story on the coming Friday, when they were to have dinner together at Laurie's expense.

Laurie felt more settled than he had for a long time. He had started painting once more and he almost had a home of his own.

More important, he seemed to have a better measure of himself. His life was beginning to fall into a more orderly pattern and so yield greater security and less loneliness. It no longer seemed mostly a lie. Some people knew about him and others did not, but in neither case was he lying any longer. He simply kept the flaw in his nature hidden from those who did not know, as one might seek to conceal a scar or wart.

Moving quickly and easily he made himself a fried egg on toast and some coffee. It was half past eight already, but it had not been too bad a day. The flat had cheered him enormously, and compensated for the uncomfortable twenty minutes with Mary earlier. He almost blushed again as he recalled his "Can I help you, Madam?" and the realisation that it was her, even as he spoke the word "madam".

She had come up from Brighton for the day. She thought that he still worked in the suburbs for that Mr. Wayne. She had looked in the door of a shop she was passing, as she always glanced in bookshops when in town, and she had seen him poised on a ladder, the same old Laurie. So she had come in, hardly feeling that she could pass without so much as a "good-morning".

She stayed for a quarter of an hour or so, inspected at odd intervals by the rest of the staff. The conversation proceeded in fits and starts: her family, holidays, his painting, Norman Wayne, apologies for not replying to letters long forgotten, a forthcoming visit to Brighton, and promises to keep in touch in the future. "I really must be off, Laurie," she had said for the third time, but she only went as far as the door. He had followed her and she had asked shyly after Susan and Tom. "They're fine, thanks," he had said, and saved a long explanation. Besides, they might have made it up since he had last seen Susan.

Laurie finished his second cup of coffee and took a copy of Grombrich's *Story of Art* from a row of books on the chest of drawers. A book-end fell over. It landed unbroken on the floor by the foot of the bed and was followed by the first few books. As he stooped to pick them up, Laurie caught sight of the portrait of Tom, still wrapped in brown paper. He put back the books and book-end, then picked up the painting, letting the brown paper peel off.

He held it in front of the mirror, and a wave of desire seized him like a fever. He could smell the nicotine on the strong, white fingers, knew the terrifying pleasure of meeting the large, brown eyes and wanted, with the intensity of a starving man at the thought of food, to feel the huge, graceful body held close to him, part of him. Whatever in him had changed, the sheer physical need of Tom remained undiluted. He would still brook no opposition to its fulfilment.

Then the wave passed and he stared coolly at the portrait in the mirror. He felt half amused and half disgusted by his feelings, but he recognised their strength. He still had far to go to reach a self-realisation that would snuff such sudden flames as easily as those of a candle. Then he heard Mrs. Murphy on the stairs and guessed that she was coming to his room. He quickly wrapped up the painting and put it behind the chest of drawers.

"Come in!"

Mrs. Murphy was panting and red in the face. "Now see here, Mr. Kingston, you know the rules of the place. No women after nine."

"I don't understand, Mrs. Murphy."

"It's near enough nine now to be after by the time she comes up."

"Who?"

"Mrs. Beeson, I think she said."

"Mrs. Beeson?—oh, Susan."

"You'll have to see her downstairs, I'm afraid."

"Of course, Mrs. Murphy." He was instantly relieved. For a moment he feared that it was someone that Eccles might have sent, though he had no specific reason for such a fear. He thanked Mrs. Murphy and hurried downstairs ahead of her. Susan was waiting at the bottom, and they shook hands. He explained that he could not invite her up owing to the rules of the house, jerking his head towards the descending Mrs. Murphy. But he offered to take her out for a drink.

She preferred coffee, so they went to a nearby restaurant. She told him straight away that she had twice written to Tom but had had no reply. By Saturday she had felt really desperate. Now the mood was passing. This morning her firm had offered her six

months in their Paris office. It was not the first time that the chance
had come her way, but she had previously refused it because of
Tom. This time they had tactfully explained that they gathered she
would welcome a change.

"I'd told Francie, a friend of mine at the office, that things had
come unstuck between Tom and me. They offered the vacancy
to her first, but she must have hinted at what I'd told her. So they
asked me. They don't mind which of us goes."

"And when do you go?" asked Laurie, stirring his coffee, half his
mind on a cheeky-looking boy at the counter.

"Monday of next week. Early," Susan answered. "It's quite easy
for me to do it. I can take most of my things and——" She paused,
and Laurie took his eyes off the boy, who was combing his hair in
the mirror over the coffee machine. "I thought you'd look after our
lamps and things, just for the moment."

"Of course." He took a bite at one of the buns he had ordered
with their coffee. It was stale and a little sour, so he put it down and
pushed the plate away.

She leaned forward towards him, the sleeve of her coat brush-
ing a tiny pool of coffee on the table. "Thanks, Laurie. I've got till
tomorrow at six to make up my mind. I've got to ring Francie then
and tell her definitely. Laurie, could you do something for me?"

"Yes," he said, "what is it?"

"Try and see Tom. Tell him I'm going. Tell him if he doesn't
come by six tomorrow, never to come." She went on in a rush. "I
won't be there after tomorrow. They've given me till Monday off,
if I'm going. I thought I'd spend tomorrow packing and the last
few days saying good-bye to friends. I thought I'd go and stay with
one of them who's asked me." She caught her lower lip between
her teeth, and continued less dramatically. "I don't want to stay
in the flat any more." She laid her arm on Laurie's. "Will you see
Tom and tell him? It's our last chance. Tell him this time it will
work. You brought us together before, Laurie. Do it again. Please!"

"I'll try, Susan," he said. She looked so frail and pathetic in
the cheap, chromium-plated atmosphere of the restaurant. He
reached out his right hand and took her sleeve out of the spilt
coffee. Then he drew his other hand away from hers and noticed
that the cheeky-looking boy was watching them.

[15]

Laurie left work at four, alleging a bad headache. His behaviour during the day had certainly borne out that he was not feeling up to the mark. He had arrived late, which was unusual for him. Twice his attention had had to be drawn to customers waiting to be served; and although he had been momentarily enthusiastic when announcing his decision to take the flat, he had hardly eaten anything at lunch and had resisted all attempts by Eccles to start a conversation.

Laurie had slept badly the night before. He had lain awake for hours arguing for and against contacting Tom within the time specified by Susan. Was it really any use bringing them together again? Wouldn't each new attempt end in a similar failure? They were not suited. They completely failed to understand one another. The gap between them would never be bridged, and if they had children matters would only become worse. Against that, what right had he to judge? How could he constitute himself the agent to deny that pathetic girl something that meant so much to her?

If he knew that behind his ceaseless posing of questions and answers there lay a bigger, more selfish argument, he refused to acknowledge its presence for a long time. He was thinking only of them. But when he awoke in the early hours of the morning after a fitful sleep, he saw the truth and knew it. Chance had so played the cards that if he willed it there would be no repetition of the night when Tom and Susan had stayed in his bedroom in the Chelsea basement.

All along the line he had had a rough deal. His mother, whom he had loved, had neglected him for his stepfather. He had been born or had involuntarily become an invert, with all the suffering and hostility that the stigma carried with it. He had been threatened by Eccles, exploited by Norman Wayne, and even the youth in Florence had cheated him. Now he was asked to cheat himself of the one experience that in some vague, mystical way would complete him. He was asked to deny himself the only person he had ever loved for the sake of the thin possibility of perpetuating a stupid marriage.

All was quiet as he had lain there, his heart beating fast, his hands clammy. It had still been dark and he had wondered how near it was to dawn. An aeroplane crossed the sky and he waited for its whine to fade. There was always the possibility that Tom would refuse to go to Susan. But he was not content to pass the initiative to someone else. This time he would take the decision himself. He began to plan a future for Tom and himself, their future, his future. At last he had fallen asleep again and had not woken until an hour later than usual.

He had already said good night to everyone at the shop when the manager told him that he was wanted on the phone. It was unusual for anyone to call him. He guessed at once that it must be Susan and wondered what to tell her. He scarcely dared say that he had so far taken no steps to contact Tom. He took the call in the packing-room. It was during the tea break and there was no one there.

"Hullo?" His stomach seemed to be drawn inwards and downwards.

For a moment he was quite unable to place the male voice replying. Then he recognised Mr. Rogers. The epidiascope would not be available this week. It had been broken at some other class. He thought that he ought to warn Laurie in advance. The bookseller thanked him for the trouble and expense of the call.

"That's all right," said Mr. Rogers. "You don't sound so bright."

"I'm not," answered Laurie. The packing-room was still deserted. "I've got a big decision to make and I just don't know which way will turn out best."

"Do what you know is right," Mr. Rogers replied with a laugh. "Your conscience won't let you down. Well, I must ring off before the pips go. See you the day after tomorrow."

"Thanks again for phoning," said Laurie. "Good-bye."

From the bookshop he went directly to the barracks. He was unable to see Tom, but they assured him that the Guardsman would receive his note before five o'clock. He had scribbled quite simply: "Desperately urgent. Please see me before 5.30 today without fail. Laurie." Then he went home, arriving shortly before five.

He made some tea, and as he drank it his resolution weakened. He would tell Tom that he had come too late, that Susan had already left. He would invent an ultimatum from Susan that contained impossible terms and conditions without which she would not resume the marriage. They would laugh at them together and go out to supper. After a visit to a cinema they would come back here for the night. Again a wave of desire gripped him. Again it abated.

He wondered whether Tom still felt as warmly towards him as on the night they had been surprised by Susan. Relationships between two human beings were always exposed to the law of constant change. By the time that a degree of feeling, caught in an instant like the rate of one's pulse, could be conveyed to the someone else, it had already undergone subtle changes. The manner of its acceptance by the other would modify it further. If only he could convey to Tom the intensity of his feelings at one of those moments when they manifested themselves so clearly.

Tom was allowed to come upstairs by himself. He was white and magnificent, his huge body moving into the room with the grace and strength of a wild animal. His eyes were wide open and inquiring, his lips slightly parted. He still had his hat on, and was inside the room before Laurie could answer his knock.

"It's about Sue?" the Guardsman asked in his deep, rough voice.

"Yes," said Laurie.

Tom moved past him and stood at the window, looking out. Laurie's eyes traced the line of the soldier's shoulders and back up to the smooth, clean neck. Their perfection belonged to his world, a world alien to most of mankind, alien to Susan and even to Tom. To exclude Tom was the most painful jab of all, but he remembered what Mr. Rogers had said. More important he remembered the example of Mr. Rogers's daily life as he stood next to the Guardsman, who was still facing the window, his weight evenly distributed. There were other ways in which he could find himself; it was a question of searching, always searching and never giving in to easy solutions. Suddenly, as a complement to his thoughts, he heard Martin's words, clear and unequivocal: "You'll regret it in the morning."

"Well?" said Tom, putting his arm round Laurie's waist and starting to fondle him unambiguously.

For a second Laurie wavered before the invitation, then: "She's leaving the country." His voice was so low that the Guardsman bent to catch his words. "Her firm has offered her a job in Paris. You won't be able to reach her after six this evening." He paused, summoning all his courage. "Tom, she needs you. She wants you more than anything in the world. She loves you, Tom." He swallowed. "Go to her, for her sake—and yours."

"Where is she?" The Guardsman broke away from Laurie.

"At the flat." Laurie crossed the room, picked up the parcel containing the portrait and pushed it into Tom's hands. "Give her this, Tom. She'll understand."

Then the Guardsman was gone. He neither stopped to say "Thank you", nor even to close the door. Laurie heard him running down the stairs, but there was no sound of a door slamming. He crossed to the window in time to see Tom hurrying along the far side of the square. A taxi came by and he hailed it. He spoke to the driver and threw the painting on to the back seat before he jumped in after it. Laurie moved away from the window; the Guardsman had never once glanced in its direction.

Laurie put the teapot and dirty cups on a tray, and brought out his paints and brushes. He set up the easel and placed the unfinished portrait of Martin on it. Gradually he started work, painting easily and fluently, never hurrying, never forcing himself. He went on like that until quite late, stopping only when he felt hungry. After a quick meal he went for a walk. As he went down the stairs he nearly tripped on a piece of worn stair carpet. He remembered now that he had had a bad fall that way as a child. His father had picked him up at the foot of the stairs. Laurie could no longer remember his face and he thought that his father had gone away on that very day. But his sudden recollection was still vague and a little out of focus, and he was not sure. It was not until he reached Marble Arch that the fog and the people and the tall Guardsmen in compact groups brought on a mood of nostalgia for the past that lasted for the whole of the rest of the week.

ALSO AVAILABLE FROM VALANCOURT BOOKS

CPSIA information can be obtained
at www.ICGtesting.com
Printed in the USA
BVOW09s0731051117
499590BV00002B/206/P